Dear Reader,

There I was, minding my own business, when Carolyn Andrews sashayed into my life. How could a classy woman like her end up in a dusty ghost town like Cold Heart? Clean and sleek, she looked as though she were heading for a cocktail party in Los Angeles. Instead she lands in Cold Heart. Population ten, not counting the wild burros. Nearest drinks served at a broken-down saloon.

She claimed she was looking for wild horses.

Cold Heart was the end of the world. With ten people in the town, I figured I'd have peace and quiet. And I did. Till Carolyn showed up.

They say that fate has a way of finding a man, no matter where he goes. They're right. Carolyn Andrews was my fate. My beautiful, brave-hearted, fire-kissed fate.

For that, I will be eternally grateful.

Respectfully yours,

Jonathan Raider

Please address questions and book requests to: Silhouette Reader Service
U.S.: 3010 Walden Ave., P.O. Box 1325, Buffalo, NY 14269
Canadian: P.O. Box 609, Fort Erie, Ont. L2A 5X3

R·A·N·C·H
R·O·G·U·E·S

WESTERN *Lovers*™

LEE MAGNER

MUSTANG MAN

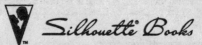

Silhouette Books

Published by Silhouette Books
America's Publisher of Contemporary Romance

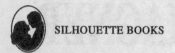 SILHOUETTE BOOKS

ISBN 0-373-30152-9

MUSTANG MAN

Chapter 1

He watched her through half-closed eyes from beneath the shade of his hat brim. She was walking toward him along the dirt street, puffs of dust rising softly behind her high heels with every leggy stride. What in hell was a woman like her doing in a place like this? Her Chinese red dress was obviously not something bought off the rack. The cut and sway of the fabric against her subtle curves had the earmarks of one of a kind. So did the matching shoes.

So did the woman in them.

He lowered the toe of his boot a little so he could keep his eyes on her as she approached. Her confident, feminine gait gave her hips a subtle, graceful lilt that was absolutely fascinating. Back and forth... He wondered what she'd look like on a beach in a string bikini, barefoot, swaying across the warm, wet sand with a flower in her hair...

She stepped onto the worn planks that served as an old-fashioned sidewalk for the sun-bleached shack. The sharp rap of her delicate shoes jarred him. There was determination in her walk. Hell! He wasn't in the mood to get up and fend off some woman bent on a mission.

She stopped in front of him and swept off the broad-brimmed, red straw hat and wiped the back of her hand against her forehead. She was hesitating, frowning a little, as if weighing her approach.

He'd been stretched out between two chairs with his weather-beaten Western hat slouched down over his forehead. Now he shoved the hat back and reluctantly eyed the attractive stranger on his front porch.

"Lost?" he asked, spearing her with a look meant to send her running to her mother. His instincts were all whispering words of warning to him. She was going to be trouble.

Carolyn Andrews ran her fingers through her hair, trying to cool herself a little. The western air felt good as it reached her head. That was what she needed now, she thought, trying to dredge up her sense of humor. A cool head.

"I'm looking for Jonathan Raider," she said clearly. She looked him over, from his unkempt head to his dusty boots. Doubt hovered in her eyes. "Are you Raider?"

"Yep."

He returned her assessment in full, taking in the ash-blond hair that glinted in the sun, the way her petite figure filled the dress to demure advantage, and the sexiest pair of legs he'd seen on a woman under five foot six.

When his gaze returned to her face, she looked a little rosier around the cheeks to him, but that was all. He grinned at her in reluctant appreciation. The girl had some grit, staring him down like that, out in the middle of nowhere.

"At your service," he added. He dropped the hat on his stomach and crossed his hands behind his head, making himself a little more comfortable while he waited to hear her story. "Well?"

Carolyn had never felt such an intense desire to hit a man as she did at that moment. The oaf was stretched out taking a siesta, looked as if he hadn't had a bath in a week, and was giving her the most blatant sexual once-over she'd had to ignore since she'd left Los Angeles two years ago. He had the gall to sprawl out in front of her like an indulgent potentate giving an audience to a harem dancer! At her service! In a pig's eye!

She lowered her eyes for a moment and stared at his disreputable hat, plopped comfortably on his work-shirted stomach. She couldn't afford to blow everything now by rising to his bait and picking a fight. She needed Jonathan Raider's help, and she'd already been told that it wasn't likely she'd get it. She didn't want to worsen the odds.

She coolly looked him in the eyes, fingering the brim of her hat to rid herself of the anger and nervous energy he'd provoked.

"I want to study the mustang herds," she said. "The man who runs the saloon said you're the expert here." So had the retired lady of the night sitting at the rail next to her when she'd asked. Then they'd both nearly doubled over laughing at the idea of Carolyn trying to talk Jonathan Raider into helping her out.

From the look on his face, they'd been dead right. His wary, slightly amused expression had vanished. Now he looked dumbfounded. His boots hit the worn wooden floor so hard that the front porch shuddered. The violence of his unexpected movement made Carolyn flinch a little, but she stubbornly stood her ground.

"Come on, lady!" he snorted, rubbing the back of his neck with one hand and half crumpling his hat in a death-grip with the other. "No one comes to Cold Heart, Nevada, to ask Jonathan Raider to take them out to see the mustangs!"

He eyed her with a steely look of dislike and suspicion. When he stood up, Carolyn had to resist the urge to take a step back. He towered over her. She clenched her teeth and put her hands on her hips in defiance.

No one in their right mind would ask Jonathan Raider for anything, she thought testily.

With great effort, she stifled the urge to tell him precisely what she was thinking. She kept telling herself not to alienate the man more if she could avoid it—even if he did deserve it!

She tried again.

"Consider me out of my mind," she suggested with a sigh of resignation. "I'm doing a study of mustang life, and I need someone from around here to point me in the right direction."

Raider obliged by pointing down the dusty main street of the old ghost town in the direction that she'd come.

Carolyn shook her head adamantly.

"That's not the direction I had in mind," she countered. "I'll pay," she added.

She said it carefully, though. She sensed that Jonathan Raider wasn't the kind of man to do things just for money. Apparently mustangs were a touchy subject for him. Money might not be the way to change his mind about helping her.

Raider hitched his thumbs in his belt and rocked back on his heels.

"Why here?" he asked bluntly. "Isn't this a little...out of the way?"

Carolyn frowned angrily. He didn't have to be so sarcastic. She fanned herself absently with the hat, trying to cool her temper as well as her body. She saw his eyes drop to her bare throat and arms. The hat stilled instantly.

"I thought out-of-the-way places were the best starting points for finding wild animals," she argued. "Lots of articles have been written about the herds farther south, nearer towns and areas with lots of ranches...." She shrugged. "I just thought the setting of a ghost town might be a good twist."

Raider scowled.

Carolyn had the sinking feeling she'd chosen the wrong approach.

"You're a writer?" he demanded.

Carolyn hesitated.

"I'm researching an article...."

"For a magazine?" He was skewering her with a look that would have rendered most people incapable of telling a lie.

Carolyn blinked.

"You have something against magazines?" she asked in surprise.

Raider snugged his hat down on his head and marched down the porch steps with a grunt that sounded as if it might have meant, "You bet your pretty butt, lady." Carolyn hurried after him. She had too much at stake to let it go at that. Besides, there wasn't much time left....

"Wait!" she shouted after him. A warm breeze eddied around her ankles and tickled her calves. "Can't we just talk a little bit more about this? Talking won't hurt anything!"

Raider was six feet tall, and when the man stretched his legs as he was doing now, his stride was impressive. Carolyn was hard-pressed to keep up without breaking into a run.

"Mr. Raider!" she called after him imploringly. "Please!"

She was dogtrotting just behind him when he came to a sudden halt. She barely avoided falling against his broad, sweat-stained back. Just when she was beginning to feel a glimmer of hope, she realized why he'd stopped. It obviously hadn't been in response to her plea. He was stripping off his shirt and dropping it into a basket on the back steps of his small shack.

Carolyn couldn't help but look at the well-muscled view he was presenting. The man was definitely built, in spite of his distinct lack of charm and parlor manners. She shook herself mentally. This was no time to be distracted by a few interesting muscles!

Then she noticed that he was pulling off his boots, tossing his socks into the basket and reaching for his belt.

"Uh...Mr. Raider..." she said, rather faintly.

He stopped, his hand on his belt buckle, and eyed her over his shoulder. A rakish grin spread slowly across his face. The look he gave her this time was unmistakable to any woman over the age of consent.

"Care to join me in my bath?" he offered casually.

She thought he was probably bluffing, just trying another crude way of getting rid of her. Of course, maybe he wasn't....

Carolyn lifted her chin and shook her head.

"No thanks, Mr. Raider. I've already had mine."

He shrugged and whipped the belt out of the loops.

Carolyn felt her throat go dry. This wasn't exactly the kind of dueling she was used to. Boardrooms...business meetings...tough correspondence or telephone calls—those were things she knew how to deal with. She watched in growing discomfort as he yanked the snap open on his jeans. Relief flooded her as he hesitated and looked at her again.

"By the way," he growled, "do you intend to tell me your name? Or are you here incognito?"

Carolyn felt another flash of anger, but this time she couldn't really blame him. The bone-tiredness she'd been fighting off began to press at her. She ran a hand through her hair. She was exhausted. She'd been driving for hours to get here. It had been days since she'd begun this trek. Before that...the months of agony...

"I'm sorry," she apologized. "My name is Carolyn Andrews. I'm afraid I've been burning my candle at both ends recently, Mr. Raider. I was just so eager to get started..."

She left the sentence unfinished. There was no welcoming warmth or understanding in Raider's eyes. They were a cold slate blue. Her desire to reach out to him, to explain a little, died instantly.

"Could we start over again?" she asked quietly.

For a moment she thought he was wavering, considering her offer. Then something hardened in his face, and she knew she'd lost.

He jerked the zipper down and began to peel off the dirty, weathered jeans.

Carolyn stood her ground and crossed her arms in front of her chest. He wasn't going to scare her off like some little schoolgirl! She had too much at stake. Besides, she had a pretty good idea what he was thinking about her, and it made her mad. She wasn't some big-city Easterner who didn't know anything about life in the raw and had to have her air conditioned and her water purified!

He yanked the jeans off and dropped them in the basket with the rest. He was wearing jockey shorts and a devilish grin that Carolyn would have loved to wipe off his face. She contented herself with smiling sweetly back at him as he walked up the steps to his back door.

"If you intend to continue this conversation," he said pointedly, "you'll have to do it in my bathtub."

The jockey shorts joined the rest of the clothes and Raider walked into his shack laughing.

Carolyn repressed the urge to stamp her foot in frustration.

"Maybe you'll be more civilized after you're cleaned up!" she shouted at him.

She whirled and marched back down the dusty street, her shoulders stiff and her back ramrod straight.

Raider watched her through his kitchen window.

There wasn't even a hint of defeat about her. Damn! He'd been right. Carolyn Andrews wasn't going to take no for an answer. The peace and quiet of the empty little town were about to go down the tubes.

He eased himself into the aged claw foot tub full of warm water and shut his eyes in pleasure. After all the riding he'd done in the past couple of weeks, it was the purest of delights to sink into the soothing bath and soak off the grime and the aches.

As he closed his eyes and drifted into a half sleep, the vision in his mind wasn't of cattle and horses and riding the range. There was this ash-blond girl in a crimson bikini with the best-looking legs he'd seen in quite some time....

Carolyn returned to her trailer, which was parked at the other side of town. It wasn't much of a walk. It wasn't much of a town. The sign next to her travel home said it all. Cold Heart, Nevada. Population 10. The "10" had been recently painted. Apparently numbers eleven and twelve had given up and moved on.

She took the trailer step wearily and opened the door. Her shoes were off by the time she was inside. It felt good to wriggle her toes again. The heels might have been fine in Reno and Winnemucca, but they'd definitely grown annoying here in the land that time forgot.

It was hot and stuffy inside the cramped confines of the secondhand trailer. Carolyn opened the windows and resumed fanning herself with her hat. It was certainly earning its keep, she thought wryly.

She wished it was all over. Funny...in all the months of planning and saving and searching for clues, it had never occurred to her that she might fail in proving Abel's innocence. Now she was so close... But was she close to success? Or to failure?

"Don't worry, Abel," she murmured. She couldn't let herself succumb to such negative thinking. "I'll find out what happened...."

Tiredness flowed over her like a slow wave. Her hat had peculiarly gained weight and was almost too heavy to lift. She let her eyes close. Just for a moment... Her hand slowly sank to her lap, and the red straw hat slithered to the linoleum floor with a soft swish. Her last conscious thought was of a slate-eyed cowboy with a build like a Greek statue's inviting her into his barn for a roll in the hay while her palm connected with his cheek in a satisfying, resounding smack.

Day faded into twilight, leaving the trailer in darkness. The soft kiss of cooler air fluttering across her thighs teased Carolyn back into consciousness. In those first cloudy moments of awakening, she thought she was back at home, and Abel was calling her name.

As she gradually came awake, she remembered where she was. She also remembered that she was alone and didn't know a soul within about a thousand miles.

She swung her legs over the edge of the couch that doubled as a bed and tried to organize her next plan of attack. There wasn't a lot of time left. That was one thing the doctors had all agreed on. The sooner she found what she'd come looking for, the better.

"'Population 10,' the sign said," she reflected. She stood up and shrugged out of her now well-wrinkled red dress. "I've met three of the locals. That leaves seven." She methodically stripped off her stockings and went into the tiny bathroom. "Maybe one of them will be more interested in my offer than Mr. Raider is."

She grimaced in disgust as she recalled his arrogant rudeness. Maybe the man had been out here in this godforsaken wilderness so long that his brain had calcified.

She poured bottled water into the basin with more of a jerk than necessary, and it splashed back onto her in rebuke. Carolyn dipped the washcloth into it with a little more finesse and sighed blissfully at her reward. The cool water felt delicious against her hot skin. She wondered what the town did for water. The area looked dry to her. Maybe that's why everyone had left it after the mining boom had gone bust.

Carolyn stared at her reflection in the small mirror tacked on the wall.

"All I have to do is find those seven other hardy souls who live here. Surely one of them will be able to tell me what I need to know."

She pulled a fresh linen skirt and a pale lemon blouse from the narrow closet. Her energy was coming back now, and so was her appetite.

Cold Heart was built low to the ground. Its rectangular skyline stood in stark relief against the harsh, rolling flatlands all around it. Now it was a graveyard of dark shapes and whispering shadows.

"I wonder if anybody goes out to eat here?" she muttered. It looked doubtful. "There's one way to find out...."

Carolyn locked the door to the trailer and jumped lightly to the ground. There were lights on at the saloon, and scratchy sounding music, as if it were coming from far, far away.

And voices, mostly men, laughing and joking...

Carolyn felt an uncomfortable stab of vulnerability. A woman alone in a ghost town in the middle of nowhere would make a very easy target. She clamped a lid on her thoughts and lifted her chin in determination. Alone or not, she had to see this through to the end.

She walked up the dirt street and onto the raised wooden sidewalk that ran beside the tumbledown buildings. A few moments later, she was pushing open the swinging doors to the old saloon and walking inside as if she did it every day.

There were a few more people there than the first time she'd dropped in. Four men were seated around a table, drinking beer and playing poker. The saloon-keeper was hovering over the radio, trying to get a new station, while the retired lady of the evening nursed a drink from her perch on a bar stool.

Conversation ceased, and everyone turned to stare at her.

"Hello," she said with her usual forthrightness. "Mind if I join you?"

Chair legs scraped the floor, and three men stood up as one.

"No, ma'am," came the chorus of replies from the poker table.

Only one man remained seated and unspeaking. Jonathan Raider, naturally.

Their gazes met, and to Carolyn it was like walking into a stone wall. He hadn't softened much, even if he did look a lot cleaner than before. She saw the sardonic glint in his eyes and blushed angrily as she realized that he might be misconstruing her staring as fascination. Men! Give them a little eye contact and they think you're issuing an invitation, she thought, feeling an annoyance far deeper than the circumstances warranted.

Abruptly, she turned her attention to the other three men. They'd been so immersed in admiring her that they didn't appear to have noticed her lapse. That knowledge helped her relax, and she smiled at them with a mild sense of relief. Of course, she was careful not to make it too personal or inviting a smile. She certainly didn't want *them* mistaking her intentions, too!

The saloon keeper had abandoned the battered black radio and turned his attention to the first new customer he'd seen in weeks, nearly months. He was a big, barrel-chested man in his mid-fifties who prided himself on knowing what was going on in the more deserted regions of Humboldt County. An open, friendly grin split his face, and he proceeded to fill the lengthening silence with his booming voice.

"Carolyn Andrews, wasn't it?" he asked her, although there was no way he could have forgotten. There weren't many afternoons when a stranger came into town, especially one as attractive as she was.

Carolyn gave him a grateful look. He was going to make it easy for her and do the introductions. She felt an unexpected sense of relief, and some of her tension eased away. She could take charge when she needed to, but she didn't want the people here to start off with the impression that she was some pushy, big city type. She needed someone to break the ice socially for her, to ease her into the small, independent circle of people that made up this lost oasis. Since Jonathan Raider had made it clear that he wasn't interested, saloon keeper Samuel Zee would do just fine.

"Yes," she replied. "Mr. Zee, wasn't it?" she inquired.

The saloon keeper laughed and shook his head.

"Only to the IRS. To everyone else, it's Sam."

He nodded toward the three men still standing and staring at Carolyn with undisguised curiosity.

"That lanky fella in the red-and-blue check shirt is Scott Longsworth. The dusty-headed man next to him is his brother-in-law, Rainey Jacks. And the old geezer next to him is Cyrus King."

The "old geezer" didn't look that old to Carolyn, maybe mid-forties, at the outside. The men guffawed at the description, except for Cyrus, who managed to look both dismayed and flabbergasted without moving more than a small muscle in his face.

"I don't know why the hell you'd tell a pretty young lady something like that, Sam!" Cyrus complained, alternately eyeing Sam and Carolyn. "After all, we don't get many pretty young girls around here. You don't have to make us any less appealing than we already are!"

"You *couldn't* be less appealing than you already are!" Sam shot back emphatically, not missing a beat.

Everyone laughed, chair legs again scraped the floor as the men started to sit back down, and Carolyn walked toward the bar. The ice wasn't exactly broken, but it sure had a good-sized crack in it.

Marlene, the retired "businesswoman," smiled lazily and swirled the ice in her drink as Carolyn sat down next to her. She glanced in Jonathan Raider's direction, her shrewd eyes narrowed in speculation.

"Evenin'," she drawled in a smoke-husky voice that strongly resembled a big cat's growling purr.

"Hi," Carolyn replied.

Sam Zee asked her what she wanted to drink, and Carolyn asked for a beer. Marlene took another sensuous sip of her bourbon on ice and crossed her legs at the knee. Her soft polyester dress clung to her like a provocative friend, suggesting everything but revealing nothing.

"Did you find Jonathan?" Marlene asked curiously as she rested her elbow on the bar. She didn't seem to be in much doubt of the answer.

Carolyn took the thick glass full of foaming golden brew and downed a healthy swallow before replying. This afternoon she had found Marlene easy to talk to, approachable. Maybe that was a remnant of her profession. Whether it was or not, however, Carolyn needed someone to confide in, and if Marlene was willing, Marlene it was going to be.

Amusement tinged with irony filtered into Carolyn's eyes. Cold Heart seemed to have a predominantly male population. Marlene's extensive experience with that sex might prove to be quite helpful.

"Yes, I found him," Carolyn admitted.

Marlene tilted her head a little to one side and waited. She seemed at once mildly entertained and fairly sure of what she was going to hear. "And?" she prodded gently.

Carolyn shrugged and gave a half laugh. ''And he said he had better things to do than talk to me.''

Like stripping naked and taking a bath. The memory flashed vividly through Carolyn's mind. She tightened her hold slightly on the heavy glass of beer. She'd tried to blot out the sight of him when it happened, and a part of her had almost succeeded. But one rebellious remnant had defiantly refused to obey the command and had looked at him with rapt attention. That traitorous piece of her now served up the glimpse again: his tall, tightly muscled body glowing in the golden sun and sporting all the endowments she would have imagined.

Carolyn stiffly returned the glass to her lips and drank. The chill, salty taste gave her something else to think about.

Marlene watched with feminine interest as Carolyn's cheeks flushed a soft coral pink.

''That's what I thought he'd say,'' she admitted. ''From the look on your face, he must have made his point quite memorably.''

Carolyn nearly choked on the last swallow.

She put the empty glass down and shook her head when Sam asked her if she'd care for another. She shouldn't have drunk it so fast, especially on an empty stomach. The beer had been cool and refreshing, but it was hitting her already, leaving her just a little light-headed and sending a warm flush all over her skin.

Carolyn turned toward Marlene again. She wanted to steer the conversation away from the ubiquitous Mr. Raider and onto fresh ground.

''Is there anyone else around here who might be willing to help me, Marlene?'' she asked.

Marlene stared at her thoughtfully. Her eyes ran slowly down Carolyn's figure, taking her in with a cool professionalism that was detached enough not to be insulting.

''Maybe,'' Marlene granted. ''You're pretty. Men do some outlandish things for pretty women. The problem is, honey, that this is a busy time.''

Carolyn looked a little surprised, and Marlene smiled in amusement.

"Just because you can't see anything happening doesn't mean nothing's going on," Marlene explained.

There was a burst of noise at the poker table, and Scott Longsworth threw down his cards in disgust. Cyrus King was happily taking in the small pile of one dollar bills while Jonathan reshuffled the deck and dealt. Scott pushed his chair back and held up his hands in exasperation.

"Next time is my time," he swore to his friends. "My pockets are empty. Rob yourselves."

Cyrus muttered, "Suit yourself," and Rainey grinned. Jonathan lifted an eyebrow and merely offered the deck to Cyrus to cut.

"They do this all the time," Marlene explained, leaning familiarly close to Carolyn as they watched the men. "This is the Thursday night poker game. Sometimes some of the other men come in, too. Mostly it's those four. You'd think by now they could read each other's minds and would be sick of playing." She was looking at the men with mild exasperation and an almost maternal indulgence.

Scott Longsworth walked over and slanted a defensive look at Marlene.

"You know something better to do with Thursday nights?" he demanded.

Marlene shrugged her soft shoulders and batted her eyes at him in affected innocence.

"No, honey," she replied. "I wouldn't have the foggiest idea."

Scott slid onto the tall, backless stool next to Carolyn and looked her over with interest.

"We don't get many visitors here," he pointed out with a smile. "Anything in particular bring you to Cold Heart, uh, Carolyn, wasn't it?" She knew he had no doubt whatsoever that her name was Carolyn.

"Yes. And it is Carolyn." She smiled back at him, a little more warmly than the smile she'd given the group earlier. "I want to study the wild mustangs around here. I'll need some help, at least in the beginning.''

If she made the job seem small and time-limited, maybe the grinning cowboy sitting next to her could squeeze it into his schedule. Scott looked harmless enough. A big, friendly, healthy young man.

''No kidding?'' His grin broadened considerably. ''What kind of a study? Not another one of those things the BLM is always doing?''

''No.'' He was right there. The Bureau of Land Management had nothing to do with this. Carolyn tried to come up with enough of an explanation to interest him. Only, what *would* interest him? Riding around the countryside would probably be a busman's holiday for him, she thought. ''I'm going to write an article about them.''

He looked at her with a mixture of increased interest and decreased respect. Carolyn found that hard to understand and rather annoying. What was it about the people around here, anyway? Did they have something against the written word, for crying out loud?

Marlene was watching Scott as if waiting to see which way he was going to go. From the look of masculine interest in his eyes, part of him would obviously have cheerfully helped Carolyn go about her business, no matter what it was. Unfortunately, another part of him didn't appear to be so rash. He was definitely hesitating.

Something was holding him back.

He sighed regretfully and glanced first at Raider, then at Marlene, and last at Carolyn. He gave her a reluctant grin and eased off the stool.

''Sorry, Carolyn. I'd like to help you. Right now, we're bringing in the stock…seeing which ones wintered well and which didn't…how many calves there are…'' He stood in front of her, arms hanging at his sides. ''Maybe later…''

There was something about the way he said it, though, that made it sound like never.

''Nice meeting you,'' he said, touching his right index finger to the side of his forehead, as if saluting goodbye. "Night, Marlene. Sam." He gave a dismissing wave to his poker buddies and ambled out of the saloon. The sound of his boots faded quickly.

Carolyn looked at the saloon doors as they slowly swung back and forth. She glanced at Jonathan and found he was watching her, a grim smile barely softening his hard mouth. It was as if he was telling her to forget it. No one around here was going to provide her with any help. She might just as well climb into her beaten up trailer and drive back to wherever she'd come from.

Determination hardened in her. She turned back to Marlene and Sam. "Is there anyplace around here to buy food?" she asked.

They looked a little surprised.

"Yeah," Sam said. "There's the General Store. But it's only open on Saturdays." He gave her an apologetic look. "Can't afford to keep it open all the time. Nobody's around. Everyone's workin'."

Marlene slid off her stool and gestured toward the doors.

"Why don't you come home with me, honey?" she suggested easily. "I was just going to go fix myself some dinner. It's just down the street." She chuckled a little. "We can trade war stories...."

Carolyn accepted the offer and put some money on the bar to pay for her beer. As she followed Marlene out, she glanced at the poker table. Jonathan Raider was watching her leave. From the veiled, dark look on his face, something was eating at him. Nothing big. But it was annoying, all the same.

A tiny streak of satisfaction shot through Carolyn at the speed of light. Good. Let him be annoyed. She found the idea of taciturn, irritating Jonathan Raider being put out absolutely delightful.

Her satisfaction certainly showed in the confident lilt it gave to her stride as she marched out into the night.

"Damn!" Raider said under his breath as she vanished. "Damn!"

Cyrus was looking at him in surprise, and so was Rainey.

"What's the matter?" Rainey asked as he looked at his losing cards, then at Cyrus'. "You don't like beating us five hands in a row? What the hell do you want, Raider?"

Jonathan was staring hard at the empty air where she had been moments before. "Peace and quiet," he muttered darkly.

Ripples of discontent swirled around him, through him. He hit the cards sharply against the table and briskly set about shuffling them together. She'd leave town soon. No one would help her. No one around here, anyway.

Then she'd leave.

Rainey and Cyrus were staring at him.

"Are you gonna shuffle all night, Raider? Or are you gonna deal?" Rainey asked, a little testy. People tended to get that way when they were losing money.

Raider dealt. Cards blasted onto the table as if shot from a Gatling gun.

"Sorry I asked," Rainey muttered.

Marlene's house was like Marlene: timeless, well-preserved and discreetly displaying its underlying talents. Carolyn could see the neatly painted exterior in the soft lamplight. Marlene had a fully functioning, antique gaslight in front that gave the lemon-lime hues of the wood frame building an incandescent glow in the moonlight.

"I feel like I've stepped into the Gay Nineties," Carolyn said, admiring the carefully restored bric-a-brac and gingerbread edging on the front porch and second-story roof.

Marlene opened the door. It hadn't been locked. The lights had been left on, too.

"I always like people to feel I'm at home," she explained, even though Carolyn hadn't asked. She smiled in welcome and stretched out one soft arm to motion Carolyn inside. "It's a quaint little house. I always wanted a Victorian home." Her smile broadened.

The interior was as Victorian as the exterior, with dark, heavy drapes swagged back to reveal delicate white gauze curtains close to the square-rigged windows. A large, dark Oriental rug woven in the heavily floral patterns of central Persia lay, a huge, melancholy swirl of colors, in the middle of the room. There were tall, stiff Chinese vases in blues and yellows, reds and whites, filled with paper flowers in eternal bloom, and stately, dark cherry furniture.

Marlene noticed Carolyn's gaze, and a look of exasperation fluttered across the older woman's carefully preserved features. "I'm going to build a greenhouse in back," she said in that sandpapery voice of hers. "Next spring I'm going to have *real* flowers in here. The house is going to smell of roses and gardenias, and every week I'll have something new in bloom."

Carolyn followed Marlene into the dining room and sat down. The table was laid for dinner for six, with a pink linen tablecloth, matching napkins folded like butterflies, and antique silverware, English bone china, and crystal stemware from Ireland. Carolyn was impressed. And curious.

"You're surprised?" Marlene asked, amused. She was leaning against the white doorjamb that separated the dining room from the kitchen.

Carolyn nodded apologetically. "I'm sorry, but, yes. I guess I didn't expect something so elegant out here."

Marlene seemed pleased.

"That's one of the reasons I restored it and moved here," she drawled. "I wanted a rebirth...a new life...fresh. I wanted...to do something outrageous." She laughed. The sound had a faintly raucous undertone, as one might expect from a woman who'd spent her life helping men live out their fantasies. "For me, *this* was doing something outrageous. It probably wouldn't seem that way to people who'd lived boringly predictable, normal lives," she admitted. She gave a live-and-let-live shrug of indifference toward those plodding souls. "Cold Heart is interesting that way. It gives us outsiders a chance to be bizarre simply by doing the normal things in life."

Her eyes narrowed slightly as she watched Carolyn. "So

tell me, what are you really doin' here, honey?'' she asked bluntly.

Carolyn blinked. Marlene's shift in topic caught her off guard, especially after the disarming soliloquy about her own motives in coming to Cold Heart.

Marlene didn't appear to be in any great hurry to hear the answer to her question, however. She turned toward the kitchen, busying herself there with making dinner. She pulled a tray of cold cuts and a loaf of bread out of the refrigerator. A few minutes later, Carolyn was custom-making her own sandwich in the dining room while Marlene poured iced tea into their glasses.

''As I said,'' Carolyn began carefully, ''I'm interested in the mustang problem. I'm here to do some research on the subject.''

Marlene nodded in obvious disbelief. She took a long drink from her glass of tea and picked up her sandwich.

''Okay. Whatever you say, honey. So... Jonathan turned you down? That's too bad. He's about the only man around here who can spend the time on this. Besides, he knows more about the herds than anyone else.'' She laughed softly. This time there was an almost tender light in her eyes. ''I tell him he's just like those mustangs. Wild and ornery, and as independent as hell.''

Carolyn murmured something noncommittal and shifted the conversation away from the mustang man.

She didn't want to talk about him. She didn't want to think about him. Jonathan Raider made her feel wary and uncomfortable and something else...something hard for her to put her finger on.

Chapter 2

Cold Heart moved gently into morning as Carolyn slept fit-fully in her cramped little bed, knees pulled up and her arms rigidly crossed over her breasts. Suddenly the harsh, triumphant shriek of a swooping bird of prey pierced the stillness, bringing her instantly upright. She was barely awake, the world just a haze. It took her a moment to realize where she was.

Outside, the fearful cry faded as quickly as it had come. The hunter, a red-tailed hawk, was already far away, its victim dangling from its spiked talons. For Carolyn, however, it wasn't over so quickly. She felt caught, like the hawk's hapless victim. Trembling gripped her like a fist and wouldn't let go.

"It's only a bird," she whispered to herself.

She sank her shaking fingers into her unruly cloud of hair. She was so tense; everything startled her. It had been like this for months on end. Ever since Abel's stroke and the insurance investigation and the night they'd lost a fortune and a lifetime all at once...

She was worn out from the struggle, but she couldn't rest yet. Not until she'd found the missing piece of the puzzle. When that was done, she'd give herself six months on an island in the sun and nothing but relaxation and pleasure.

"Ah...for some relaxation and pleasure..." she murmured wistfully.

The image of a tall, muscular, dark haired man, stretched out in the sun next to her, made her smile. He had a warm, even tan that gave his virile contours a deep, golden glow. And the trunks he was wearing might just as well have been made of invisible thread for all they hid!

Then it dawned on her whose body she'd conjured up in her fantasy vacation, and the smile died on her lips. She tossed the tangled sheet off and got out of bed. Grumpily, she reached for her jeans on the hook on the back of the closet door.

"Get out of my vacation, Jonathan Raider!" She muttered the warning out loud for extra emphasis.

She yanked the jeans on, one leg at a time. That was all she needed! Jonathan Raider and a desert island. What had happened to her taste in men, anyway? The sun must already be baking her brains.

"Maybe it's just been too long since I went on a date," she grumbled. Dating had certainly been one of the numerous casualties of the past twenty-four months. And before that... She recalled the man she'd been planning to marry not so long ago and grimaced even more.

"Maybe I'm one of those women who have great instincts about everything except men."

It was not a comforting thought. She brushed her hair with a punishing vengeance, as if it would purify her of her stupidity where the opposite sex was concerned. She firmly believed that if you knew your shortcomings, you could overcome them. Unfortunately, sometimes it took some effort to do the overcoming.

"There." She sighed approvingly as she put down her instrument of torture and turned her thoughts toward the day that lay ahead.

"First, breakfast…"

She was in the miniature kitchenette in two steps. It took only a few minutes before her toast and juice were half-finished. She was beginning to get used to the claustrophobic feeling of the place. It certainly was a far cry from the house in Long Beach, though.

Her lips curved in a soft, affectionate smile. She and Abel had lingered over breakfast on many a morning. He was forever arguing with her to take over more of the firm's operation so he could pursue his investments more closely. And she'd parried that she had her own interests to pursue and didn't relish being the tough businesswoman at the top of their mini-corporate ladder.

The cramped metal and linoleum of the present closed in on her from all sides, and her tender reminiscence was swallowed up in bitter reality. The firm was bankrupt. His investments were in escrow. Only her own trust fund and financial assets were supporting them now.

How had the world gone so topsy-turvy on them? Despair gnawed at her anew. She loved Abel more than anything or anyone. She'd been loyal, as only an adoring daughter could be. In spite of all the evidence, she couldn't believe that Abel, her godlike father, could have done what his accusers claimed.

She'd stood by him when even his oldest friends and closest business associates had fallen silent, beset by doubts and the preponderance of the evidence marshaled against him.

And she'd stood by him when the man she was going to marry had given her an ultimatum: give up her stubborn refusal to accept her father's guilt or give up the marriage. With anguish and fury, she'd thrown his engagement ring in his face.

It was then that she'd realized something inside her had died. The love and affection she'd felt for her fiancé had been fading for weeks. She had watched him back away from her, a step at a time, in her hour of need.

"That's the one good thing that's come out of this disaster," she said, addressing her feckless love. "I found out what you were really made of, Gary. And, unlike most women, I was lucky enough to find out before it was too late."

Disillusionment had given her a steely kind of strength. Even when she was mentally and physically exhausted, that strength was there for her to draw on. Now, after losing so much, she was more determined than ever to find the answers that would set Abel Andrews free. For those answers would not only liberate him, they would free his daughter, as well.

"I'll prove it, Abel," she vowed. "Even if I have to spend every last dime we have, and we end up spending the rest of our lives in this mousetrap of a mobile home!"

She could just imagine his disgust at having to do that, and she laughed as if he were there with her.

"I'll just have to see to it that we don't end up here!" she reassured the absent Abel.

To do that, she was going to need a few things that she didn't have. It was about time she phoned the man in McDermitt she'd talked to last week.

Sam had a telephone.

Carolyn headed for the saloon. In Cold Heart, it was always open.

Jonathan Raider saw her as she was leaving Sam's a little while later. He was walking down the street with a bridle slung over his shoulder just as Carolyn came through the swinging doors and stepped onto the dirt street.

Most people wouldn't have noticed the slight hesitation in her walk as she recognized him. Raider wasn't most people. He noticed.

"Morning," he said.

Never had Carolyn been greeted with such dispassion. Not even by her enemies. She bristled. That annoyed her even more.

"Good morning, Mr. Raider," she responded, coolly polite.

She refused to slow down, which meant that she met him in the street and had to walk alongside him for a few strides.

"Got a big day planned?" he asked. He eyed her curiously, shifting the leathers dangling over his shoulder into a more comfortable position.

"That all depends on your definition of big."

Carolyn decided that she could be just as uncommunicative as he could. If this was the way the man carried on conversations, so be it.

He skipped defining "big" in Cold Heart terms and went straight to the point. "I figured you'd be long gone by now, lady."

Carolyn wasn't aware that she was stretching her stride and walking faster to keep up with the long-legged cowboy.

"I can't imagine why," she retorted. "As you pointed out yesterday, I didn't just happen to run into this little town. It took some effort to get here. I'm not about to leave just because the first person I asked for help isn't interested."

Raider's expression darkened. "I heard the second and third persons weren't exactly jumping up and down with joy at the prospect, either."

Carolyn glanced up at him in surprise. "News travels fast," she said, a little sarcastically.

Raider strode on, unperturbed. "It's a small town."

That had to be the understatement of the year.

Raider turned the corner and headed for an old barn. Carolyn's trailer lay in the opposite direction. There was no point in pursuing Raider. He'd made his position perfectly clear. Carolyn turned stiffly toward her mobile home.

She would kill some time looking at the maps again. The man from McDermitt ought to arrive this afternoon, which meant that tomorrow she could start searching. On her own.

The airport in Denver was crowded. A fast-moving storm was dumping snow in the Rockies, leaving airplane schedules in chaos. A slim man in a neatly pressed, charcoal-gray suit was pacing back and forth, frowning now and then at one of the numerous computer monitors suspended from the wall behind the airline ticket counter.

The green lettering flickered and changed. The man halted and stared intently as the newest flight information appeared on the screen.

"It's about time," he muttered darkly.

He pulled out a cigarette and wandered over to one of the lounge areas. The flight he'd been waiting for was finally going to arrive. An hour and a half in the airport hadn't improved Gary Lord's temper, and his temper had bordered on the unbearable for several weeks, as it was.

Lord ground the cigarette out in the tall steel ashtray and gave the plump teenager next to him a black scowl. He wasn't in the mood to see people who were so obviously happy. The gum-smacking adolescent snapped her fingers and hummed off key to the music in her earphone radio. Lord got up and walked over to the baggage claim area where the man he was meeting would soon be.

"Hurry up, damn it all, Gagan," Lord muttered to his soon-to-arrive associate. "If you'd taken the flight I told you to, we'd already be in Elko! And I'd know exactly what Carolyn is doing."

That was why Gary Lord had been making life miserable for just about everyone recently. Carolyn had dropped out of sight without a word to anyone. He'd spent quite a chunk of money tracking her down, and he didn't want her getting any farther on her little jaunt without his knowing exactly what she was up to.

If the stubborn little witch had only done what he'd told her to, they wouldn't be tearing all over the country like this. He would have had everything under control. That was the way Gary Lord liked things: under his control.

Carolyn pulled a heavy, wine-red sweater over her head. The cable stitched wool rippled over her as she tugged the bottom down around her hips. The added warmth felt good. The temperature was dropping as the sun went down. The unseasonably warm weather had blown on to Utah, and the cooler temperatures of early spring in Nevada were returning with a vengeance.

The sound of an engine and tires drew her attention outside. A glance through the window confirmed what she'd expected to see. Her four-wheel-drive Jeep had arrived from McDermitt. The driver's partner was parked nearby in a battered, once-green pickup. Apparently he wasn't planning on staying long. He was keeping the engine idling.

The Jeep driver was at the door when Carolyn came out of her trailer. He pushed back his stockman's hat and smiled the easy, open smile of a native-born Westerner.

"You Carolyn Andrews?" he drawled.

"Yes."

"Would you mind signing this?"

He held out the papers verifying that the delivery had been made. Carolyn signed her name quickly.

The driver touched his finger to his hat brim. "Thanks, ma'am. Nice doin' business with you."

With that he sauntered over to the waiting truck and swung up into the passenger seat. The two men pulled out, raising dust as they went, heading back up the road toward far-off McDermitt.

"Nice doing business with you, too," Carolyn murmured, immensely pleased that her wheels had finally arrived. "Now I can get started."

With that heartfelt statement, she opened the Jeep door.

Jonathan watched the battered truck disappear down the road, heading east. He noted that the Jeep wasn't making the return trip. Obviously the lady wanted to drive while she was vacationing here, he thought. A dry smile creased his face. Northern Nevada in early spring was a pretty unlikely vacation spot. That brought him back to the question he'd never gotten an answer to: what was Carolyn Andrews doing here?

Curiosity ate at him. That annoyed him to no end. He didn't want to be curious about that ash-blond beauty. She was out of place here. She belonged in a city or on an estate some-where, with gardeners and chauffeurs and servants to do the dirty work.

That wasn't the kind of life that interested him.

Real life: that was what he respected.

And he certainly wasn't going to permit himself to be curious about a writer, of all things! He'd been roasted over a slow fire by writers five years ago. They'd taken pieces of facts and arranged them to suit themselves. The stories had made sensational reading. The newspaper and magazine owners must have been grinning all the way to the bank from the avalanche of sales that had resulted.

The fact that they had destroyed some innocent people along the way had gone unnoticed.

He was standing in front of his shack, the lariat he'd been mending still dangling from his hand. Angrily, he twirled it up over his head. It whipped the air vengefully. In one quick snap, the length of it coiled out and snagged the hitching post off to one side of the building.

Raider gave the lariat a savage tug.

He wasn't ever going to completely rid himself of the fury he felt over that disaster and the writers who had fed on it. They'd cost him enormously. The fact that he'd outsmarted them at the end and managed the legal maneuvers to protect the property under dispute was small consolation. It hadn't saved the lives of two of the people he'd loved.

Nothing could change that. Kimra was dead. So was his brother. And he was an outcast.

The lariat was rigid from the force of his anger. The strands bit into his hand, close to cutting the flesh. The pain finally broke through the rage that had engulfed him.

He snapped the rope loose and dragged the loop back to him, coiling the braided length methodically, coolly.

He heard an engine start a few blocks away, across town.

Raider draped the coiled lariat over the peg on the front porch and ambled toward the Silver Dollar Saloon. He'd be damned if he'd listen to the carefully groomed Ms. Andrews gun her Jeep!

She'd blow out of town soon enough. Then things would return to normal. He could hardly wait. In the meantime, he'd have a beer and a sandwich with Sam and Marlene. The sound of Sam's jukebox should drown out everything else within earshot.

And what he didn't hear, he wouldn't think about.

Carolyn left early the next morning, when the sun was barely above the horizon. The soft, rustling sounds of awakening wildlife stirred over the rolling landscape as she drove over an old dirt trail leading northward.

The map was sketchy, though it had all the terrain markings an engineer could want. The map under it was more conventional, but just as full of big, blank sections.

"That's why they call these the wide open spaces," she joked under her breath.

The Jeep bucked over bumps and ruts, but Carolyn was relieved to endure them. She'd rather bounce over a rough road than have to cut her own way through the sagebrush and underbrush that spread across the land as far as the eye could see. When she ran out of road, as surely she would, she would be ready.

On the seat next to her lay binoculars, a compass and a photograph of what she was looking for. It was a picture of a horse standing on a ledge hung over a slender, twisting river. It was an aerial photo taken six months ago by a Bureau of Land Management mustanger.

The horse in the picture was hard to see clearly. One thing was beyond question, however. The horse didn't look like a mustang. He looked like a Thoroughbred.

Raider spent the day in the barn in town. It served as a livery stable as well as a blacksmith's shop for the tiny community. It had come in handy during a couple of surprise snowstorms and any number of rainstorms. The blacksmithing business had been pretty brisk for the past five years, too, ever since Jonathan had come to town and taken it over.

Scott Longsworth rode in, leading a limping mare by a rope tied to a hackamore. He slid off his horse and approached the corner where Raider was mending a damaged saddle.

"Morning," Scott said easily. "Here she is," he added, pointing to the palomino gingerly resting the tip of one hoof against the straw-strewn floor.

Raider eyed the mare and nodded. The horse belonged to Candy Jacks, Scott's sister and Rainey's wife. She was everybody's kid sister. Except for Rainey, that is. To him, she was one hot little number.

Scott admired the skillful repair work on the bridles and saddles spread around the shop.

"When did you learn to do this, anyway?" he asked curiously.

"When my saddle and bridle broke when I was growing up," Raider replied shortly. "My old man said fix them or walk." Raider shrugged eloquently.

Scott laughed and led the limping mare to a stall and closed her in.

"That's what they call necessity mothering invention, huh?" he joked. "This country's too big to walk in."

Raider nodded and snipped off the excess strand of leather from the bridle he'd been working on.

Scott swung up into the saddle and looked down at Raider before departing.

"Say, I saw that pretty girl driving across the range about twenty miles from town as I was coming in. What's she doing out there, anyway?"

"Looking for mustangs," Raider replied sarcastically.

Scott chuckled. "Not in the direction she's heading."

"Good," Raider said. "Maybe when she doesn't see any broomtails in a couple of days she'll get tired and go home."

Scott looked a little wistful as he reined his gelding and backed the horse slowly out of the barn.

"That's too bad," he said forlornly. "I was hopin' we could get a little dance going one Saturday. She looked like she might be a pretty good dancer...."

Raider glanced up sharply, but Scott's horse was already turning away, and he couldn't see the young man's face. Raider leaned on the bellows and worked up the heat in the fire by the blacksmith's anvil.

"See ya, Raider," Scott called out as he disappeared from view.

"Yeah."

Raider pumped harder. The coals turned white-hot under the continuous blast of oxygen-rich air.

A good dancer. Raider envisioned her swirling around a dance floor, effortlessly in rhythm with her partner's every step. He could imagine what she would feel like in a man's arms, too. She'd be light and curved in just the right places, her softness brushing elusively against him....

Raider pumped the bellows vigorously, raising a brilliant fire that blasted the air with a burning shower of red and gold ashes. The heat building inside him had no place to go, however. It just burned.

"You keep that up and you'll burn the place down." Marlene chuckled as she wandered into the big barn. It was quite a sight, Jonathan Raider beating the blacksmith's furnace into flames like that.

Raider stopped. "What can I do for you, Marlene?" he asked.

He picked up a horseshoe with a pair of long black metal tongs and heated it in the small furnace.

Marlene watched in amusement. She wasn't fooled by his cool, tough exterior. The man showed all the signs of frustration. He was tight and stiff-jawed and not too sociable. Not that Jonathan usually won any sociability contests. But even for him, this was a little short and unfriendly. After all, they'd known each other for a very long time. And quite well, at that.

She walked over to one of the box stalls and caressed the nose of the horse that came to greet her.

"I was wonderin' how my little mare was doing," Marlene said.

"She's fine. I'll shoe her this afternoon. You ought to be able to ride her again tomorrow."

Marlene held out an apple, and her horse greedily crunched it up. Marlene glanced at Raider. "Guess she decided to go it alone..."

Raider grunted. He knew who she was talking about. He wasn't the kind of man to pretend otherwise.

"I imagine she'll have a hard time getting close to any mustangs."

"I imagine so." Raider didn't bother to look at Marlene. He concentrated on bending the shoe on the anvil.

"Of course, she'd be gone sooner if someone would take her to them."

Raider took the shoe off and plunged it into a bucket of cold water. He held the tongs out in front of him and examined the shoe carefully. It was exactly how he wanted it. He put it down and turned his full attention to the mischievous Marlene.

"She'll be gone sooner if she has no luck," he countered.

Marlene looked skeptical.

"Why are you so interested in this, anyway, Marlene?" he demanded. His annoyance showed through this time.

Marlene's face softened. Small crow's-feet appeared at the powdered corners of her eyes as a tender smile warmed her aging face. "I had a long talk with her the other night at my place." She shrugged philosophically. "I liked her, Jonathan. I think you would, too."

Raider's annoyance deepened. He knew what Marlene was doing, and he didn't want any part of it.

"I came here five years ago to enjoy the solitude, Marlene," he reminded her. He spoke curtly, warning her off the subject.

"I know that, honey...."

"When I want female companionship, I know where to find it."

Marlene grimaced in the earthy way only she could.

"Don't try putting me off with that, Jonathan Raider! I know exactly what kind of motives send men to hunt up that kind of female 'companionship,' and I also know you too well to swallow that line."

Raider reached for his jacket and tugged it on, ignoring her. "Believe what you want, Marlene. I'm not interested. Not in Ms. Andrews, and not in her so-called study."

Marlene pulled her full-cut winter jacket around her and followed Raider out of the barn. "You don't believe her, then?" Marlene asked curiously.

"Nope."

He didn't miss a stride in answering.

Marlene fretted over his reply.

"I have to agree with you there, Jonathan. She never would open up and tell me anything different, but I had the same feeling myself when I was talking to her. But what could it be, honey? There's nothin' here but a ghost town and a bunch of livestock."

Raider pulled up short, and Marlene's head snapped up to see why.

A big truck was pulling into town. A very big truck. Two men were in the cab, peering through the windshield.

"Now who the hell are they?" Raider muttered, his face darkening in a frown. "We've had more visitors in the past few days than we've had in the past few years!"

The truck's engine was cut. The two men pushed open the doors of the cab and stepped down, stretching their legs a bit. They looked as if they'd been traveling for some time. From their well-laundered appearance, they didn't look like men who drove a truck for a living.

"Is this Cold Heart?" one of them called out, forcing a superficial smile onto his face as they approached Raider and Marlene.

''If I told 'em no, do you suppose they'd go away?'' Raider muttered under his breath.

''I don't think so,'' she replied softly.

Marlene frowned slightly. There was something familiar about one of the men. She couldn't quite place him, though. Where had she seen him before?

The slimmer of the two newcomers stopped a few feet away as Raider finally replied to his question. ''Yep. This is Cold Heart. Who are you?''

The strangers didn't seem to mind Raider's directness.

''I'm Gary Lord. This is Rance Gagan.''

There was a moment of silence as Lord and Raider sized one another up. When it was obvious that Raider felt no obligation to continue the conversation, Lord cleared his throat and resumed speaking.

''We're looking for a friend of mine. She should have arrived here within the last few days. You wouldn't happen to have seen her, would you? She's about five foot five, blond hair, brown eyes.''

Carolyn Andrews.

Raider studied the two men a little more closely. Yes. These two could well have stepped straight out of Carolyn Andrews' fast-track world.

They wore designer-label, tailor-made leisure clothes. They smelled of expensive cologne. Even their hair was a giveaway. Men didn't get cuts like theirs at a corner barber shop on a Saturday morning. They walked and talked like ambitious young urbanites.

There was something else, though, something that bothered him. There was an underlying predatoriness about these two that set them apart from her. Carolyn Andrews might be a huntress, but in Raider's estimation these two men were raptors.

''Her name is Carolyn Andrews,'' Lord added, growing a little annoyed at the lack of response to his previous question. ''Has she been here?''

The two men stared intently at Raider and Marlene. The

obvious nonverbal pressure tactic angered Raider. He didn't like being pushed around.

"Were you supposed to meet this woman someplace specific?" Raider drawled, staring back at them with a hard look in his eyes.

He was uneasy giving them information about the irritating Ms. Andrews. He found his protective instincts rising in spite of his determination not to have anything to do with her. After all, she was a woman alone in the midst of a vast, empty land. Maybe it was his old shepherd's instincts coming to the fore. You didn't throw a young ewe to the wolves.

Lord didn't appear to be very pleased. Raider still hadn't answered his question. Gagan was harder to read. A blankness had settled over his features, thoroughly masking his feelings.

"Have you seen her?" Lord repeated, ignoring Raider's question as Raider had previously ignored his.

Carolyn was discouraged. The sun was low in the west, and the eastern sky was growing dark. She hadn't seen anything that resembled a mustang all day. She'd passed some stray cattle, a little gaunt from winter and still wearing their shaggy, cold-weather coats. There had been a few calves, more than a few jackrabbits, miles of uneven terrain, and endless stretches of undulating gray-green sagebrush.

But no horses.

She saw the tiny cluster of buildings grow larger as her four-wheel-drive vehicle ate up the distance between her and Cold Heart. She was looking forward to getting back. It was getting colder, and it had been several hours since she'd finished the lunch she'd packed.

"You didn't expect to find him on the first day, did you?" she chided herself aloud. "Look on the bright side. Now you know a few square miles where the horse *isn't*."

Considering how big northern Nevada was, that wasn't a terribly comforting observation. Besides, mustangs were notorious gypsies and weren't known to be impressed with man-made state boundaries. The horse she was searching for could have wandered up into southern Oregon. He could be almost anywhere. It was like looking for a needle in a haystack, especially since she didn't know the first thing about the territory or the mustang herds.

Carolyn grimly shook off the feeling of defeat that threatened her. Finding that Thoroughbred stallion was a long shot, but it was the only shot she and Abel had left, so she was just going to have to take it, whether she liked it or not.

She'd reached the edge of one of the dilapidated buildings of Cold Heart and put the Jeep into second gear. As she drove up onto the flat, hard dirt, she saw the four people standing in the middle of the street. Her heart froze.

"Gary…" She was barely aware of saying his name. She was stunned to see him here. Stunned and appalled. He must have followed her. No one had ever done that before. It was a chilling thought.

The sound of Carolyn's Jeep had caught their attention; they were all staring in her direction. As soon as Lord and Gagan recognized her, they broke away and approached her. Carolyn braked twenty feet from Raider and Marlene, frowning suspiciously at her ex-fiancé and his associate.

"Well, Gary," she said as he reached her. "Isn't it a small world? What brings you to northern Nevada?" Her sarcastic tone and the flat look in her eyes made it clear that she knew exactly why he was here and didn't like it one bit.

Gary put his hands on the door and leaned through the window to kiss Carolyn on the cheek. She didn't move. The touch of his lips left her cold, and angrier than ever.

"Please don't do that, Gary."

There was a hardness in her usually soft voice that conveyed the depth of her feelings. She didn't want him to touch her with such familiarity anymore. She found it deeply offensive.

Raider was watching. That bothered Carolyn almost as much as Gary's unwelcome gesture. She didn't want taciturn, arrogant Jonathan Raider to think that a snake in the grass like Gary was close to her. She didn't want anyone to think that. Even at this distance, she could see the cynical glint in Raider's eyes as he observed Gary's welcoming kiss. That made her even angrier. How dare he look like that! Especially since she'd done nothing to invite Gary's attentions.

Gary withdrew a little, but he obviously wasn't about to accept defeat so easily.

"I was worried about you, Carolyn," he said in the low, husky voice that used to thrill her so. "As soon as I heard you'd come here, I took some leave and caught the next flight out of Los Angeles."

"Why?" she asked curiously, leaning back to study him as he answered. She couldn't imagine why he would suddenly become concerned about her welfare. It certainly hadn't been uppermost in his mind the last time they'd talked at any length.

"This is no place for a woman alone," he replied smoothly. "I know how tough things have been for you recently, Carolyn. Running away like this isn't going to help."

She looked at him in honest bewilderment. He sounded like his old self: protective, possessive, polished and suave. He'd always been good about blending those traits in the amounts guaranteed to fascinate a woman. For a moment, she was tempted to believe him.

"Running away? I'm not running away, Gary," Carolyn protested. She was surprised he'd think that of her. Surely he knew her better than that.

"What are you doing here, then?" he prodded, speaking in the soothing, intimate voice one uses with a person who needs to be calmed down.

But Carolyn had developed a finely tuned ear during the past tumultuous two years. It was a sixth sense, and it served her well now. There was a shrewdness in him that came through the carefully stated question. Carolyn heard it, and her defenses tightened. Her initial confusion vanished. For a moment she'd almost believed him again.

No. Gary Lord wouldn't have rushed out here to save her from making a foolish mistake in a moment of depression.

Gary would be here to protect Gary's interests. Whatever they were...

"I'm on vacation, Gary," she replied. There was a steely tone in her voice this time. "I'm thinking of taking up writing as a career, since the last career I had is apparently on the rocks. So why don't you fly back out to California on the next available commercial airliner going that way. I'm fine. Thanks for your concern, but I can take care of myself."

His cheeks reddened in anger, and the warmth left his eyes with remarkable speed. "Just because things didn't work out between us, that doesn't mean I don't still care about you, Carolyn."

Carolyn put the Jeep in gear and nodded, but the look she gave him was skeptical. "I wish you hadn't troubled yourself, Gary," she said. "Now, if you don't mind, I'd like to get going."

He stepped back and let her pass.

Carolyn managed to smile at Raider and Marlene as she drove slowly by them. Marlene looked curious. Raider looked as if he couldn't wait for all of them to be long gone.

I won't be staying a moment longer than necessary, Mr. Raider, Carolyn thought grimly. She pulled up in front of her trailer, locked the Jeep and marched inside.

She had the feeling that Gary wasn't going to turn around and go back to California right away. What a perfectly nauseating thought. Now, in addition to having to search for that stallion on her own, she was going to have to evade Gary Lord and his friend Rance Gagan while she was doing it! She didn't know why Gary had come here, but she was sure that it wasn't to help her out.

"Nobody said life was going to be easy, Carolyn," she muttered as she put her kettle on to boil and reached for a can of soup to warm up.

Her life was certainly proving that saying to be true.

Raider was standing at Marlene's parlor window, holding back her drapes a little as he stared through the sheer curtains.

The dark streets were empty. Even the saloon was quiet tonight. Sam was doing his bookkeeping, and he got annoyed
when people interrupted his arithmetic to ask for drinks, so
people stayed away as a rule.

When Marlene had suggested he come by for supper, he'd
taken her up on her offer. Her front windows had a view of
one corner of Carolyn Andrews' trailer. Of course, that hadn't
had anything to do with his decision. That was just coinci-
dental, he told himself.

Marlene ladled out the stew she'd been simmering all afternoon and carried the wide, shallow bowls of steaming supper to the dining room. She couldn't help the discreet chuckle
that escaped her when she noted the direction of Raider's
intent gaze.

"Dinner's on the table, Jonathan." She sat down and del-
icately shook out her pearl-gray linen napkin. As he joined
her, she glanced at him askance. "Did anybody go to her
trailer?" she asked innocently.

Raider sat down. "Nope."

"Did she go out?"

"Nope."

The silence that ensued was broken only by the sound of
soup spoons touching china.

Marlene took a sip of her ice water, then turned her wide-
eyed, guileless look on Raider as he sat back in his chair.

"Why don't you just go down there and knock on her door
and make sure she's all right before you turn in?" she suggested reasonably.

Raider glowered at her. "She's a big girl. She can take care
of herself."

Somehow Marlene managed to keep a straight face. "I
see," she drawled. "Is that why you've been watching her
trailer like a cop on a stakeout, honey?"

Raider shot her a quelling look, but Marlene just chuckled
good-naturedly.

"How about a hand or two of blackjack before you go?"

she suggested, reaching for the deck in the table drawer nearby. "It'll cool your temper."

"My temper's never been cooler," he growled. "Deal."

And he'd be damned if he'd look through that parlor window again!

Chapter 3

Carolyn rose a little after dawn, ate a cold breakfast, packed a lunch and filled a large Thermos with coffee. She drove out of town to resume her search and returned at sunset empty-handed. The following day, she did it all again. The pattern was repeated over and over as she patiently covered the land in a grid pattern.

As the days wore on, she began seeing small bands of horses in the distance. As soon as she got within a half a mile of them, however, they'd gallop out of sight. They seemed to be heading toward the low mountains that lay northeast of Cold Heart. Day by day, Carolyn pursued them, methodically covering new ground.

She didn't know how Gary Lord and Rance Gagan were faring, only that they were still in town. She was so tired when she got back to her trailer in the evening that she just ate, washed and fell asleep. All she saw of them was their truck.

Raider, on the other hand, always seemed to be crossing her path, to her everlasting consternation. One morning he'd be leading a mule toward the barn when she was leaving, another morning he was walking past her car. He rarely said much, just a grunt of hello and an off-putting frown.

After a while, she made a game of smiling sweetly at him as she drove by, bundled up in her crimson hunter's cap and lambskin coat. There was a perverse pleasure in smiling at the man when he so clearly still thought she should go back where she'd come from.

Late in the week she caught sight of Scott Longsworth and Rainey Jacks rounding up cattle in one of the quadrants she'd covered the previous day. They hailed her, but were too busy to ride over and talk.

It was about then that she realized she hadn't had a real conversation, or even spoken aloud, for nearly a week!

Late in the day, just when she was beginning to succumb to despair again, she saw a mare running along the horizon. The colt at her side was what interested Carolyn. She lifted her binoculars and focused.

The mare was clearly a mustang. She was small and wiry and moved with the feral instincts of a wild animal. She was a bay with black stockings and no redeeming grace or beauty in the shape of her head, shoulders, barrel or legs.

The gangly-legged colt, however, was a horse of a different color, literally and figuratively. He had the long, spindly legs she'd seen over and over at foaling time in Kentucky and California. The haughty tilt of his head, the refinement in his tiny face, the lift of his tail as he tripped and ran alongside his dam, marked him as a blue blood of the horse world.

His color was familiar to her, too. It was the juvenile version of a beautiful shade of chestnut: precisely the color of the stallion photographed on the ledge.

That colt hadn't been sired by a mustang stallion. He was the offspring of a Thoroughbred.

"You're out there somewhere!" Carolyn cried triumphantly into the wide, rolling emptiness of the range.

Her discouragement had metamorphosed into exultation. She was close. Very close. Her slender thread of hope grew a little stronger.

"I'm going to find your papa," she vowed, watching the colt and his dam tear pell-mell over the small hill and out of her sight. "And when I do, somebody is going to pay for what they did to us."

It was then that she noticed she wasn't alone anymore. As she swept the horizon with her binoculars, searching for some sign of the stallion, she saw something else. It was a small pickup truck, almost too far away for her to see.

It wasn't moving. When Carolyn turned back to town, heading toward the pickup, it roared out of sight. It, too, was going in the direction of town. When she got back, she saw it again—parked behind Lord's oversize truck.

He was following her.

That night, Carolyn didn't sleep well in spite of her exhaustion. She didn't like being stalked. Worse, it made her go back over the last two years, trying to remember where Gary had been just before the fire, and just after. It made her wonder whether she'd misjudged him even more than she'd thought. The idea made her feel ill.

Surely he couldn't have been involved in *that*.... Gary was ambitious, she knew, but he wouldn't have gotten involved with something so crude, so illegal, as arson...would he?

Carolyn tried not to think about it. She flopped over on her stomach and pulled the pillow on top of her head, wishing she wasn't quite so alone. At a moment like this, the companionship of a friend would be worth more than gold.

But her friends, the few that remained, weren't here.

After a restless night, she set out again. The temperature was rising a little, staying in the sixties. At least the sun was on her side, she noted with a sense of optimism.

To her surprise, Raider wasn't around when she left this time. She slowed down and looked for him, even though she was a little embarrassed to find herself doing it. Funny. She'd come to enjoy their little nonverbal exchanges every morning. The clash of wills had been...invigorating. And then he'd been around in the evenings, too. It had made for a strangely comforting end to the day.

"You're really hard up, Carolyn," she muttered in exasperation. She gunned the engine and bounced over a bump and onto the open range. "If you miss Jonathan Raider's nasty temper, you've been away from civilization for too long!"

Even so, she wished he'd been there.

Where was he?

Raider was sitting on a rangy, ten-year-old gelding and watching the sky turn from purple and rose into pale, powder blue. He liked it here in the foothills. Their beauty always awed him, especially at times like this, when the night was passing into day and winter melting into spring.

The land was rich with promise. New growth was budding in the trees. The yellow flowers of the antelope bush were ripe and full. The brilliant red Indian paintbrush was splashing its last dabs of blossoming color higher up.

He stood in the stirrups and stretched his legs a little. He'd gotten stiff doing odd jobs around town for the past week. It felt good to get out and ride again. Off to the west he could see Cyrus, Scott and Stoneface George bringing in more Longsworth stock. To the south he could make out the telltale haze of dust made by Carolyn's Jeep.

"Good morning, Ms. Andrews," he said under his breath. "Sorry I missed you this morning."

He had intended to be sarcastic, but as soon as the words were said, he knew that he'd meant them. He *had* missed seeing her stubborn little chin and that ridiculous red hat and the way she jounced around inside the Jeep when she flew over that bump. And he'd missed that butter-wouldn't-melt-in-my-mouth smile she shot at him like an arrow from a bow.

He sat down in the saddle and urged the gelding down toward the cattlemen.

Maybe it was just as well he hadn't been there this morning, he thought. A man could make quite a fool of himself over a woman. And Carolyn Andrews was the kind of woman that almost any man would be tempted to do idiotic things for.

The gelding gingerly picked his way through clumps and thickets of sprawling creosote bush until he reached a narrow trail that cut through the sagebrush and scrubby plants that flourished as far as the eye could see. Raider touched the horse lightly with his heels, and the gelding broke into a rocking-chair lope.

He told himself that he wasn't going to think about her anymore. He was going to concentrate on cattle. He shook his head and made a sound of disgust. Like hell he was.

Carolyn drove straight to the rugged, low-rising mountains. The photograph had been taken in this vicinity five months earlier. If she was lucky, maybe the Thoroughbred had taken a liking to the range and was still here, returning as spring melted the snows higher up.

If he'd survived the winter, that is.

That was the one thing she feared most. Was the stallion still alive? A Thoroughbred who'd spent his life in stables and on racetracks wasn't prepared for the harshness of life in the wilderness. If predators hadn't killed him, rival stallions might have. Or he could have sickened from eating something poisonous, or starved to death because he didn't know how to forage.

In two hours she'd reached the sparsely treed foothills.

Since she planned to spend as much time searching as daylight allowed, she'd brought along extra food, a sleeping bag and a couple of gallons of water. She would camp out in the Jeep overnight. That would give her all of today and part of tomorrow to scout the area.

She drove the Jeep up as far as she could. Within a half an hour it became clear that the ground was too overgrown to be traversable by vehicle.

"This is where I get to stretch my legs a little," she told herself as she climbed out.

Carolyn shrugged out of her coat and left it in the Jeep. By now the temperature had risen into the high sixties; her sweater was warm enough. She fastened the canteen onto her belt, looped the binoculars around her neck and reached for the compass she'd laid on the dashboard.

She squinted a little and shielded her eyes as she searched for a natural trail to follow. Then she strapped on the revolver she'd brought along.

There was a lot of ground to cover. If she could get a good lead, though, she'd come back later with a horse and pack mule.

As she began hiking up through the piñon pine and juniper, she wished again that she wasn't alone. She hadn't been out in the wild like this since she was a teenager. With every crack of a branch or flap of wings, she felt herself tighten defensively.

Most animals would go the other way if they were aware of her presence. It was the one that she came upon by surprise that might turn and attack. Her hand slid down over the small revolver holstered on her right hip. She was counting on scaring any attacker off before either she or it came to harm.

Much as she hated to admit it, she wished Jonathan Raider had accepted her job offer. She had the feeling that nothing on God's green earth would have the temerity to attack *him*.

"Nasty-tempered man," she muttered under her breath.

She took one last glance back in the direction of Cold Heart. There was no sign of Gary Lord.

"Wherever you are, Gary, stay there. Much as I'd like some help, yours I can do without."

A stone loosened beneath her boot and slid down the sparsely covered slope on her right. Carolyn felt a premonition of danger and frowned as she watched the small landslide of pebbles cascade down to a dry riverbed fifty feet below.

The sound had startled the animals in the vicinity, as well. Birds flapped frantically into the air, and small furred animals rustled the bushes as they dashed for cover. Another sound instantly attracted Carolyn's attention. She jerked her binoculars up and peered in the direction it had come from.

"Bingo!" she murmured happily.

The snort and stamping of hooves had been real. She glimpsed three frightened mares jump up and over a fallen yellow pine, then nearly trample one another in their eagerness to gallop up the twisting mountain trail on the other side of the riverbed. Before she could get a good look at them, they had disappeared behind huge boulders.

Carolyn quickened her pace. The horses had come back. If only the one she wanted was among them…

Scott Longsworth lit the small portable stove he always brought along at times like this. It had been a long, hard day, and they were all ready to sit down on something other than a horse and have something fresh and hot to eat. Rainey was tying the horses nearby, and Cyrus was hunting for the big metal coffeepot in back of the pickup truck. The sun would be down soon. Already the temperature was beginning to drop.

He looked up to see Stoneface George lead a fresh horse to Jonathan. Raider, who'd just unsaddled the horse he'd ridden all day, was obviously not sticking around for supper.

Scott shoved his hat back on his head, perplexed. "Hey…I thought you were camping out with us, Jonathan."

Raider, who was managing to look as stone-faced as their Paiute friend, tightened the cinch on the mouse-colored horse he'd just tossed a saddle on.

"I changed my mind," Raider said curtly.

Scott stood up and watched in consternation as Raider swung up into the saddle. "You're coming back later, aren't you?"

"Yep. Later tonight, or sunup tomorrow."

"Where're you going? If you don't mind my asking," Scott inquired sarcastically. Damn it all! Raider could have told him…

Raider checked to see that his bedroll was securely tied to the back of his saddle as Stoneface George brought him a rifle and slid it into its leather case strapped on the front.

"Our big-city visitor hasn't left the mountains yet. She's been there all day, and she never went back to town." Her telltale dust had never appeared in the sky signaling her return. "I'm going to ride over and make sure she hasn't done anything terminally stupid."

The others all immediately volunteered to come along, but Raider shook his head. "If I need help, I'll shoot you a signal." He snorted in disgust. "There's no point in all of us wasting our time baby-sitting."

There was a chorus of good-natured male laughter as Raider turned his horse away.

"It's a good thing the women around here didn't hear you say that, Raider!" Rainey Jacks shouted out as Jonathan rode out of camp. "One of these days some girl's gonna lasso you and show you just how tough a pretty little thing can be!"

Carolyn looked at her watch. She only had about an hour of daylight left. She picked up her pace a little as she hiked back down the mountain trail, retracing her steps from earlier in the day. She was sorely tempted to drive back into Cold Heart, even if she had to do it in the dark. She needed a horse to track the mustangs. Trying to gauge their habits on foot was going to take forever.

She wondered whether the Longsworths might be willing to rent her one of theirs. She didn't relish the prospect of having to buy, feed and stable a horse while she was here.

A coyote howled, sending a chill down Carolyn's spine. It made her think how large a horse was and how big it could make its rider feel. At the moment, she wouldn't have minded that one bit.

Carolyn descended the twisting trail as rapidly as she could. Finally she rounded a bend, and she could see the range again. Her Jeep was less than a quarter of a mile farther down.

She was just beginning to relax, thinking that the toughest part of the day was behind her, when a sharp crack ominously shattered the wilderness's tranquility. She stopped immediately and searched for the source of the sound. Surely no one

was out hunting? It wasn't the legal season for the more pop-
ular game.

Of course, not all hunters concerned themselves with such
details....

Another shot rang out. The bullet struck the wall of rock
fifteen feet away from her. Bits of dirt blasted in all directions.
The next shot hit the dangling limb of a western juniper growing from a ledge above her.

Carolyn crouched as she looked up, raising her arm to ward
off anything falling on her. It was too late.

There was another sharp report. This time the high-powered
rifleman hit the boulder just overhead and to her left. The
scraggly branch tumbled down, accompanied by a shower of
small rocks.

Carolyn had no time to react. The shrubby juniper branch
hit her shoulders and the rocks mercilessly pummeled her
back and hips. She felt each razor point as she cringed, pro-
tecting her head with her arms.

"Hey! Stop shooting!" she screamed at the top of her
lungs. Couldn't the idiot see her red hat, she wondered furiously. It wasn't even dark yet! She dropped onto her stomach.
"Cut it out!" she shouted. She could only pray that whoever
was out there could hear better than he could see!

The next shot whizzed by just inches above her back.

Carolyn rolled without thinking. She had to get out of the
hunter's line of fire before he killed her.

"Stop!" she shouted again, as loud as she could. This time
her voice was shaking.

Another shot bit into the dirt barely a foot away from her
head. Carolyn flinched and twisted away. Suddenly there was
nothing beneath her, and she was falling through the air. Falling, falling, falling...

Raider was walking his horse around Carolyn's car, relieved that everything looked in order, when he heard the first
shot. He reined the horse to a standstill and frowned. At the
second shot, he pulled out his binoculars and tried to see who

was doing the shooting. After the third shot, he heard Carolyn scream faintly in the distance.

He dug his heels into the horse's sides and rode as hard as he could up the trail in the direction of her voice. With each of the next shots, he flinched a little. He hoped like hell that none of them had hit her. He reached for his rifle to fire some warning shots, hoping it wasn't too late.

Carolyn felt the cold water envelop her. She was plunging downward, feet first, into a deep, natural well. The springwater closed over her head, and the shock of it kept her from breathing at first. Then, instinctively, she kicked and stroked, pulling herself upward. When her face broke through the surface, she was gasping for air to fill her bursting lungs.

Her hands brushed over the rough rock wall that encased the pool on all sides, searching for a hold.

Carolyn shook her head and opened her eyes, grasping the bumpy rock with aching fingers. It wasn't much to hold on to, but it was better than nothing. Her heavy clothing was soaked. She would have very little chance treading water in it.

She heard a rifle again, this time very close. Three shots rang out in sharp succession.

"I'm down here, you son of a..."

She lost her grip and got a mouthful of water before kicking back up and regaining her precarious position. She was sputtering and choking when she heard the unmistakable sounds of hoofbeats on the trail and a man jumping to the ground.

"Get me out of here!" she shouted furiously.

The cold was awful. She began to shake uncontrollably.

"Hur-ry up!"

"Yes ma'am!" called the insolent male voice she'd been hearing in her dreams lately. Not in her wildest nightmares, however, had she ever expected to see him like this.

"N-n-not y-y-you!" she groaned. She leaned back and looked up. Sure enough, Jonathan Raider was sprawled out on the ledge on his stomach and staring down at her, a rope in his hand.

"None other," he growled. "You're hardly in a position to complain about who rescues you, lady," he pointed out angrily.

He tossed the lasso neatly around her shoulders.

"Don't c-call me lady!" she shouted back. The way he said it made it sound like the worst kind of insult.

Carolyn let go of the rock with one hand at a time and wriggled her arms through the loop. Her fingers, rigid with cold, couldn't hold on any longer, and suddenly she was floundering in the water again. It was harder to kick her way up this time. She was feeling numb all over, and her hands and arms wouldn't react anymore. She felt the rope tighten and bite into her, but it was as if it were happening to someone else very far away.

The furious male bellowing, however, was unmistakably aimed at her.

"Hold on to the rope, damn it! Carolyn!"

It was his shouting her name, oddly enough, that got through to her. She could hear the note of pleading buried beneath that furious order, and something deep within her responded. In an act of sheer will, she managed to get her other arm up and hold on to the rope.

She was still in the water, but he was pulling hard enough to keep her from sinking. Then she was being hoisted up into the air like a sack of potatoes, lurching upward and upward and upward. At last she felt his arms around her, and she was unceremoniously hauled over the lip of the trail and dumped on the ground.

"I—I...never...knew...ten feet c-c-could...s-s-seem...so f-f-far..." she said. It took great effort and concentration to say it, too, considering how hard her teeth were chattering.

Raider yanked the lasso off her and quickly coiled it over the saddle horn. He gave the patient horse who'd just obediently pulled Carolyn out of the water a quick pat on the neck, then grabbed the bedroll from the back of his saddle.

Carolyn was making an effort to get out of her wet clothes, but her fingers were so stiff, it was an uphill battle.

"Hold still," Raider ordered roughly as he snatched her soaking-wet sweater and pulled it up over her head. He was none too gentle about it, either. Her boots, jeans and shirt followed immediately, but Carolyn was too cold to care.

He wrapped her in his blanket and squatted in front of her, looking her over with a mixture of anger and exasperation. Carolyn stared defiantly back, still feeling more frozen than thawed.

"Did you find any mustangs down there?" he asked bitingly.

"Why were you sh-sh-shooting at m-m-me?" she demanded angrily.

For once he looked speechless. A dull red crept into his cheeks. He was furious. "If *I'd* been doing the shooting, *Ms. Andrews*, you'd be in the happy hunting ground right now."

His hard words hurt her, but she was relieved to hear him deny having shot at her. Carolyn's shoulders slumped a little in exhaustion and reaction. If Raider hadn't done it, whoever had was still out there and wasn't coming forward to see if she was all right. That was an ominous thought.

"I'm s-s-sorry," she murmured. Her voice had dropped to a whisper. The trembling was getting worse. "I j-j-jumped to the wrong c-c-conclusion...."

Raider was scanning the rocky cliffs and piney ridges surrounding them on three sides. He didn't appear particularly interested in her apology.

"I don't think this is the best place to talk," he pointed out grimly. "Come on. I'll give you a ride back to your Jeep."

He stood up and offered Carolyn his hand. She took it and weakly got to her feet. On the way to his horse, he scooped up her damp clothes, which he tied onto his saddle.

"Do you ride?" he asked skeptically. He looked as if he'd need to be convinced of it if she said yes.

Carolyn's temper flared anew. "Yes! As a matter of fact, I *do* ride, Mr. Raider," she snapped.

And with that she mounted the startled gelding and lightly settled in the saddle, gathering the reins with the ease of an experienced horsewoman.

Raider could see that she knew how to ride. He could also see the enticing curve of her thigh a few inches in front of him where her blanket had pulled back.

Carolyn blushed and yanked the blanket over her leg.

"If you've seen enough, would you mind if we left?" she asked sharply.

Her gibe didn't help his temper at all. "I've seen *more* than enough," he retorted darkly.

He stalked over to pick up her binoculars, revolver and holster, and red hunting cap which had been flung off during her mad roll over the cliff and subsequent high-speed disrobing.

"Here." He shoved them at her and mounted, sitting behind her.

Carolyn sat stiffly, clutching the blanket, as Raider took the reins and urged the horse back down the trail at a steady walk toward Carolyn's Jeep.

She could feel his thighs and knees brush hers from time to time, and the heat from his body warmed her back. She was still angry with him, although it was becoming difficult to recall precisely why. She just could *not* seem to carry on a normal conversation with Jonathan Raider, no matter what the circumstances.

His arms touched hers, and she was surprised at how much she enjoyed the contact. He was strong and muscular in a loose-limbed, rangy way. He was like the mustangs...tough and wiry and strong. It was so tempting to think of leaning back against him....

Just for a little while...

"You planning on sleeping in the saddle?"

His voice was a warm rumble just behind her ear. Groggily,

she dragged herself awake. With a sudden rush of embarrassment, she realized that the warmth enveloping her wasn't just the blanket. Jonathan Raider was holding her in his arms. They were still riding double, but the horse wasn't moving anymore.

They'd arrived at Carolyn's Jeep.

Carolyn sat up straight and pulled the blanket tightly around her. "I'm sorry," she said quietly, flustered by their unexpected intimacy.

He was sitting there, not moving. She wished she could see his face, know what he was thinking. "Raider..."

"Hm?"

"Thanks for coming to my rescue. I...I'm sorry for what I said earlier...I mean about thinking you might have been the person shooting at me."

Carolyn clenched her fingers. Why was the blasted man still sitting there, not saying anything? What was he thinking?

"You saved my life...." She turned and looked at him, eyes open and honest. There was no more anger there. "Jonathan...thank you..."

He didn't look angry anymore, but Carolyn wasn't sure how to read the enigmatic expression that had replaced his fury. His slate-blue eyes were darker, and there was a grimness in the set of his jaw and the tightness of his mouth. His mouth... She wished...

No. She wouldn't let herself think that. Not even for a tiny fraction of a second. Because he might see it in her eyes and put his arms around her and kiss her. And right now, she wasn't sure what she'd do if he did. No. That wasn't true. She knew *exactly* what she would do, and it frightened her.

She dropped her gaze and waited for him to dismount. As if feeling a similar need to put a little distance between them, he did just that.

"You're welcome," he said tightly.

She dismounted and freed her wet jeans from the bundle tied to the saddle horn. She retrieved her key from the damp pocket and unlocked the door.

Raider watched, perplexed, as she searched through a small pile of things in the back.

"I brought other clothes," she explained. She glanced at him, trying to sound calmer and more confident than she felt. "Uh, would you mind turning your back?"

He shrugged and turned away, but not before Carolyn saw the gleam of amusement in his eyes and the barest hint of a grin beginning to curve his mouth.

"*You* didn't," he reminded her.

Carolyn scrambled into the jeans. "I don't remember having much of a choice!" she retorted. She couldn't help smiling, though. The nerve of him! She buttoned the blouse as fast as she could. "Did you think I'd leave town out of shock?"

His short laugh was muffled by her heavy sweater as she pulled it over her head.

"I don't know what I thought," he admitted, somewhat reluctantly. As he recalled, thinking hadn't been uppermost in his mind that first day.

She backed out of the Jeep and looked at him, her arms folded protectively in front of her.

"You can turn around now," she said awkwardly.

He wasn't exactly smiling, but there was definitely an amused cast to the way he was looking at her. It was hard for her to remember that they didn't particularly like one another when he looked at her like that.

Her heart warmed, and she decided that it must have showed in her face, because something subtle changed in him. He was a little too still, and his gaze had become more intense in a subtle, elusive way.

"Would you like something to eat?" she asked, seizing on the first rational thing that came to mind. They couldn't just stand here and stare at one another like this, she thought rather desperately.

She didn't wait for his answer. She leaned back inside the Jeep and started prying open the bag containing what was to have been her supper and breakfast.

She turned, food in hand, to find Raider scanning their surroundings with her binoculars.

"Can you see anyone?" she asked.

He shook his head and turned his attention back to her. "No. I don't suppose you have any idea who might have been taking potshots at you?"

Carolyn shook her head. "I thought it might have been a hunter..." She wished she could still believe that.

Raider didn't say anything. He put the binoculars on the front seat and took the sandwich Carolyn was holding out to him.

"You don't think it was a hunter mistaking me for some kind of game?" she asked when it became obvious that he wasn't going to comment without being prodded.

He raised his eyes to hers and held her gaze. "No. I don't."

Carolyn poured some coffee into a Styrofoam cup and handed it to him. She wasn't looking forward to staying out here alone tonight. She turned a little away and put her sandwich back in the bag. She'd lost her appetite, too, it seemed.

Raider saw her sleeping bag and supply of water and looked at Carolyn in consternation. "Were you planning on camping out?" he demanded.

"Well...yes..."

"Alone?"

He made no effort to disguise his feelings on the subject, she noticed. Obviously he thought she was out of her element, not to mention her mind.

"Yes. Is there a law against that?" she asked testily. She was too tired to put much punch into the retort, though.

"They don't pass laws for things like that! You're supposed to have enough common sense not to do them!"

Carolyn put her hands on her hips and faced him, drawing herself up as tall as she could. It didn't help a whole lot. She still had to look up at him, since he was six foot and she was five foot five.

"I didn't *want* to do it, Mr. Raider," she informed him. "And right now, I want to even less than before. But I have to. If you'll recall, I did ask for help when I first got here. I even offered to pay for the help. No one's interested. What do you want me to do? Pack my bags and leave? I can't do it.'' She said each word slowly and distinctly. ''I can not do that.''

He moved toward her, trapping her between his body and the Jeep, pressing his palms against the door so she couldn't slip away. She couldn't have moved, anyway. She was so startled by the suddenness of his attack and the nearness of his body that she stood as if mesmerized.

''What the hell is going on?'' he demanded, raking her face with a searching look. ''Someone tried to kill you. Don't give me that drivel about writing about the mustangs, either! People don't get shot at for that.''

Carolyn was holding her breath. The tension in him was filling the air around her. She felt it like hot electricity running through her. It was intimidating and exciting all at once. It made her feel vividly alive.

He lowered his head slightly. For one long moment, she thought he was going to kiss her. She could almost feel the hard warmth of his mouth on hers as she remembered the sensation of his muscled arms and solid body pressed against her.

He stopped a few inches away, as if struggling with himself.

''Cold Heart was a quiet little town before you got here, Carolyn Andrews,'' he muttered. ''I don't appreciate strangers showing up and destroying that.'' His eyes narrowed. ''Now, tell me the real reason you're here. If it makes any sense at all, I'll try to help you.''

She searched his face.

Could she trust him with the truth?

Chapter 4

The tension built as the silence lengthened. Carolyn could see the impatience growing in him as she hesitated, weighing the risks in answering him honestly.

She wanted to trust him. He had the qualities of toughness and aloof independence that would make it very hard not to rely on him in a tight spot. And he couldn't very well be a friend of her enemies. Living out in the middle of nowhere as he did, he probably knew very few people at all.

Raider was still staring hard at her, a frown tightening inexorably on his face as his patience withered away. His square jaw was clenched a little to contain his temper. She could see a muscle working in the flat plane of his tanned cheek. His eyes were turning the color of flagstones at midnight, and looked just as impervious to appeals for sympathy.

"You're asking a lot, Jonathan Raider," she said quietly, biting her lower lip in indecision. She'd made a serious mistake in judging the character of at least one other man in the recent past. Was she about to make a similarly disastrous blunder now?

Raider's mouth hardened in anger, and his brow furrowed in warning. "Maybe," he conceded. There was no discernible sympathy in his voice, however. "As I see it, lady, you don't have much of a choice. You need help. I'm willing to consider giving you mine. Do you want it or not?"

She saw something else in his eyes then. It was a warmth buried deep inside. He quickly closed it off, keeping his feelings veiled beneath a veneer of toughness and logic. But she'd seen it. That glimmer swayed her. Yes. She'd risk it.

Carolyn took a deep breath to steady her resolve and leaned her head back a little, resting it against the Jeep. Exhaustion was sapping her strength, and now that she'd decided what to do, she let herself feel her weakness and her physical need to lean on something.

Before she answered him, though, she had a question of her own to ask. It had been bothering her ever since they'd reached the Jeep and she'd begun to think more rationally about what had happened that afternoon.

"How come you were so close when I was drowning in that pool?" she asked curiously.

Her question caught him by surprise, and it showed in his eyes. The look was gone as quickly as it came. He wasn't pleased she'd asked, though, and that showed clearly.

"I saw you go out this morning. I never saw you return. I've told you before, I like the peace and quiet here. I wanted to make sure you didn't spoil that by getting into trouble while you were wandering around."

Carolyn eyed him thoughtfully. He wasn't being entirely honest with her. If he were worried about her, though, why wouldn't he just say so? He didn't strike her as the kind of man who would be cautious about telling a woman that he cared about her. He didn't appear to be the kind of man who would be cautious about anything, as a matter of fact. Quite the opposite—he was blunt and outspoken to the point of rudeness!

"Why don't you want to say you were worried about me?"

she asked in genuine consternation. "If you expect me to be honest with you, you'd better be honest with me!"

"All right, damn it!" he bit out angrily. "I was worried about you! I didn't want you breaking your stupid neck or getting trampled by an angry stallion or falling off a cliff or being bitten by a rattlesnake! Now, what in hell are you doing out here?"

If she could have stepped away from him, she would have. His blistering anger was overwhelming her. As she leaned back to get away from his fury, she found herself pressed against the metal of the Jeep door.

He closed his eyes and sighed. "Relax," he muttered. He straightened up and crossed his arms in front of his chest. "I'm not going to attack you."

"I know that," she said softly. She was shaking a little, and it wasn't from exhaustion, or the cool night air.

Her eyes opened wide, ingenuous and a little shocked. The shock came from suddenly discovering her own complex feelings about him. Even as she'd instinctively sought to escape his superior strength, she'd yearned for him to come after her and overwhelm her with it.

What was happening to her? Desperation rushed over her as she struggled to ignore the upswell of primitive feeling he was evoking. She didn't want to have to face that. She didn't want to feel this way about him. It was the wrong time, the wrong place, and Jonathan Raider was most definitely the wrong man! But her heart was still pounding heavily, and the blood was singing through her veins, igniting her with knee-weakening thoroughness. She closed her eyes and tried to concentrate on the feel of cold metal against her shoulders and back. Anything to regain the strength in her spine.

When she opened her eyes again, she was a little more in control of herself than she'd been before. Raider hadn't moved. He stood like the mountains nearby, carved from the earth with a giant chisel and waiting for her reply. He was as enigmatic as ever.

"I'm searching for a dead horse," she said, forcing a cool and businesslike calm into her voice through sheer willpower.

His eyebrows shot up in obvious skepticism.

She shrugged and gave him a small, grim smile. "Everyone believes he's dead, that is," she explained. "Everyone but me. I think he's alive, and I came out here to prove it."

Scott Longsworth was staring in the direction Raider had gone hours earlier.

"I still think one of us should go and check on 'em," he protested, frowning anxiously at his bone-tired friends. "I don't like those rifle shots."

Stoneface George grunted and poured himself another cup of black, overcooked coffee. "He didn't signal," the Paiute reminded Scott.

"Maybe he didn't have a chance to," young Longsworth argued worriedly. "What do you think, Rainey?"

His brother-in-law stood up and stretched. "I already told you what I think. About fifteen times. I think he's okay, and if he wanted our help, we'd have heard him ask for it." A sly grin slid over his boyish face, and he poked his thumbs arrogantly into his belt. "What's more, I think if one of us rides over there uninvited, we might wish we hadn't. If you want to risk having your face flattened, Scott, you go right ahead, but me...I'm going to let Raider have all the time alone that he wants with pretty Miss Carolyn."

Stoneface George chuckled and held the frying pan over the gas burning stove. "He's okay, Scott," the Indian said calmly. "No buzzards in the sky. No signal shots. No horse running loose. Don't worry about it. Pass me the bacon, huh?"

Scott tossed a slab on the skillet, and it hit with a sizzle.

"All right," Longsworth muttered, unconvinced. "It's not like him, though. Raider steers clear of other people's problems."

"Maybe this is different," George suggested.

"Maybe," Scott said thoughtfully. "Maybe."

* * *

Raider lit the tinder under the camp fire they'd built and gently fanned the flames to life as twilight painted the sky a shimmering deep blue.

Carolyn sat down and stretched out her hands to warm them. Raider joined her, sitting a few feet away. He was watching her, remembering what she'd said and the way she'd said it. Carolyn Andrews was turning out to be more complex than he'd thought. And so were his growing feelings for her.

He frowned and slowly brushed the dirt off his hands.

"Why didn't you just tell me this to begin with?" he demanded. "Why the smoke screen about the mustangs?"

Carolyn tried to explain. "The horse was...is...worth millions of dollars. I'm trying to keep my search...secret."

His look sharpened. "Why?"

"Because if he is still alive, whoever tried to make it look otherwise may try very hard to see that I don't succeed."

"Shooting you would certainly accomplish that," Raider observed curtly. He gave an uneasy look around them. The range lay in darkness. Nothing was moving. He turned his attention back to Carolyn, who had turned pale. "Who owns this horse?" he asked, pinning her with a hard gaze.

"About a dozen people owned shares of him."

"Owned?" he asked, zeroing in on the past tense.

Carolyn sighed in frustration. "It's all tangled up with the lawyers now. The insurance company is refusing to pay the claim, since they think the horse was killed to get the insurance on him. A lot of people had high hopes for that horse. He was insured for a *lot* of money."

"What happened?"

"I wish I knew," Carolyn said unhappily. "There was a fire in the stable one night two years ago. The remains of a Thoroughbred stallion were found in his stall. The poor thing was burned beyond recognition. Everyone assumed that it was Firefight. There was no reason to think otherwise."

Carolyn hated having to remember. She'd watched Firefight grow from a gangly foal cavorting at his mother's side into a magnificent, winning three-year-old. Her father had always been amused at her vehement affection for the horse. To him, Firefight had been a highly promising financial property. To Carolyn, the prizewinning champion had been a mischievous friend and a creature of imperial beauty.

Raider picked up a piece of dead sagebrush and tossed it onto the crackling fire. Burning ashes burst upward in a fiery cloud. He didn't want to see the sadness in Carolyn's face. Grimly, he pushed the image away.

He didn't want to be Carolyn Andrews' knight in shining armor. That was what she obviously needed, she of the swaying walk and the rich girl's eyes. If he let himself get involved with her, friendship was not the kind of involvement they would have. There was something about her that ignited the fires of longing in him. The heat in his body had been making that uncomfortably clear for the past couple of hours.

Friendship was out. On the other hand, he couldn't just leave her to wander around alone out here. He wanted to keep her in one piece and help her finish her business as fast as possible. All he had to do was keep her at arm's length. Think of her as…an unruly and stubborn filly…

The frown that was becoming a permanent fixture on his face faded into a slight grin.

"What's so amusing?" Carolyn asked sharply, frowning in annoyance at his unexplained expression of humor. "Have I said something funny?"

Raider wiped the smile off his face and stared flatly at her. "Nope."

He didn't think she'd find his image of her as a stubborn, unruly filly as amusing as he had. As exhausted and bedraggled as she looked now, he wasn't sure how she'd react. He decided it might be kinder to change the subject. Not that he was doing it out of affection for her, of course. It was simply…good livestock management.

"I take it the insurance company thinks the fire was arson?" he asked pointedly.

"Yes." She sank back in discouragement.

"Who do they think set it?"

Carolyn raised her eyes to his, a world of pain and a life-time of determination reflected in them. "My father," she replied stoically.

She shivered and rubbed her arms vigorously to ward off the sudden chill.

Raider threw another large branch on the fire, building up the blaze. "I take it you don't agree with them?" he asked slowly.

"You bet I don't!" she exclaimed. "He's an honorable man. He never would have done something like that. And... it's destroyed him...."

She couldn't go on. The break in her voice had made that clear. She took a minute to regain control of her emotions. Raider waited silently, staring thoughtfully into the fire.

"My father is an accountant. Some years ago, he began managing financial properties for people. One of the special-ties he developed was Thoroughbred racehorses. Our firm managed Firefight and a number of other horses for a con-sortium of owners. We handled the financial planning and supervised the execution of all the necessary legal details. The buying and selling of investors' shares of the horse, insurance, tax liability calculations, things like that... After the fire, there was an investigation, naturally. That's when they accused him."

Raider was perplexed by her description. It didn't sound as though her father was in jail, or even in court.

"Where is your father now?" he asked.

"He's in a nursing home. The day after the formal charges were made, he had a stroke. He's been unable to speak or get out of bed since."

There was a long moment of silence.

"I'm sorry," Raider said softly.

Tears gathered in Carolyn's eyes. Angrily, she brushed them away. She couldn't afford to dwell on the tragedy. All the tears she'd shed over it in the past hadn't changed any-thing. She refused to waste any more of them.

"Thanks," she said stiffly. "I'd rather not go into that, if you don't mind. Are you still willing to help me?"

She looked at him a trifle belligerently. She felt very exposed to him. Raider, on the other hand, was still a virtual stranger to her.

"Yes. Although I have the feeling I may live to regret it."

Carolyn shook her damp, matted hair and awkwardly attempted combing it with her fingers.

"Here." Raider pulled a comb from his back pocket and tossed it to her.

"Thanks," she mumbled warily.

"There are a few other things I'd like to know before we go on this wild-goose chase of yours."

"It's a horse I'm after, Raider, not a goose."

There was a hint of laughter in her eyes, even though she still looked like a woman beaten halfway to her knees. He couldn't help grinning a little in return.

"I'll give you this, lady," he conceded with some reluctance. "You've got grit."

Carolyn laughed and nodded, running her hands over her hair and arms in disgust. It had been a dirty day, all the way around.

"I'm afraid you're right about that."

Raider tore his eyes away from the enticing curves lurking beneath the blanket she'd pulled around her and tried to recall what he'd been going to say.

"Uh, the two men who came to town after you did... What do they have to do with this?"

The humor left her. "I wish I knew. I don't know how, but somehow they followed me. I tried to leave quietly on this trip, so they must have done some digging just to have found out that I was gone. Tracking me here took professional help, I'm sure."

"A private detective?"

"Probably."

Raider liked them less than ever.

"I take it you know them." He remembered the air of

intimacy that Gary Lord had worn when he'd approached Carolyn.

"One of them better than the other…"

Carolyn blushed. She hated having to admit her past relationship with Gary. He'd turned out to be so different from the man she'd thought he was. She felt like a complete fool.

"Yes. I know them. I…was engaged to Gary."

She had Raider's full attention. That only made her feel worse.

"We broke up two years ago." She obviously didn't want to talk about it.

"Before or after the fire?" Raider drawled, leaning back on his elbows and watching her curiously.

"After. Look…I don't think that has any bearing on this at all."

Raider looked at her in unconcealed amazement.

Carolyn hurried to explain. "That…was personal."

"Why the hell is he here, then?" Raider demanded incredulously.

"I don't know! He was, or is, one of Firefight's investors. Maybe it has to do with that."

"That sounds like a dandy reason to me," Raider growled, his frown returning in full force. "Whose idea was it to break up?"

"I don't think that has anything to do with this!" Carolyn shot back testily.

"You can think what you want, lady," Raider rejoined, not even slightly deterred by her objection. "But if I'm going to lead you around, I want to know if a jealous boyfriend is going to be upset about that fact."

Carolyn sat up as straight as she could, gathering her boardroom dignity in a last-ditch effort to control the direction of the conversation.

"Gary isn't my boyfriend. He isn't even the jealous type. He's just not the kind of man to make a scene over a woman. Does that relieve you of your worries, Raider?"

Raider remained unconvinced. To add to that, he was more

than a little mystified by Carolyn's past attachment to Lord.
What kind of a relationship had they had if she could describe
her ex-fiancé in those terms? He couldn't conceive of such a
cold-blooded relationship with a woman he was promising to
marry.

"What did you see in him, then?"

Carolyn blushed in a combination of frustration, anger and
embarrassment. "That's none of your business," she said
flatly. She drew the blanket up a little higher and gripped the
front folds tightly in her fist as she rose to her feet. "It's been
a long day, Raider. I'm going to sleep. Help yourself to the
front seat, if you want."

Before he could object, she marched to the Jeep and yanked
out her bedroll, spreading it out on the back seat. As soon as
she'd crawled inside and pulled up the zipper, the day's events
caught up with her. Exhaustion set in, and within moments
she was sinking into a deep sleep.

Raider followed her a little while later, wrapping himself
in his blanket and trying in vain to find a comfortable position
for his six-foot frame on the narrow front seat. The cramped
quarters made it difficult to sleep. He was forced to listen to
the soft breathing of the woman lying a few feet behind him,
whose shape and walk he'd committed to memory in spite of
himself. He wondered what it would feel like to kiss her,
although he was uncomfortably aware of how he imagined it
would be.

Most of all, he wondered what kind of man Gary Lord was.
He must have had something going for him, to attract a
woman as classy as Carolyn Andrews. Or maybe he was just
good at projecting an image of himself. Raider had met people
like that before.

And he'd despised them.

To the soft torture of listening to Carolyn breathe, Raider
gradually fell into an uneasy sleep.

"Carolyn."

She heard Raider say her name, but everything was black.

She was in the depths of sleep and deeply reluctant to leave it.

"Carolyn."

This time, he sounded a little more imperious. With regret, she struggled to wake up.

The sun filtered through cold gray clouds that had rumbled across the skies overnight. The shady, early morning light was a grim welcome for the day as Carolyn groggily opened her eyes.

Tentatively, she stretched her stiffened arms and legs while Raider leaned over the front seat and eyed her doubtfully.

"I know I look a little worse for the wear and tear I've had lately," she said testily, sitting up and rummaging around for a scarf to cover her disreputably tangled hair. "Look the other way if it bothers you!"

Raider grinned. "I hadn't noticed."

"Well, then, why the dirty look?"

His grin broadened, and a mischievous glint shone in his eyes. "Sorry. I didn't know my look could be considered dirty."

Carolyn jerked a triangular red scarf over her unstylish locks and tied it defiantly behind the back of her head.

"Whatever kind of a look it was, please don't shoot it at me first thing in the morning."

"I'll try to remember that."

There was a subtle change in him as he spoke, a deeper timbre to his voice, a trace of darkening in his eyes. Carolyn looked away and began searching for the bag of paper cups buried beneath the jumble of things that had landed on the floor last night in all the confusion.

"Carolyn."

She reluctantly looked back up at him. She wished she didn't look like a drowned rat. She suddenly had the deeply feminine urge to look nice for him. Not that she wanted any masculine attention from him, she hurried to tell herself. But it was always better to look your best for people you were doing business with. Yes. That was it. They were partners. In a way.

The look in his eyes had become more businesslike, although she had the impression it had taken a conscious effort on his part to accomplish that. When he spoke, it was in a no-nonsense tone to match.

"I've got to go back and help out Scott and the boys. They're expecting me to work on the range with them all day today."

She tried not to let disappointment rise in her, but it did.

"Look," he said, almost kindly. "Why don't you drive back to Cold Heart, clean up and pack whatever you'll need for a week? I'll be back tomorrow, most likely. We'll work out a plan then. Okay?"

"I could keep looking on my own until you can join me…" Carolyn suggested hopefully.

"Forget it." He was back to frowning at her furiously again. "I don't have time to come fish you out of mountain springs on a daily basis!" Carolyn's face had a rebellious expression, and she stubbornly stuck out her chin. "That won't happen again," she argued.

"Not if you stay in Cold Heart, it won't." He drew in a breath and through nearly gritted teeth added, "Please."

Carolyn had to suppress the laughter that rose in her. Saying please clearly did not come easily to Jonathan Raider. Her heart softened, and she grinned in spite of herself.

"When you put it that way, Raider," she said softly, "how can I refuse?"

Raider accompanied her halfway back to town, riding alongside the Jeep while Carolyn drove.

"Remember, keep an eye out for riflemen," he shouted as he reined his horse away from her.

Carolyn nodded and waved. "Right," she shouted after him.

He pressed his heels lightly against the gelding's ribs, and the horse broke into a lope.

Carolyn put the Jeep into a higher gear and stepped on the gas. Now that Raider was gone, she wanted to get back to town as quickly as possible. There were lots of things she could do if she had to cool her heels for a day. Besides, in spite of what she'd said to Raider, she wasn't all that eager to be out in the wilderness alone.

First on her list were a couple of phone calls. One to a nursing home. The other to a pilot at the Bureau of Land Management.

"Do you see her?"

Gagan was standing at the edge of town, anxiously looking over Gary Lord's shoulder, while Lord stood looking through high-powered binoculars into the rangeland.

Lord lowered the binoculars but kept staring into the rolling sagebrush. "Yeah. I see her."

"Are you sure?"

"I can see her. She's driving."

Gagan began tapping his left heel arrhythmically against the dirt. It was a habit he'd had for years, an outlet for nervous energy. "Well, now we know where she is," he observed.

"Yeah," Lord agreed drily. "But what's she been doing all night? We don't know that, now, do we?"

Gagan shrugged. "I don't think it's too hard to figure out," he argued. "She must have spent it with the local cowboy in her Jeep."

Lord scowled. "She isn't the type."

Gagan laughed unpleasantly. "They're all the type, Lord. When are you gonna grow up?"

Lord whirled to face him. "If I were you, I wouldn't say another word on that subject," he warned, eyes glittering with fury. "Not one more word."

Then he walked rapidly in the direction of their truck, leaving Gagan to ponder his threat.

Gagan, not one given to much pondering, merely shrugged and shielded his eyes, turning back to watch Carolyn's tiny Jeep grow larger as it approached town, a telltale flag of dust rising in her wake. Gagan had long ago decided that Gary Lord was not a man to be relied upon in times of stress. He was too much a servant of his own irrational impulses when under a great deal of pressure. And those impulses weren't the right ones.

Of course, with a good-looking woman like Carolyn Andrews, it was understandable that a man might get annoyed when she refused to accept him as her lord and master. It hit a man where it hurt the most: in his ego.

Gagan grinned. That was funny. Gary Lord still couldn't swallow the fact that Carolyn Andrews had rejected his offer of lordship. Gagan started laughing.

That was how Carolyn found him when she drove into town. Standing there all alone. Laughing.

Carolyn turned her back to Sam, who was wiping glasses behind the bar. She curled her fingers more tightly around the telephone receiver and bowed her head covertly. Ring... ring...ring.

"Hello. Winset Nursing and Convalescent Center. May I help you?" answered a nasal feminine voice.

"Yes. May I speak to Frances Barnes, the head nurse in—"

"I know who Ms. Barnes is," interrupted the switchboard operator in a reprimanding tone. "Just one minute, please."

The call was put through. The next hello that Carolyn heard belonged to Nurse Barnes. Anxiously, she identified herself. "Frances, this is Carolyn Andrews..."

"Carolyn! Where are you?" The normally unflappable, fiftyish nurse in charge of Abel Andrews' round-the-clock care sounded mildly alarmed.

"East of the Sierra Nevadas and west of the Mississippi," Carolyn replied, trying to speak quietly enough not to be overheard by the one other person in the saloon.

"That's not too specific," the nurse pointed out in amusement.

"I know. I'm sorry, Frances. I think it would be wiser to leave it at that for the time being."

"Hm. Sounds like something a smuggler would say," Ms. Barnes observed, obviously itching to know what was going on, but mature enough to know how to survive without having her curiosity satisfied. "I suppose you'd like to know how your father's doing?" she asked, briskly moving along to what she correctly presumed was the purpose of Carolyn's call.

"Yes. How is he?" Carolyn asked anxiously.

"He's holding his own. He's been sleeping well and eating much better than before." There was a slight pause. "He keeps looking at the door, though."

"Yes?" Carolyn prompted her.

"We think he's wondering why you haven't been coming, dear," the nurse explained gently. "Did you tell him you'd be gone for a while?"

Carolyn rubbed her forehead, trying to dispel the headache gathering there. "Yes. The last afternoon I spent with him, I...tried to explain. I told him what I was doing, and why. I told him it might take several weeks...maybe more...."

The nurse remained silent.

"I don't know if he understood," Carolyn said softly. "There were moments when I was sure he did. His eyes would look fierce and strong, just like before he got sick." She sighed and closed her eyes, shaking her head in frustration. "Then the light would fade, and he'd look at the curtains, and I wasn't even sure if he knew I was there or not...."

"Ummm. Well, perhaps he did understand," Frances mused. "He seemed agitated the day after your last visit. The aides were sure he was trying to tell them something, but no one could understand. He became so frustrated at his inability to speak, we were afraid he'd have another stroke. His blood pressure really started to soar. The doctor has kept him sedated ever since."

Carolyn rested her forehead against the bare saloon wall. "How is he now?"

"Much better. As I said...sleeping, eating. He just

seems...preoccupied. It's not like the frustration and despondency brought on by his strokes.''

"Could...could I speak to him? Would hearing my voice help?'' Carolyn asked tentatively.

"It's hard to know for sure, but in my opinion, it would only upset him more, dear,'' the nurse said kindly but firmly. "If you were here, it would be wonderful. He could see you and be reassured that you're all right. But to hear your voice...he'd be trying to tell you whatever it is that he's been trying to tell us.''

"In other words, it's not a good idea,'' Carolyn said, disappointed.

"I'm afraid so.''

Carolyn felt defeated. "Abel's always been protective,'' she murmured. "You're probably right. If he understood anything that I told him, he'd be worrying, thinking that he should be the one doing this...not me.''

The nurse murmured understandingly. "Well,'' she said, in an effort to be reassuring, "the doctor *has* restricted his visitors, and we're *trying* to keep the court people off the premises. Whenever they come by, he always has a setback. We're doing our best to keep him free of any additional stress and anxiety.''

"Thank you, Frances. I don't know what I'd have done without you all....'' Carolyn really meant it.

"Perhaps *I* could reassure him in some way that you're all right,'' the nurse suggested thoughtfully. "It might relieve some of his worries.''

"Oh, please...would you, Frances? Tell him....'' Carolyn wrapped the telephone cord around her index finger. The image of a tough and taciturn cowboy crossed her mind. "Tell him I'm safe and sound, and that I've found someone who's going to be helping me for the next few weeks. Someone I trust...someone he'd like, I think...''

The nurse sounded pleased. "Wonderful!'' she said briskly. "Now, I've got another call coming in. I'm afraid I'm going to have to go. Keep in touch, though, will you, Carolyn? I'm sure that would help."

"I'll do my best," Carolyn promised.

Her best might not be too great, she thought as she hung up the phone. They didn't have too many phone booths where she was going. Resolutely, she redialed, giving the operator her telephone charge card number and the number of the Bureau of Land Management. She couldn't help Abel by sitting at his bedside. The only way she could do either of them any good was by doing her best to find Firefight.

"Bureau of Land Management. May I help you?" said a voice.

"May I speak to Ted Weston?" Carolyn crisply replied.

"Just one moment, please..."

Scott Longsworth waved an arm in welcome as Jonathan Raider rode up to the wranglers that morning. There was no need for small talk among the men. Raider went to work without explaining how he'd spent the past twelve hours. No one asked, either.

The men worked hard, as they always did. That was one of the things that Raider enjoyed about life in Cold Heart. When you went to work, you didn't go halfway. Everyone worked their tails off until it was time to quit.

By evening, Scott was sitting on his horse, tired, but proudly surveying the cattle spreading out on the range.

"I think that about does it," he told them.

Stoneface George was already unsaddling his horse. He wanted to get the animal rested. He was leaving at dawn for the long ride back to his uncle's ranch south of Denio. Rainey had already left. He was eager to chase Candy around their big double bed and didn't care if it was obvious to the others or not.

Raider walked his horse over to Scott's and rested his hands on the saddle horn. "I think I'll leave tonight, Scott, if it's all the same to you," Raider said.

Young Longsworth's mouth fell open. "Now?" he asked incredulously.

"Yep."

"You'll be in the dark for the last half of the ride back!" Scott exclaimed. "Are you crazy?"

"I've ridden in the dark before," Raider said drily. "So've you."

Scott slung his right leg over the saddle horn and scratched his head. He'd found Raider downright perplexing recently. If he didn't know better, he'd think Raider was attracted to Carolyn Andrews.

"Yeah," Scott said, conceding Raider's observation about their nocturnal riding. "But I don't do it unless there's a damn good reason for it," he pointed out. "What's yours?"

Raider's face was about as informative as a slab of granite. "I'm ready to go," he said. There was finality in his voice. "See you around, Scott."

He turned the gelding toward Cold Heart and set off at an easy pace. He figured they'd make town about an hour and a half after dark. Right about the time Carolyn was having dinner...or maybe taking her bath...

He cursed himself for a fool. Why the hell was he thinking something like that now?

"Arm's length," he muttered under his breath. "Keep her at arm's length..."

Chapter 5

Carolyn saw Raider when he rode into town.

She was standing on the front porch of the Silver Dollar Saloon when he walked his horse into the barn that served as a livery stable. She'd had sandwiches and beer with Sam and Marlene, and had been hanging around, making idle conversation with them for over an hour.

She could have left right away. That was what she'd told herself to do. But somehow, when she got to the porch, she'd lingered, letting her gaze wander over the tidy and prim main street so at odds with the character and history of the little ghost town, not to mention its fiercely independent citizens.

She'd told herself she was just soaking up some of the local color, and that it was a commendable use of her time. Carolyn had spent her entire life doing commendable, sensible, constructive things just like that. She thought she knew sensible and commendable when she saw it.

She'd never been the type to pine and swoon over men. That was why she was absolutely sure that she hadn't been standing around on the porch just in case she could glimpse Jonathan Raider's return. That was just...coincidental.

Carolyn Andrews didn't do things like that. That would be too...forward.

So why had her heart felt as if it had skipped a beat when she finally caught sight of him, sitting tall and indomitable on that rangy, rawboned horse of his? That was the question bothering her now. It bothered her enough to worry about it. At least, it worried part of her. Another part of her, however, seemed to find it all rather amusing.

So my heart skipped a beat? So what?

It doesn't usually do that.

He took me by surprise. I was just startled for a minute.

It didn't feel like you were startled. It felt more like excitement. Anticipation.

Baloney! I'm too old for that kind of adolescent reaction.

Adolescents don't have exclusive rights to that sensation.

*I've **never** felt that kind of sensation! Not even as an adolescent!*

Maybe you're just a late bloomer?

Carolyn shook herself loose from her mental wrestling match and made a conscious effort to forget all about Jonathan Raider and his peculiar effect on her circuitry. She marched straight back to her trailer and slammed the door behind her. There were a few last minute things to do, so she set about doing them with the absorption and concentration of a Hindu mystic.

By the time she quit to survey the results of her labor, all the things she needed for the horse hunt were neatly wrapped, tied and piled in a corner. The place was tidy. The dishes were washed. The notes and maps and photographs were all on the table, ready for discussion when the time came.

Carolyn wandered over to the window and pulled back the curtain a little. The light was still on in the barn. She could tell from the shadows being cast behind the buildings. Every once in a while there was a flicker, as if Raider had walked in front of the light and the shadow cast by his body had rippled across her line of vision.

Raider and his darned body! Why did the man have to be built like a prototype for the male of the species? she wondered despairingly.

Carolyn resisted the idea of walking over and talking to him, although, she had to admit, it was tempting. But he must be tired, and he probably wouldn't be interested in her company, in any event. She certainly had no intention of humiliating herself by running over to visit him the moment he showed up in town.

A soft blush crept across her cheeks.

That was the real problem. She was afraid he'd see through her conversational excuses and realize why she was really there: to see him. Just to see him. To be in the same room with him.

She found herself wanting his company, even though at times he could be the most irritating man she'd ever met. Still, there was something about him that drew her, even though she told herself quite reasonably that it wasn't smart to be drawn to a man like Jonathan Raider.

"I don't seem to be paying much attention to myself lately," she sighed. She pulled the curtain back across the window, closing out the view of temptation. "Why don't you just get cleaned up and go to bed, Carolyn?"

This time she took her own advice.

Fifteen minutes later, she was lying in her narrow bed, her hands behind her head, staring at the ceiling just a few feet above her, still wondering about Jonathan Raider. What kind of a man was he? Why was he living here, playing the role of everyone's hired hand? He had no ties that she was aware of, and she'd been careful to listen for any hint of them.

It didn't add up.

Raider just didn't strike her as the kind of man who would spend his life as a drifter, living on the edges of society. He possessed an intelligence and inner strength that wouldn't be satisfied with that, in her opinion.

Jonathan Raider might enjoy playing the lone wolf much of the time, but when he ran with a pack, he would be at the front of it. He was a leader, not a follower. Carolyn would have bet her last dollar on it.

There was a determined smile glimmering at the corners of her lips as she fell asleep. Raider might be accustomed to keeping people in the dark, but she was just as familiar with unearthing the truth.

It might be interesting to see which of them was better at the game....

Raider turned out the light in the barn and closed the big swinging doors. He dropped the heavy wooden latch in place and ambled through the darkened street. He was walking in the general direction of his shack, but he wasn't taking the shortest route. He was going by way of Carolyn Andrews' trailer.

Her lights were out.

That was good. That meant he didn't have to argue with himself anymore. He'd certainly had enough of that for one night. He'd just spent half an hour pacing back and forth in the barn and its environs trying to decide whether to check on her.

He had just wanted to make sure she was all right.

Well, maybe that wasn't it exactly. He'd seen her standing in front of the Silver Dollar when he rode into town. She'd looked perfectly all right then. He doubted that much could have happened to her on the short walk from the saloon to her tiny home to change that.

Raider hunched his shoulders and stuffed his hands into the pockets of his heavy coat, resolutely striding past her darkened trailer and forcing himself not to look at it. He'd see her soon enough. Tomorrow morning. And he'd be seeing more than enough of her for some time after that.

His frown deepened.

Arm's length. Remember, Raider, arm's length...

* * *

Raider arrived at her doorstep the following morning, determined to get on with the search for Carolyn's missing horse. The sooner they got started, the quicker she'd be gone. Since that was what he had wanted ever since he'd laid eyes on her, the thought should have cheered him up. It didn't.

Instead, he felt distinctly torn over it.

That angered him, and this time he directed the anger toward himself. In spite of the fact that he hadn't actually spent a lot of time with her, she no longer seemed like a stranger to him. Mysterious and elusive, yes. A stranger, no. There was a warm, seductive allure about Carolyn Andrews that compensated mightily for the fact that he really knew very little about the facts of her life. As a matter of fact, it made knowing the details seem close to irrelevant.

His jaw tightened, and his brow furrowed. He resented the effect she was having on him. He hadn't planned on Carolyn Andrews, and he was going to hustle her out of his life before she left any traces of herself in it.

He rapped his knuckles smartly on her door. The thin metal barrier shook wildly. Raider stepped back, startled and annoyed at the excess of force he'd used.

Carolyn flung open her door, more than a little annoyed at the unexpected assault he'd just executed on her entryway.

"For crying out loud, Raider!" she exclaimed testily, examining the door hinges for any evidence of bending. "This isn't a stable!"

He almost looked embarrassed, but then the expression was gone, and he was staring at her in the tactless, mocking way that was becoming irritatingly familiar to her.

"It's a good thing that it *isn't* a stable," he drawled. "This place is so flimsy a stiff breeze could heave it on its side."

Carolyn's annoyance rose. Damn him, anyway. They couldn't even say hello without arguing! How was she going to remember to keep her temper and manage a decent business relationship with him? When he wasn't ignoring her outright, he was insulting her, taunting her, or telling her to go back where she'd come from.

"Could we skip your evaluation of my living quarters?" she asked crossly. She motioned him inside.

Raider stalked past her with a grunt, which she assumed substituted for yes, and came to a temporary halt in the middle of her tiny living room.

He surveyed her compact home with no great show of social interest, just a mild, rather detached, curiosity.

Carolyn's hand was cold as she closed the door after him. Now that he was inside, she wished they were having this meeting somewhere else. She felt overwhelmed by his presence. Raider filled the trailer both literally and figuratively. He'd had to duck through the doorway and was now standing with the ceiling barely an inch above his head. There was hardly room for them to move more than a few feet without brushing against one another. Worse still, there was an aura of leashed tension about him that was producing a peculiar, tight sensation in her chest.

She tamped down her nervousness and briskly moved around him to sit in the cane-backed chair. The feeble old thing didn't look as if it would survive an intimate acquaintance with six-foot Jonathan Raider. Besides, the chair allowed her to have her back to the door. That gave her a reassuring sense of control over the situation. If she didn't like the way things went, she could always get up and go outside. She wouldn't be trapped.

Raider sat down on the couch. It looked like doll's furniture under him.

There was absolutely nothing doll-like about Jonathan Raider, however. He was wearing a brushed-cotton work shirt that had once been a dark red-and-black tartan but had long since faded. That didn't matter. The lean, rolling muscles of his shoulders and arms gave it all the appeal any shirt would ever need. His jeans had faded naturally from the sun and were now the stone-washed shade that designers charge hefty prices for in Beverly Hills. And he looked as succulent in them as any male model Carolyn had ever seen. He had the flat, hard belly and tightly muscled thighs that made otherwise perfectly normal women dream of being carried off into the sunset.

Raider stretched his long legs out in a vain attempt to avoid being cramped, crossing his booted ankles for balance. Then he awkwardly rested an arm along the back of the tiny day-bed. He looked over in discomfited annoyance at Carolyn and was surprised to see a glassy expression in her eyes.

Carolyn cleared her throat and quickly looked down at the materials she'd spread across the table between them. "Shall we get straight to business?" she suggested.

"Suits me."

He was struck dumb. He was willing to swear that glassy-eyed look she'd had was one of unadulterated female interest. Heat rushed through him from his face to his feet.

She held out the photo, and Raider leaned forward to take it from her. It was the picture of the stallion on the ledge.

"You think this is your horse." He made it more of a statement than a question.

"Yes. It was taken by a friend of a friend who works for the BLM as a pilot and photographer."

Raider, who'd been studying the picture, looked up at her from beneath his dark brows.

"A friend of a friend?"

"Ted Weston. He was practically engaged to a close friend of mine in college. When I found out that the horse might have been brought to this area, I called him up and asked to see any aerial photographs he could loan me. This one had never been published."

Raider's eyes had never left her face. "He knows what you're doing?"

"No. I told him that I was interested in the land here...told him something vague about needing more facilities for some of our investors. I asked him to keep it quiet. I'm sure he has."

Raider tapped the corner of the photo thoughtfully against the palm of his hand. "Okay," he said neutrally. "What made you think the horse was around here in the first place?"

Carolyn pulled out another photograph. This one belonged to her. She handed it to Raider.

"Is this you?" he asked.

"Yes. That's Firefight next to me. On the other side, a little bit in the shadows, is Firefight's groom, Elias."

Raider studied the photograph. She looked very happy and relaxed. Her ash-blond hair was blowing a little in the breeze, and she'd been caught in the act of catching a wisp that threatened to veil one of her eyes. She had on a crisp white blouse, tailored and plain, but of obvious quality. The shape of her bra was subtly showing beneath the fabric. She was wearing light brown whipcord jodhpurs and black riding boots, which gleamed in the sun. She looked clean and lighthearted and breathtakingly beautiful.

"Elias saw them switch horses," Carolyn whispered. She'd never told a soul that, for fear poor Elias would be killed if anyone found out.

Raider frowned. Elias. That was the small figure haunting the other side of the photo. He tore his eyes from Carolyn's enticing image and studied the small, wiry youth.

"He looks about thirteen," Raider said. He didn't like the idea of a kid being involved in this mess.

"He was sixteen when that was taken," Carolyn said softly. "By now he'd be…eighteen, I guess."

Raider's attention shifted to the flesh and blood Carolyn sitting across from him. "Your voice got very soft talking about Elias," he said carefully. "Is he someone special to you?"

Carolyn smiled affectionately and nodded. "Yes. Elias is…different. He's like a lost, hurt animal. He doesn't fit in most places. People, society, don't know what to do with him. But he's an earnest, loyal, intensely loving boy when he trusts someone…or something."

Raider heard the tenderness, the kindness, in her voice, and felt a small crack form in his defenses. He'd been tough all his life, but that sweetness he kept getting glimpses of in her got through to him. He found it disconcerting.

"Yeah. Society can be pretty tough on a kid who doesn't fit in," he agreed at length.

Carolyn looked at him in surprise. There had been no emotion whatsoever in his voice, yet she'd sensed there was something behind his words. He wasn't just talking about Elias. He was relating it to something in his own life. Before she could decide whether or not this was a good time to pursue that possibility, Raider spoke.

"I take it that the horse—" he looked up at her "—and you became…important to him."

Carolyn nodded. "Yes. We were his friends. That was why Elias hid and watched when Firefight was loaded into a trailer that night. He held on to the back…" She still shuddered to think of him doing it. "He managed to ride like that for half a day, but lost them when they stopped for gas. When he got off, he couldn't get back on again without being seen. But he could see the direction they were going, and he kept going on foot, hitchhiking."

"That's some devotion," Raider said quietly.

"Elias is still looking for him. He sent me a postcard shortly after it happened, so I knew to start looking in the northern half of Nevada. Every once in a while, I get another card." She looked sadly out the window. "Poor kid. He's panhandling or working odd jobs just to be able to stay in the vicinity."

"How did you know they wouldn't just keep driving—up to Montana, say, or out of the country?" Raider asked.

"I didn't know. The photograph that Ted gave me was the first reassurance I'd had that Firefight might still be here." She was serious now and leaned toward him. "I've been hoping that Firefight somehow managed to get loose and stay that way. If he's running with the wild horses, maybe he can stay free."

Raider shook his head. "That's a big if, and a whale of a maybe," he observed. Another thought occurred to him and made him frown. "Why didn't you just have the authorities look for the horse after you first heard from Elias?"

Carolyn lowered her head. "The authorities in California were convinced Firefight was dead," she explained. "It would have taken very persuasive evidence for them to undertake a massive search for a horse they firmly believed wasn't alive."

"But the kid…"

Carolyn pressed her lips together, then caught her lower lip between her teeth. "Elias wouldn't have been believed…" she said.

Raider's eyes narrowed suspiciously. "Oh? Why not?"

"He's been in and out of juvenile psychiatric programs for years. He's had some…breaks with reality."

Carolyn spoke reluctantly. She didn't want to divulge Elias' private hell. The poor kid had always been deeply ashamed of his illness. He knew he was different, and he'd hated it with the profound, heartrending loneliness that only a child can feel.

"He'd just begun to have some confidence in himself," Carolyn explained. Pity saddened her eyes and softened her voice. "Nobody had ever expected much of him before he started working around the stables. Everything he'd said had always been taken with a grain of salt." Her eyes hardened in anger against the callousness people could show one another, the damage their unthinking words had done to that child. "In this case, you can just imagine what people would think." She released a short, harsh sigh of frustration. "They'd say that he lost the most important thing in his life. That he couldn't deal with it. That he hallucinated the whole thing to keep the reality of his loss at bay." She focused on Raider, seeking his understanding. "That's why I couldn't drag Elias in as a witness."

Raider wasn't entirely persuaded. "All right. But now you've got the photograph of the stallion on the ledge. Wouldn't that add credibility to the kid's story?"

She gave him a small, wan smile. Raider had a cool, logical mind, the kind that was a pleasure to do business with. Too bad the rest of the world wasn't more like him.

"I'm afraid not everyone would see Firefight in that picture," she reluctantly had to admit. "And...I wouldn't be tremendously surprised if quite a few people thought *I* was starting to hallucinate in claiming I saw Firefight in that stallion." A bitter smile tinged her lips. "The insurance investigator avoids me like the plague. He's convinced I'm so devoted to my father that I couldn't see the truth if it were staring me in the face." She looked back at the photo, and her expression saddened. "Unfortunately, this is just a picture. It won't serve as positive identification. And considering the lack of enthusiasm the authorities have shown every time I asked for a more vigorous investigation, I doubt very much that they would do more than put the print in their files."

"Sometimes we see what we want to see," he said slowly, studying her as if to determine whether she was indeed so desperate to free her father that she'd lost some of her capacity to judge.

Carolyn's eyes flashed. "Yes," she agreed angrily. "But I've made my livelihood being able to distinguish between wishful thinking and a reasonable gamble, Raider. I'm putting everything I've got into chasing down this horse." She tapped a carefully manicured fingernail on the photo, although she held Raider's eyes all the while. "I'm seeing what I want to see. But I'm seeing it because it's really there!"

"All right," was all he said, but Carolyn sensed he was willing to give her the benefit of the doubt and trust her judgment on this one. For some reason his silent vote of confidence filled her with a sense of buoyant relief.

"Thanks, Raider," she said softly. Her eyes were dark, glimmering pools of heartfelt appreciation.

He felt desire surge through him like the winds blowing through the sage. He realized that she must have shouldered everything on her own for a long time now to be so hungry for his small show of moral support, a simple gesture of belief in her judgment. He was staring at her, wanting to touch her, wanting to taste her mouth, wanting to hold her comfortingly. The urge came as a shock to him. Because unlike the day before, when he followed her into the mountains, he had no ready excuse to rationalize the urge. This urge was visceral, like an instinct from a long forgotten age when a male held his female to him in a hard and lustful embrace and never paused for rational thought.

He saw the color rise in her cheeks. The silence between them was swirling with unspoken words. She seemed to tense, even though she didn't actually move. His eyes slid down across her beautiful cheekbones and graceful throat, caressing her breasts and waist with a glance so light that he might not actually have been looking at her.

But he *was* looking at her, looking at her the way a man looks at a woman in the instant when he's first fully aware of her as a woman, desirable and warm and not yet his. Carolyn saw the expression in his eyes and felt herself melt inside from the heat of that look. She wondered what it would be like if he touched her, really touched her. Because right now she was tingling from her shoulders to her knees, and he wasn't even near her.

She forced herself back into her carefully crafted shell. Raider saw her polite, socially correct posture and expression, and tried to get his mind back on the business at hand. Rich girls from the big city didn't have a place in a life like his, he reminded himself cynically. He considered what she'd told him, rolling it around in his mind, thinking.

"Why didn't you hire a private eye?" he asked at length. The rest of his unspoken thought was clear from the hardened look that had returned to his face. A woman of Carolyn's obvious financial resources would have had no problem hiring help. She could have kept her manicured hands clean.

Carolyn squelched her resentment of his attitude to her. The man seemed to have a problem with moneyed people, or maybe it was just moneyed women, she wasn't sure. She would have to deal with that later. Right now, she wanted to focus on the facts. They were disheartening, and she wanted to get them all out on the table and disposed of. Then, she hoped, she and Raider could move ahead.

"I *did* hire a private eye," she replied, her bitterness and frustration showing again. "He spent five thousand dollars of my money and came up with absolutely nothing. Now that I'm this close, I don't need one. I need someone who knows the mustang country, someone who can help me track this horse down."

Her eyes sought and held his. The heat that flowed between them was almost palpable. And through the bond of attraction, the obvious sexual chemistry flowing between them, she was asking him silently for his reassurance.

"That's why I need *you*, Raider." Her voice was steady enough, calm and smooth, like that of a woman who was accustomed to handling decisions. But her eyes...

Her eyes showed the small glimmer of fear that filled one far corner of her mind with doubt. Was he going to keep his promise? Was he going to come through for her? Would he keep the bargain they'd struck, or was he going to back off now in the cold light of day, far from the scene of her near drowning, her near shooting.

Carolyn held her breath, without actually realizing she was doing it. Deep down, she was scared that everything was going to slip through her fingers again. She was so close. She could almost taste the triumph. But she couldn't do it alone. Much as it galled her to have to admit it, she needed Raider. Without him, she stood to lose everything. If the horse was out there, and her search became known to the kidnappers, Firefight might be whisked away, and she would be back where she started. No leads. No horse. And no one believing her theory.

So it all came down to Raider, she thought uneasily. He wasn't predictable. Raider, the man who'd stripped that first day to chase her off. She'd gotten glimpses of the man beneath the hard facade he wore. And the way he looked at her sometimes... Yet she hardly knew anything about him. Of course, she'd known a lot about Gary Lord, and that hadn't done her a bit of good. When the chips were down, Gary had walked out without a second glance.

And she'd never felt the strange, heavy currents of electricity with Gary that she felt with Raider. It was a peculiar, intoxicating experience, being in the same room with him. One look into his fathomless, dark gray eyes and she could feel an odd glow begin deep in her abdomen.

"Well, Raider." She forced herself to say it since he obviously wasn't going to say anything more. "Do we still have a deal?"

She needed him, and they both knew it. It was naked in her eyes. So was her determination to go it alone again if he'd had a change of mind.

Raider's jaw tightened, and his brows furrowed in an angry V. What kind of a man did she think he was, anyway? The look on her face made him want to crush her in his arms, and her obvious lack of faith in his commitment made him want to take her to the floor in the most primitive form of conquest. If he didn't know better, he would have thought he was going nuts. He couldn't recall ever having such violent emotions where a woman was concerned. In a way, he did regret having promised to help her. Because now he was going to have to spend night and day with her until God only knew when.

He wasn't sure how long he could survive living in a constant state of semi-irritation, semi-arousal. Obviously, he was soon going to find out.

"I told you I'd help you," he growled irritably. "I don't know what kind of men you're used to dealing with, but let's get one thing straight at the start. I never welsh on a promise. As far as I'm concerned, we've got a deal."

He unfolded himself from Carolyn's midget-sized couch and absently massaged a cramped muscle in his left shoulder. Arm's length was turning out to be mighty damn short.

"I don't know how long this is going to take," she blurted out, having abandoned her search for an easy way of saying it. "And I know that means I'll be taking you away from your regular jobs around here." She ignored the sardonic amusement that glinted in his eyes at that. "So I insist on paying you. Would a thousand dollars a week plus expenses be all right?"

Carolyn tried to make it sound like the most natural thing in the world, perfectly neutral, strictly business. Inside, however, she was a little nervous at how Raider might take the offer of money. She had to make it, though. For one thing, she wanted him to know this *was* business, and for another, she didn't want him to go broke on her account.

When she saw the cold, steely look in his eyes, her heart sank. She lifted her chin defiantly and glared back. So it had been a mistake to mention money. He didn't have to be so unreasonably touchy about it!

"Look," she said defensively. "Stop trying to intimidate me with those glowering looks! This is *business*. There's nothing wrong with your taking money for spending your time on this, Raider! You do it when anybody else asks you to do something for them. What's wrong with taking my money?"

Raider's glower grew even more formidable. Business? Not to him. And although he couldn't for the life of him tell her what was wrong with taking her money, he wouldn't have touched a dollar of it to save his soul. It was because it was hers. And he knew it.

"Keep your money!" he said tersely. "I'm not interested in it. And, for your information, this is *not* a business transaction. The *only* reason I'm helping you is that I don't want you getting yourself killed. I want you and your... friends...out of town as fast as possible. Period. Now, have you got that?"

Carolyn flinched as if his words were blows. "They aren't my friends," she retorted hotly. "I thought I made that plain the other day."

He stared at her moodily. "One *was*."

Carolyn closed her eyes and pressed her fingertips to her temple to ease the throbbing pain that was threatening to become a full-blown headache. She didn't want to get into the depressing subject of her failed engagement to miserable Gary Lord.

"Look," she said, regaining her aplomb with an effort.

"I'm sorry I offered to pay you. I withdraw the offer. Okay? But couldn't we be civilized about this?" She opened her eyes and dropped her hand to her side. "How about a drink to seal our agreement?"

He looked surprised. "Isn't it a little early in the day?" Some of the anger left him, though, and he looked as if he was on the verge of smiling at her. "Maybe you're more of a Nevadan than I'd thought...."

Carolyn was so relieved that she laughed. It was surprising how good it felt, too, as if the end of her troubles was in sight, and everything was going to work out. She knew it was idiotic, unrealistic, but she felt that way all the same.

"I was thinking of coffee," she admitted, slanting him a quick, apologetic smile. "Sorry to disappoint you. I'm afraid that's all I've got."

He shrugged his indifference to the lack of liquor and watched her as she gingerly brushed past him.

Because of the close quarters, their elbows touched briefly as she passed by. A burst of electricity seemed to leap from the point of contact and run down her spine, leaving her even more on edge than before.

Carolyn kept her back to the silent Raider and stepped up to the small stove, turning on the fire under the kettle. She tried to push away the physical awareness that Raider had aroused in her, but the only result was a jerkiness to her motions as she reached up to open the narrow cupboard to search for mugs. She tried to smooth her movements out, but it took an effort.

Raider slouched against the wall and watched as she fumbled nervously among the china, then in the drawer of mismatched silverware. She was wearing a dark gold blouse with very feminine tailoring, and neatly pleated, cocoa-colored twill slacks cinched at the waist with the slimmest black belt he'd ever seen. It had been pleasant enough seeing her seated a few feet away moments earlier. Now he was getting glimpses of her delectable body as she stretched and bent, twisted and turned. The slightest movement brought the carefully fitted clothing into intimate contact with her skin, revealing in enticing detail the precise curves of her breasts and bottom.

He was picturing her stripped when her voice pierced the fantasy, and he blinked, frowned, then focused on her startled face.

"What?" he asked blankly. No hint of apology there, just annoyance at being dragged away from his fascinating tour.

"How do you take it?" she repeated. His eyes darkened, and her cheeks followed suit as she guessed his thoughts. "Your *coffee*," she clarified, adding a little bite to her voice by way of self-defense. Everyone knew men disliked sharp-tongued women. Although, from the lingering tension in Raider's slouch, she was beginning to have her doubts about that.

"I take it any way it's offered," he replied. He ran his eyes over her in desultory appraisal, but there was an underlying glimmer of humor that took some of the threat away from the look. That is, until his eyes returned to hers. He was interested, all right. And not in her coffee.

Carolyn's hand trembled a little, much to her disgust, as she measured out the coffee into the faded green mugs and poured the boiling water in. She mixed slowly and laid down the spoon. Black. No sugar. That ought to jolt them back into reality. Her lips felt dry, but she grimly pressed them together. She handed him his mug, then raised hers and bumped his lightly in a toast as he straightened up.

"To a successful partnership," she said bravely, meeting his eyes steadily over the raised mugs.

"To our success," Raider responded.

They drank. Then Raider stepped forward, put his mug on the countertop and slowly, deliberately, took Carolyn's mug and put it next to his. They were a foot apart, and he was looking down at her in a dark and brooding way that was doing peculiar things to her breathing.

"There's just one more thing we have to take care of before this goes any further," he muttered.

"What's that?" she asked, barely breathing, hardly recognizing the whisper that was her voice.

He pulled her into his arms, burying one hand in her hair and holding her around the waist with the other. His mouth hovered tantalizingly over hers, saying, "This…" and then his lips touched hers, and she knew the talking was over.

Chapter 6

She stood in his arms, trembling a little in spite of herself, feeling the heat of his body as he drew her more tightly into his embrace. His mouth was hard and warm, demanding her acquiescence, demanding that she respond. She didn't need any prompting. His mouth was too tempting. She closed her eyes in ecstasy, savoring the texture of his lips as they moved sensuously, erotically, against hers. Kissing couldn't be this good, she thought in a small, swooning part of her astonished mind. But it *was* that good. It was sensational.

"Where did you learn to kiss like that?" she whispered foggily, her eyes still closed to hold in the hot sweetness of it.

She felt him smile against her cheek; then he was rubbing his mouth enticingly over the sensitive spot in front of her ear and on down the tingling side of her neck. She arched against him like a cat, exquisitely pleasured by his soft caress.

"You don't want to know," he murmured roughly.

Her eyes flickered open, and she stared at his dark, bent

head. "I want to know *everything* about you," she whispered unsteadily.

He raised his head, a veiled, wary look in his passion-darkened eyes. Even the way he looked at her made her soft and damp, eager to cling to him, to feel him take her.

"Later," he muttered, cutting off further conversation by recapturing her mouth with a hungry kiss.

The touch of his lips was like velvet fire. He made her feel vibrantly, vividly alive. The swirl of nerve endings rocketing to life spread from her lips downward like fireworks. She wanted to tell him what he was doing to her, but there weren't any words for this. Instinctively, she pressed herself against him, hard. It wasn't close enough. Nothing could be close enough to satisfy the raw need that he had ignited by his touch.

She felt his body grow taut in reaction to her movement. His fingers tightened against her head, drawing her closer still. Carolyn felt an overwhelming need to hold him, and her arms slid around him, pulling him more tightly to her. She purred with pleasure at the hard, insistent contact of their bellies. A purely feminine thrill of delight shot through her at Raider's instantaneous reaction to the provocative sound.

He was murmuring something hot and unintelligible against her lips, tasting her with his tongue and twisting her erotically against him. Carolyn didn't understand the jumbled words, but she had no trouble getting his message. He wanted her. Just as fiercely, just as primitively, as she wanted him. The power of it was frightening in its intensity, but the pure strength of it crushed any chance of her hesitating. She was swept up into a steaming vortex and didn't want to turn back. She needed him to love her.

Raider kissed her hungrily, moving against her with coaxing, then hard, demanding motions, determined to possess her. Carolyn kissed him back as hotly, as sensuously, as he was kissing her. She knew she was being provocative, but she didn't care. She wanted him. Oh, how she wanted him.

She opened her lips, and their mouths melted together in a

fusion of desire. Intimately, rhythmically, again and again he explored her mouth.

Her breasts were flattened against his hard, muscled chest. Even through their clothing, she could feel the strong, well-formed contours of his pectoral muscles against the pebble-hard tips of her breasts. He was as strong, as resilient, as wild, as the land. He was like the untamed stallions that captured and mated and held their mares through raw, brute strength. In his embrace, Carolyn felt incredibly soft, but wildly, fiercely, female.

He lifted his head and looked down into her passion-hazed eyes, breathing a little roughly. He spread his legs and leaned back against the counter, pulling her to him so she could feel his hardness. Her eyes closed, and she leaned forward. Tenderly, lightly, she grazed his neck with her teeth. He sucked in his breath and pulled her harder against the bulging male ridge of his arousal, rocking her soft cleft urgently against him.

She teased his throat and collarbone with her teeth, shivers of delight coursing over her skin as he groaned softly at her erotic play, and pulled her harder and harder against him.

Raider splayed his hand against the small of her back and began a slow, sensuous massage that sent wave after wave of warmth and relaxation through Carolyn's body. The sensation pooled in her thighs and legs, increasing her urge to lie down for him. She moaned softly, and her head fell back a little as desire flooded her, making her weak with wanting him.

"I want to see you," he muttered, his voice harsh with passion.

He bent her back across his arm a little and deftly unbuttoned her blouse, then yanked it free from her slacks and pushed aside the material. He flicked apart the front opening of her bra, and she was exposed to his hungry view.

She gasped as he lowered his head and ran his tongue over the soft, swollen mounds of flesh, first one, then the other, kneading her flanks all the while. She sank her hands reflexively into his hair as he ran his damp, rough tongue round and round each stiffened nipple, sending ripples of fire spiraling inward.

"You're beautiful," he murmured thickly, teasing her breasts again and again. He ran his hand down her in a long, slow caress from her shoulder to her hip. Then, easing her away from him a little, he slid his hand up the inside of her thigh. Gently at first, then harder, he pressed his hand against the part of her that ached for his touch.

Carolyn moaned in pleasure, half afraid he'd stop, half afraid he wouldn't. She felt his hand move to her waist and search for her belt buckle. Even through the haze of passion that had enveloped her, she knew they were going too fast. At least, the rational part of her mind was trying to get that message across. But the voice of reason sounded very faint, very far away.

Raider was burning up. He wanted to shove himself into her soft flesh and drive them both into the mindless ecstasy that he knew lay only a few minutes away if they kept this up. He was so firecracker hot for her that he was half inclined to take her standing up, with their clothes still on. The hell of it was, he hadn't meant it to end up like this when he'd started kissing her. But the moment his lips touched hers, he'd forgotten whatever it was he'd been trying to prove to her. Now, all that mattered was taking her, making her burn for him the way he was burning for her.

There was just one problem. Afterward...he didn't want her to regret it. He didn't want her to feel used. She was soft and sweet-smelling, and sensational in his arms. They had nothing in common. He was sure of that. But their bodies fit together like the two halves of one whole.

And he cared for her, damn it. That was the unsettling part. He'd been trying not to, but... Raider took a deep breath and raised his head to look at her bed. It was likely they'd break the thing to smithereens if he carried her over there and took her on it.

Then a movement at the trailer window caught his eyes, and he froze, instantly alert.

Carolyn felt the change in him immediately. He was tense, but it was the coiled tension of a man preparing to fight, not the unreleased tension of a man desperate to pour himself into a woman's soft and yielding body. She tried to focus her swirling mind and looked up at him. She blinked a couple of times to bring him into focus.

She found him staring angrily over her shoulder. At least he wasn't mad at her, she thought, as her sense of humor came to her rescue.

As Carolyn turned a little in his arms amusement deserted her, and she paled in shock. Then her color returned in a rush, as embarrassment and anger tinged her cheeks a dark shade of rose. Gary Lord was staring through the window at them. And from the stunned and disbelieving look on his face, he'd seen quite clearly what had been going on between Raider and Carolyn.

"Looks like your old friend's come to call," Raider drawled. He looked down at Carolyn, his eyes distinctly cooler than the last time their gazes had met.

"I'm getting tired of telling you, Raider, he's *not* my friend," she retorted, annoyed at his persistent misinterpretation.

She pulled away from him, quickly rehooked her bra and hurriedly began trying to rebutton her blouse. Her fingers were shaking, though, and it was uncomfortably slow going. Raider brushed her hands away and did it himself. She looked up at him in surprise, but he ignored her, concentrating on her buttons instead, which were dispatched with remarkable speed. Next he proceeded to tuck in her shirt.

He looked at her, then, an amused gleam in his eyes.

"You're very good at this," she observed, a little testily.

It obviously wasn't the first time he'd dressed, or undressed, a woman. Carolyn wasn't sure how she felt about that. Since they weren't exactly contemplating a dating relationship, she decided it would be a good idea to stop thinking about his expertise with women altogether. She had to admit, though, it was going to be a little difficult insisting that theirs was strictly a business relationship after what had just happened.

"It's the least I can do," he explained, keeping a remarkably straight face. "After all, I was the one who undid everything."

Carolyn lowered her eyes and resisted the temptation to laugh, in spite of the fact that her cheeks were burning at the memory his words evoked. He was a hard man to fence with. One moment kissing her into oblivion, the next calmly buttoning her blouse as though nothing had happened. If it weren't for that gleam in his eyes...

The sound of her trailer door opening interrupted Carolyn's train of thought. She turned to see Gary Lord stepping inside.

"Sorry to interrupt," Lord said. His eyes went from Carolyn to Raider and back. He didn't sound sorry at all. And he didn't look it, either. "I'd like to talk with you, Carolyn."

He'd decided to ignore Raider and was turning his full attention on Carolyn. The crisp, businesslike edge to his voice was intended to command.

That was one of the things about Gary that had always annoyed her. She was relieved that she no longer had to gloss over it, or pretend it didn't bother her.

"I don't believe I heard you knock," she said coolly, staring at him in an unwelcoming way.

Gary's eyebrows rose ever so slightly. "I didn't realize that was necessary between us, Carolyn."

Carolyn made a most unladylike sound of disgust. "Oh?" she said in clear disbelief. "Are you sure you weren't having such a fascinating time peeping through my window that you just decided to forego the social conventions?"

Her contempt for him was obvious, and Gary stiffened, then flushed in anger.

"That's not like you, Carolyn," he said angrily. "You don't let your temper get the better of you. Don't you think you've had enough of this...whatever this is? Why don't you quit before you've made even more of a fool of yourself than you already have?"

He shot a cold look at Raider.

"You're not the saddle-bum type, Carolyn. You need clean sheets." He ran a disgusted look up and down the length of Raider's deceptively relaxed frame. "I can get you on a plane whenever you like. Just say the word." His eyes returned to Carolyn's. They were more than a little warm. "For old times' sake…"

Carolyn felt the anger in Raider. They were only a foot apart, and his fury was like electricity crackling in the air. He didn't like Gary. And she was sure he didn't intend to put up with any more of Gary's insults, either. Carolyn had a brief, nightmarish vision of what her small trailer would look like if Raider got angry enough to fight Gary. She closed her eyes wearily. She didn't need that.

She marshaled her strength and tried to keep the situation under control. "For old times' sake," she said, sounding more like her old self, "just let me work this out my own way." Her eyes begged him silently. "Please, Gary?"

Raider's jaw tightened in anger. He didn't like to hear her say Lord's name. Especially the way she was saying it now, softly, evenly, pleading with the jerk! It reminded Raider that she'd been engaged to the guy and had no doubt said his name any number of times, and probably with a great deal of tenderness and warmth, sometimes with passion. Passion! If that didn't raise his blood pressure…

It galled him to think of her in Lord's arms, kissing him, going to bed with him. Raider forced the image out of his head before he completely lost his temper. He'd taken an instant dislike to the man the moment he'd laid eyes on him. And although he had no idea what had caused Lord and Carolyn to break their engagement, he had absolutely no sympathy for Lord's loss.

Lord didn't deserve her.

The dark flare of anger deep inside became more recognizable to Raider, and he was even more put out with himself than before. He was jealous of Lord, and of any tenuous hold he might still have over Carolyn Andrews. Raider shifted forward and crossed his arms in front of his chest.

Carolyn glanced up and was surprised at the look of near disgust on Raider's face. If being in her trailer had become so distasteful, she thought angrily, he could leave! He was an ornery, unpredictable man. Even if he *could* kiss like the Don Juan to end all Don Juans!

She got a grip on herself and tried to give Raider a businesslike look. "I'm sure you've got lots of things to do today," she told him. She saw his startled reaction, but she kept looking at him expectantly, even so.

His eyes narrowed. He didn't like to be managed. Besides, he wasn't about to leave Carolyn alone with Gary Lord.

"Nope. Not a thing," he said succinctly. He reached over and finished his now lukewarm coffee while Carolyn stared at him as if he had lost his mind.

"Why, sure you do," she pointed out, wide-eyed and daring him to contradict her again. "You told me you did." Well, not in so many words, but surely the man would take the hint and leave her to deal with Gary.

Raider smiled coldly and slowly shook his head. "I've got *plenty* of time. Besides…" He fixed a hard look on Gary. "I have a few questions I've been meaning to ask your friend here."

Carolyn muttered under her breath. "I told you to quit calling him that, Raider." Raider ignored her.

Gary, perplexed at the undercurrents and suspicious of Raider's intentions, hadn't heard her comment. "Oh?" he asked cautiously. "What did you want to ask, Raider?"

Carolyn felt a sense of defeat. The men were focusing on each other now. She just hoped they'd keep the argument verbal. She had no doubt that Gary would. It was Raider that she wasn't so sure of. Sometimes she had the distinct impression that he wasn't completely civilized.

Raider looked Gary up and down, as if taking his measure. "First, where have you been this past week, Lord? People around here haven't seen much of you, or your friend Gagan.''

Gary blinked and stretched his chin forward slightly. Carolyn recognized the nervous habit and stared in surprise. He always did that when he was trying to be evasive about something.

''We drove back to Winnemucca so I could transact some business, then drove around some of the hunting areas southeast of Cold Heart.''

Raider didn't look particularly impressed with the explanation. ''You planning on settling down around here, Lord?'' he asked, a little sarcasm showing through.

''No,'' Lord snapped. ''And I don't owe you any explanations, either, Raider. Look, I came here to talk to Carolyn. Why don't you take the hint and leave, so I can do that?''

Carolyn closed her eyes. Gary had never been very bright when it came to reading people. Once again, he'd put his foot in it.

Raider stepped forward, and his hand closed slowly around the front of Lord's jacket. He was rigid with barely controlled anger. He lifted his hand up slowly, forcing Gary to lift his chin to avoid choking.

''I don't suppose you or your friend know anything about some rifle shots that were fired at Carolyn when she was out in the mountains the other day?''

Lord looked totally shocked. ''What?'' he gasped, his eyes seeking Carolyn's. Fear and disbelief were mingled in his face. ''Someone shot at you?'' he said. ''That can't be...''

Raider released his grip on Lord's coat. ''If you happen to hear anything about that, you'll let me know, right?''

Gary had lost all his color and appeared to be thinking hard. He ran a slender hand nervously through his light brown hair and nodded. ''You shouldn't be here, Carolyn,'' he murmured anxiously.

Raider leaned toward Lord again. ''You'll tell me, right?'' Raider repeated, quite clearly.

Lord nodded nervously. ''Right,'' he murmured. He turned

toward the door. "I'm leaving tomorrow, Carolyn," he said. He looked as if he'd aged five years in the last five seconds. "I can't stay here any longer. I came because..." He looked embarrassed. "Because I felt badly about the way our engagement ended. I wanted to try to make it up. But...if you won't come back...I guess you're going to have to chase your demons until they catch you."

Raider didn't like the sound of that one bit.

Before he could press Lord for an explanation, Carolyn had flown across the room and thrown her arms around Lord.

"Thanks, Gary." She just wanted him to leave. Putting her arms around him wasn't what she particularly wanted to do, even if his sorrowful speech had seemed genuine and made her sad for a moment at the mess her life had become. Mostly she just wanted to get him out of the trailer and out of her hair.

Gary felt himself moving toward the door and wasn't quite certain how he was getting there. Then the door was open, and Carolyn was handing him out with a tight little smile.

"'Bye, Gary. Thanks for trying...."

The door closed, and she fell back against it in relief.

"Very touching." Raider was looking at her in a cold, contemptuous kind of way, as if she were a new species of poisonous insect.

"What?" she asked, confused by his sudden venom.

The old cynical look was back in his eyes in full force.

"He must still be smitten to tear out here after you like this. Hire a private detective to find you, rent a truck and a car to follow you around, offer to fly you home, ask you to give up your crazy behavior. You must be one hot little number to keep him—"

He never finished the rest of the sentence. Carolyn had crossed the room, and her hand connected with his cheek as her eyes blazed with wounded pride and a deeper, more troubling kind of hurt.

"You don't know what you're talking about, Raider," she

whispered, furious at his words and crushed that he would talk to her like that.

She marched over to the door and opened it for him, waiting for him to go. "Just let me know when I should be ready to leave," she said stiffly.

Raider stalked by her. He hesitated when he reached her and looked into her eyes, as if searching for something. She thought she saw a flicker of doubt, perhaps remorse, in his. Then he closed up again and turned grim. "Sunup," he snapped.

She closed the door after him and leaned against it, shaking a little in spite of her best effort not to. She knew what had happened to Raider, and it upset her. He didn't like the idea that she'd been involved with Gary. And now she was going to spend days on end with him in the wilderness, fending off his jealousy, his contempt and the incredibly powerful attraction they felt for one another.

She wished she could remember her childhood prayers.

Unfortunately, she had the sinking feeling that only giving in to the desire to be in his arms was going to help where Jonathan Raider was concerned. She wasn't sure if she could handle that. He didn't seem interested in a long term relationship, and she was afraid that an affair might bring her more sorrow than delight.

"Damn you, Jonathan Raider," she murmured in frustration. "Damn you!"

Carolyn collected her things and dropped them outside her trailer door. They fell with a heavy, dull thud onto the cold, hard ground. Nothing was moving. The town lay in chilly darkness, the early morning silence broken sporadically by the soft cooing of mourning doves and the occasional shrill *whit* of a lonely kingbird.

She locked the trailer and picked up her belongings, then resolutely walked toward the barn, which was swathed in deep shadows, ghostly in the eerie quiet.

It had been a long night. She'd paced and fidgeted at the

stove and fixed herself food that she threw out barely touched. It hadn't been easy contemplating going into the rangeland and low-lying mountains with Jonathan Raider. A cougar she could shoot at. She couldn't very well shoot Raider if he threatened her. And threaten her he did, though in a very different way.

Over the fifth cup of coffee, consumed some time around midnight in the darkness of her bed, she'd faced it. Raider wasn't like the other men she'd known. He was completely on his own and obviously determined to keep it that way. He apparently disdained owning anything. He was content to rent what he needed, when he needed it, and return it when he was done, according to easy-talking Sam Zee.

She wondered if he treated women that way, as well. Since she hadn't seen that part of his life, she had no way of knowing for sure, but she had the feeling it was probably the same. Rent her for the hour, or the night, and leave when he'd had enough.

She trudged through the quiet, her pace slowing significantly as she drew close to the barn's great doors. She'd never been so physically attracted to a man. Why on earth did it have to be him?

Raider heard the doors swing open and straightened. He was standing next to a ten-year-old mare that had been left for shoeing the day before. He ran his hand down her sturdy leg, coaxing her to lift her hoof. He wasn't in the mood to be pleasant. He was frustrated, and furious with himself for letting things get out of hand with the beautiful Ms. Andrews. She could damn well open the door and drag her own things in, as far as he was concerned. Besides, he wasn't sure he was ready to see her face this morning.

That beautiful, expressive face of hers…he'd been seeing it in his dreams. Along with the rest of her thoroughly kissable anatomy.

He frowned and concentrated on the horse's hoof. It was perfectly all right. Of course, he'd been fully expecting that it would be.

"Good morning." Carolyn tried to get things off to a normal start. She was standing just inside the doorway, her bundles on the ground on either side of her.

Raider put the horse's hoof down and straightened up. He stepped out, closed the stall door and turned a cool, measuring look on her. He was a stranger again. Carolyn's heart sank a little, even though she knew she should be relieved. At least she wouldn't have to fight with him to keep his mind on business.

His eyes flickered, going to her things and then back to her. "Is that everything?" he asked flatly.

"Yes." She couldn't help it—the cool look in his eyes angered her. She wanted to melt some of the ice between them, even if she had to do it the hard way. "Did you think a rich girl like me would be bringing steamer trunks and suitcases piled five feet high?"

His eyes burned for a moment, but then the fire was banked, and he merely shrugged. "I was thinking a smart girl like you would have reconsidered the whole plan," he said. He leaned against the closed slat door of the stall behind him and studied her. "I can travel faster without you," he pointed out. "The fastest way to find your horse, assuming he's out there, is for me to go it alone."

Carolyn took a couple of steps toward him, her hands clenched. "I'm going." She was determined, and she was a woman accustomed to winning the struggles she took on. She stared at him hard. "I'm going, even if I have to go by myself, Raider."

He didn't look pleased. "You're *not* going alone," he growled. "I thought we'd settled that."

Carolyn drew a breath and pushed the issue into the open.

"I thought you were having second thoughts," she said. She had to force the words out, although they sounded steady and even.

"Why would I be doing that?" Raider asked darkly. He didn't look as if he was eager to hear her reply, though.

Carolyn's cheeks acquired a deeper hue. "Because of yesterday…" she said, trailing off rather lamely.

He wasn't making this any easier, she thought angrily. In all fairness, however, she wasn't sure there was an easy way to discuss the events of the previous day. The unblinking, unreadable way he was staring at her wasn't helping one bit, either.

He shook his head and slowly expelled air from his lungs, as if trying to ease his own discomfort.

"Ah, yes," he muttered. "Yesterday. That seems as good a reason as any for you to stay here." His eyes held hers, and this time she saw the danger in him. "Yes, I still want you. And you still want me, Carolyn Andrews." His mouth twisted in something that was part smile, part grimace. "And if we spend night after night alone together, how do you think things are going to end up between us before we're through searching for your lost horse?"

He straightened. Then he closed the distance between them with the deliberation of a predator stalking its prey. He stopped a foot away. She could feel the warmth radiating from him, even through her heavy jacket and his. It was more than just the heat of his body; it was the heat of her longing for him, her body's traitorous recognition that he was near.

He radiated an aura of sexuality that made her mouth, as well as a few other spots, tingle. She had no doubt that half the women on the planet would have the same reaction to the man. She would be willing to bet that a sizable percentage of those west of the Mississippi probably already had.

She couldn't let this sink all her well-laid plans, even if traveling with Raider turned out to be a new form of exquisitely painful torture. Everything depended on her finding Firefight. Everything. She couldn't turn back. They'd have to find a way to work things out between them.

"I think you've been out here in the middle of nowhere for too long, Raider," she argued, meeting his threatening gaze without flinching. "Besides, being out in the wilderness doesn't exactly bring out a woman's beauty," she pointed out.

A teasing light softened her eyes, and she smiled a little, as if they were friends. "Believe me, you have nothing to worry about. The longer we're out there, the deeper I'll be buried in trail dust." At his dubious snort, she raised her eyebrows. "And so will you," she added with emphasis.

A glimmer of humor threatened to show through his cynical expression. "We'll see," he said. "But if I hear any complaints, you're coming back," he warned.

Carolyn shrugged, as if that wouldn't be a problem. "Can I help saddle up?" she asked briskly.

Raider led her to the horses and mules they were taking and pointed her toward the tack hanging nearby. The mules were patiently waiting for Carolyn's bundles to be added to their packs. Nearby, a horse noisily blew air out his nostrils and stamped a hoof as if to relieve the boredom.

"Do you know how to bridle a horse?" he asked bluntly. The mask had settled over his face again.

Carolyn stifled the urge to shake him for that. She knew what would happen if she put her hands on him, even in exasperation. She could recall exactly how he'd felt beneath her touch. With an effort, she shoved the memory away and tried to ignore her edginess.

"I can manage," she muttered.

She lifted the bridle from its wobbly hook on the wall and entered the stall of the horse he'd indicated was hers. Straw crunched, thick and brittle beneath her boots. Pungent stable scents wafted around her as a startled barn swallow flapped into the upper rafters.

She eased up next to the gelding, who turned to look at her with calm dark eyes.

"Hello," she said soothingly. The horse stretched out his neck, and Carolyn smiled, reaching out in return to rub his soft black nose affectionately. "I think you and I are going to be friends."

She slid the bit into his mouth and lifted the headstall over his ears. The horse accepted the bridle without objection, grinding his teeth as if to pass the time.

"What's his name?" she called out over her shoulder as she fastened the small straps and reached for the saddle.

"Kettle."

Carolyn laughed and settled the saddle on his mottled, coppery-brown back. The horse was the color of an old copper kettle left too long on the stove without polishing.

"Hello, Kettle," she said, patting him reassuringly before she tightened the cinch. He nosed her hip and eyed her as she drew the cinch up to a good, snug fit. She smiled at him and gave his nose and neck another series of friendly rubs. "We're going to get along just fine," she said quietly. Which was more than she could say about the man standing not too far away.

Raider had turned his attention to the pack mules, deftly adding Carolyn's two equally balanced bundles to the animal that had the least to carry. He stood so he could watch Carolyn as he worked, telling himself that he wanted to make sure she knew what she was doing.

That was partly true.

It didn't take him long to realize that she was more than competent when it came to saddling and bridling a horse. He kept on watching her anyway, following her lifts and bends, seeing her move around the horse, talking to him all the while in a low, soothing voice. The sound reached out to him like warm honey on a sun-drenched day in spring. His body stirred. He wanted to feel her hands on him like that, wandering over him, caressing, playing....

His jaw tightened in frustration.

If only she hadn't come to town. He'd picked Cold Heart because it was the end of the world, and still she'd stumbled into it. The ache in his groin deepened, and he swore silently. The sun wasn't even up yet, and he'd be lucky to get out of the stable without pushing her down into the straw and picking up where they'd left off the night before. Suddenly the reality of the next few days and weeks became excruciatingly vivid to him.

He'd told her that he wanted her. He almost snorted in

derision. That was turning out to be one hell of an understatement. He was becoming obsessed with her, with the need to take her. He was dead certain that once wasn't going to be enough, either.

If he could have found some way out of this, he would have taken it. Unfortunately, he couldn't. Even for his own physical comfort and peace of mind, he couldn't leave her to go it alone. The memory of finding her drowning in that bone-chilling spring was still too fresh. For a moment, he'd thought he would have to jump in after her. She'd been slipping away, frozen from the cold. Then he'd called her name, and, miraculously, she'd done what he'd asked of her.

He hadn't called out a woman's name like that since...not since Kimra had died.

"Raider?" Carolyn was standing in the stall doorway looking at him oddly.

He blinked and frowned, his cheeks darkening in embarrassment. He didn't usually space out like that. It was uncomfortable to be caught at it, too, especially by the subject of his daydreaming.

He finished tying a knot and slapped the saddlebags slung over the mule, as if sealing the job.

"Let's go," he growled, striding toward his own tiger-striped dun and swinging up into the saddle without looking back at Carolyn.

She wondered what he'd been thinking about. For a moment she stood in the stall door, staring at him, as if she could figure it all out if she just looked at him hard enough. The expression on his face had made her want to run to him and put her arms around him and hug him to her as tightly as she could. It had been a shock to her, seeing that mixture of shock, pain and anguish on Raider's usually cynical, stoic face.

Raider had picked up the rope of the lead mule and was heading toward the barn door. Carolyn shook herself into action and mounted Kettle. There was plenty of time to find out why he'd looked that way. Time enough to learn all she wanted to about Jonathan Raider. Time enough to learn more than she should, unless she used some sense.

Then a thought occurred to her. Talking could be useful on this trip. Maybe she could kill two birds with one stone. If she could draw him out, keep him talking, she'd find out what she wanted to know about him and, at the same time, keep him out of her bedroll. She had a lifetime of practice in keeping men out of her bed by talking them out of their interest. Once she'd figured out how to do it, it had been amazingly simple, even with the most narcissistic and determined men.

It had worked before, and it would work just fine again.

She hoped.

The sky was paling into a soft shade of blue along the horizon as they started out of town. Carolyn looked in the direction of Gary's truck and saw him standing there, his hands shoved in the pockets of his heavy jacket, staring at her in silence.

She wasn't surprised. She'd guessed he might do that. A sort of final farewell gesture. She waved at him, and she saw him wave back in the distance.

Then she noticed another figure, standing in the shadow of the big truck. A shiver ran down her spine, and she couldn't help feeling relieved that he wasn't going to be hanging around anymore.

Gagan made her nervous. He aroused a primitive instinct of alarm in her that was too strong for her to ignore.

"If you're finished saying goodbye, we can pick up the pace," Raider said, his voice as hard as the chilled, rocky ground.

Carolyn smiled at him, the same sweet smile she'd dished out all those mornings when she'd driven past him in her Jeep.

"By all means," she said pleasantly, as if they were going out to play a social round of golf.

Raider touched his heels to his horse's flanks, and Carolyn followed suit; they loped onto the range, Raider leading the way.

Chapter 7

The land was a sagebrush sea dotted with islands of rabbit grass. Here and there a twisted tree rose stubbornly above the scrub, standing tiredly beneath the warmth of the rising sun. The soil was parched. The sandy dirt thirsted for quenching spring rains and melting mountain snows. The horses and mules seemed indifferent to it all as they twisted methodically left, then right, stoically picking their way over the barren trail, ears twitching from time to time.

They were heading toward the low-rising mountains that Carolyn had searched earlier, but Raider was approaching them from a different route, a few miles farther east. Maybe Raider knew a better way. Or maybe he had his own reasons for taking this path. Carolyn had never enjoyed repeating herself, so she welcomed the change.

The gradually awakening countryside was fascinating to see. By midmorning Carolyn had spotted two groggy lizards, a couple of panicked jackrabbits and a foursome of startled chukar partridge. As she began thinking that Raider had chosen this trail for its safe footing, her horse lurched sharply to one side to avoid stepping into a gopher hole. Carolyn, thrown onto his shoulder, kept her seat through sheer instinct and razor-sharp reflexes honed by years of riding experience.

"Watch where you're going," Raider warned sharply. "I don't want that horse's leg broken."

Carolyn tried not to laugh. He was going out of his way to try to prick her with a comment like that.

"I don't imagine you'd appreciate having to shoot me if I break mine, either, would you, Raider?" she shot back.

He sent her a glance intended to shut her up, but Carolyn smiled her sweetest, wealthiest smile and ignored the silent threat.

The rhythm of hoofbeats was soothing. Only that and the occasional cry of a bird or *whrrr* of an insect broke the peacefulness of the range. There were no cattle here. No sheep. No men tending them. Just the wild and untamed land, and its tough and cagey spawn.

Raider fit in. There was a seamlessness in the way he sat his horse and loped across the wilderness. He was straight and relaxed, his hands holding the reins as if he'd been born to it, his strong legs gripping the horse with the oneness of a centaur. Man and horse moved confidently through the garden of dangers, hidden and silent, awaiting the unwary.

Raider would never be that. For all the easy relaxation in his manner, he was as alert and aware of his surroundings as anything that lived in this unforgiving land. Tough as rawhide, smart as a hawk. Carolyn felt her admiration for him swell, and she reluctantly savored it in uneasy silence. Maybe this *was* where he belonged, she admitted, even though she could easily visualize him in more civilized surroundings. This was where he fit.

Raider, who had been well aware that she'd been studying him, glanced at her in annoyance. The fact that annoyance wasn't the only reaction her steady gaze was arousing in him merely made things worse.

"If you stare at me any harder, I'll be left with a brand," he objected irritably.

Carolyn laughed. He sounded strange, touchy. His reaction made her perversely pleased.

"I doubt if you're brandable, Raider," she retorted, not the least embarrassed at having been caught watching him. "As a matter of fact, I was just thinking that you're as unconquerable as the land around here." She swept the panorama with her outstretched hand. It was unfenced as far as the eye could see. "Besides, no one wants his brand on an animal as ornery as you."

Raider was annoyed. "Ornery!" he exclaimed. "For a rich girl, you have pretty poor manners," he grumbled.

She obviously didn't appreciate how fortunate she was that he'd decided to be ornery instead of amorous, he thought with irritation. The fact that his own strategy was proving highly successful didn't occur to him for a moment. Then he remembered. Let her think of him as ornery, he decided. The way things were going between them, he'd have no trouble whatsoever keeping up his image.

"Keep that in mind," he advised tersely. Maybe if she thought of him as an ornery bastard, she'd keep her distance!

"It will be easy," she assured him testily.

They settled back into an uneasy silence, and, after another hour, they passed the remains of an abandoned gold mine. Its wooden buildings, darkened and weathered, stood in shabby disrepair, a fading testament to failed dreams. Not far away, the crumbling skeleton of an old stock pen leaned beside a rusting spur of the Central Pacific Railroad. Once it had been a link to the outside. Miners, stockmen, farmers and wagon trains had used it as a lifeline, buying the goods they needed and selling what little they had.

That had been ninety or a hundred years ago. Now there was nothing but disintegrating buildings and rusting railroad ties. They were links in the middle of nowhere, going no place.

Raider pointed toward the blue-green foothills rising a couple of miles away. "We'll take a break at noon, when we reach the pines."

Carolyn nodded. Not that her agreement mattered, of course. She grimaced at his overbearing back, covered by a weathered sheepskin coat. Raider wasn't asking. He was telling.

"You must have read my mind," was all she said.

He heard her, all right, but Carolyn couldn't have proved it. He was shutting her out again, restlessly watching the land like a wild animal instinctively keeping a sharp eye out for predators.

The only predators that Carolyn was concerned about were of the two-legged variety. Gary would be halfway to the nearest airport by now, and with him Rance Gagan. Surely the unidentified rifleman wouldn't be following them, she mused, frowning.

She stood up in her stirrups and scanned 180 degrees behind them. There was no place for a man on horseback to hide. A four-wheel drive vehicle would be even easier to spot. A man on foot wouldn't have a prayer of keeping up with them. She sat down in the saddle again, rocking a little in rhythm with the horse's loose-limbed gait. So what was Raider looking for?

"Can I help look?" she asked, raising her voice authoritatively over the deadened beat of the horses' hooves.

"Sure."

"What am I looking for?"

"Trouble."

He still wasn't looking at her, just riding, the mules trailing behind him on the long, thick rope, his stockman's hat pulled straight over his brow.

Carolyn kept her mouth shut until her temper subsided a little.

Raider was doing a good job of being obnoxious. She wondered fleetingly if that was his way of dealing with sexual frustration. She began to give the idea some serious thought. Maybe that *was* it. She felt both better and worse. Better because she wasn't going to be riled by his reluctance to talk, his absolute refusal to be sociable. He wasn't ignoring her out of some deep-seated distaste for her company. Quite the opposite. She also felt worse, though, because she *did* want to talk to him. To be friends, as much as they could be, for the short time they'd be traveling together. Even if it were a wary friendship.

She wondered if this was how Eve had felt in the Garden of Eden, staring at that delectable, juicy, forbidden apple. She stiffened her spine and reminded herself not to let him make a fool of her. She also forced herself to recall that she had a pretty poor track record when it came to judging men's true characters. Undoubtedly, Raider would turn out to be just like the others. Not what he seemed to be. A big disappointment.

"Raider," she said coolly, "why don't you just tell me, in plain English, what you're looking for? We're partners, remember? Not adversaries."

He wasn't sure he'd agree with that. He felt a little more in control if he thought of her in a distinctly adversarial way. Partners... That was riskier. He sighed in resignation. She was as stubborn as ever. It would probably be easier just to tell her and get it over with. Otherwise she'd keep pestering him about it. She wasn't dumb. And she wasn't the dependent female type, either, happy to ride blindly along behind him, letting him do all the thinking for them.

"I want to make sure no one's following us," he said bluntly.

Carolyn was surprised. She'd half expected him to say he was watching for mustangs or coyotes.

"Have you seen anyone?" she asked.

"Nope."

"But you think someone will?"

"Yep."

"Because of the rifle shots," she added, a little more faintly, less confidently.

"Right."

Carolyn started paying closer attention to everything in sight. She began to empathize with the wild animals that spent their entire lives wondering if something was hunting them down and about to devour them. She didn't like the feeling at all.

Twenty feet to her right, a startled sage grouse flapped pell-mell into the sky, clucking in disgruntlement at having been flushed.

"Easy for you to say," Carolyn said under her breath. If someone flushed Raider and her, they wouldn't have such a ready escape. "Too bad we don't have wings."

Raider glanced over his shoulder at her. "Talking to yourself already? Most people hold out at least a few days."

"I could talk to you…" she suggested with her sweetest, most innocent smile.

He just turned away and urged his horse and the mules upward, through the outcropping of piñons that had spilled down the hillside. Carolyn followed. They made their way up the hill and into the mountains.

Carolyn was surprised by how fast the day went. Lunch was short and simple. They rested the animals, then fed and watered them. Their own meal was dried meat, dried fruit and bottled water consumed in silence as Raider sat across from her on a rock overlooking the range.

They spent the afternoon picking their way up an ancient trail rising through the twisted nut pine trees and antelope bush. Now and again a patch of wildflowers erupted in the middle of the forest floor. Balsam root, mahogany-colored wild peonies, white and yellow Indian potato.

"Is this an old trail, Raider?" she asked curiously.

"Yeah. The Indians used it. Then the trappers. The miners, the settlers. Now, mostly hunters or people who want to get away from civilization for a while." He twisted in his saddle, as if easing a muscle in his back that was cramping a little.

"Are you okay?" she asked.

"Yeah." Nothing a good massage wouldn't help later on tonight. But he wasn't going to dwell on that. Grimly, he settled back, looping the mules' lead rope more comfortably around his palm.

"Want me to lead them for a while?" Carolyn offered. She

guessed that the uncomfortable position of trailing the mules was the cause of his stiff back.

Raider eyed her doubtfully. "You can ride," he admitted with obvious reluctance. "But I'd just as soon wait until we're on the way back to find out if you can lead pack animals."

Carolyn gave him a look that had struck lesser men dumb. "Afraid I'll lose them?"

"You got it."

"Tell me, Raider, do you treat all the women around here like this, or have you singled me out?"

"The women around here grew up in the saddle, leading stock." He cast an eloquent glance at her Calvin Klein jeans, the same shade of midnight blue as the day they were dyed, and her well-oiled, custom-fitted Argentine leather boots in a unique shade of light mahogany. "You look like you belong in a privately owned riding stable."

She couldn't really blame him for his assessment. It was very close to the truth. Not all the truth, of course. But a piece of it.

"Looks can be deceiving," she pointed out, in a tight, cool voice. "But I don't think that's the problem here."

He eyed her warily. He didn't trust that underlying tone of determination. "No?"

"No. I think you're afraid to see me as I really am, Raider. I think it's safer for you to keep me as a stereotype, the spoiled rich girl who doesn't know how to do anything."

He frowned deeply. He wanted to say something cutting, something that would keep her away. But she'd put her finger right on it, damn it. He wasn't about to be a hypocrite. He could always stall her for a while, he thought, mentally estimating the number of days he'd have to do that. It wasn't an encouraging number. Well, miracles occasionally *did* happen.

"If you don't mind," he said sarcastically, "I'll wait to eat my words. If they run off on the way back, we'll all end up in Cold Heart about the same time, not too hungry if we're lucky. If they get loose before we've found your horse, we're really going to be roughing it." He gave her another acid look, underlining his lack of confidence in her ability to make it in the wild. "I'd rather not find out how well you handle that."

Carolyn laughed angrily and shook her head. "Sooner or later, Raider, you're going to realize that I can take care of myself. This *isn't* the first time I've camped out."

"I didn't ask."

"I noticed. I figured you were just being polite. I decided to tell you anyhow."

"Thanks," he muttered unappreciatively. "Watch out."

Kettle stepped gingerly over a fallen lodge pole pine, and Carolyn had to abandon conversation as the horse picked its way through a rock slide that had littered the trail.

They spent the afternoon with their heavy coats tied behind the saddle cantles. The warm spring sun shone down on them, reaching out to touch the tree-covered land with revitalizing golden fingers. Late in the day, however, the temperature steadily dropped back down again. As Carolyn put on her fleece-lined, antelope leather jacket, she discovered why Raider had chosen to come this way.

They were approaching a semicircle of buildings: three lean-tos and a rudely constructed log cabin.

Raider stretched and stood in his stirrups.

"Here's where we camp for the night," he announced.

By nightfall, all the work had been done. The mules and horses had been fed, watered and bedded down for the night in the lean-tos. Raider and Carolyn had gathered some wood and now were enjoying the crackling warmth of the fire in the fireplace. An old iron kettle that Raider had filled with springwater was just coming down from a hissing boil. The squat round pot next to it, blackened from use, was sitting on an iron rack, simmering a thick beef and vegetable soup. It was remarkable how tasty dried food could smell, especially with a little seasoning, Carolyn thought in admiration. She inhaled slowly, savoring the tasty aromas that filled the small shelter.

They'd brought their packs inside, removing only what they needed for the night. Two bedrolls were spread out on the bare wood floor, on opposite sides of the open fireplace, as if facing off for a duel. The rough-hewn plank floor was a little cleaner than it had been when they'd walked in. Carolyn had used a homemade whisk broom that she'd found hanging on a hook behind the door to clear away the dust and dirt.

"What is this place?" Carolyn asked as she sat down in front of the fire and fixed them each a cup of instant coffee. "It doesn't look that old, and it seems to be well kept up." It clearly wasn't an abandoned homestead or camp from ages past.

Raider pushed the heavy wooden door closed. Reluctantly, he turned to join her. His boots beat a sharp tattoo on the hardwood flooring. Like an executioner's drumroll, Carolyn thought wryly as she put his coffee on his side of the fireplace.

She sipped her own coffee and glanced up at him. There was an odd expression on his face, just beneath that stony facade he was so adept at wearing. It was the expression of a man who'd lost what he'd treasured most in all the world. The look was fleeting, though, and gone before she could be sure.

Raider picked up the broken branding iron that served as a poker and coaxed the small logs into a fuller blaze. He stood there, staring at the flames for a moment.

"Who built it?" Carolyn asked softly.

He laid the old branding iron against the wall.

"I did."

There was an odd note in the way he said it. It was a forced toughness meant to cover pain.

"By yourself?" she probed cautiously.

"No." He seemed reluctant to answer.

"No. It's a big project for someone to tackle alone," she agreed thoughtfully, her gaze running over the neatly chinked walls, the carefully finished ceiling. "Who helped you?"

She thought at first that he wasn't going to answer. He was half turned away from her, and the firelight was dancing on his face. Was it anger she saw there? Or just a trick of the flickering light? He shook off whatever brooding thoughts had been plaguing him and leaned one shoulder against the cabin wall, turning to look down at her.

"My brother," he replied evenly. He reacquainted himself with the room, as if seeing it as they had seen it together. "We used to come up here fairly often. After a few years, we got tired of sleeping on the ground and shaking the insects out of our sleeping bags. We wanted something a little more…civilized."

His gaze, which had wandered over the rough panels with something akin to affection, moved back to Carolyn. A bitter, crooked smile formed on his mouth.

"You aren't the only one used to the creature comforts," he admitted.

Carolyn smiled at him. It wasn't the fencing smile she'd given him morning after morning on her way out of Cold Heart. It was a smile of warmth and camaraderie. She wanted to reach out to him.

"Why, Raider," she teased, "I think that's almost a compliment of some sort."

He shrugged noncommittally, but he was comfortable with the idea. "A pack trip goes a lot more pleasantly if the packers try to get along," he pointed out reasonably.

He moved away from the wall, squatted down in front of the fire and reached out to ladle the thick, hot soup into their bowls.

"Do you still come here a lot?" Carolyn asked carefully. She didn't know exactly what was touchy about this subject, but something obviously was, so she went carefully with him.

He handed her one of the steaming bowls and a spoon. "Several times a year."

"And your brother…does he still come?"

She wasn't exactly holding her breath, but her spoonful of soup was suspended in front of her mouth for an inordinate length of time as she blew on it to cool it.

He was staring into the fire, blindly spooning his dinner into his mouth. "No. Not anymore."

Carolyn was swallowing her next spoonful of soup, having decided that closemouthed Raider had said all he was going to on the subject of his brother. She was wrong. He was still staring into the flames, so his words didn't really register at first.

"He's dead."

When it finally sank in, she blinked and nearly choked on her food. There had been no trace of emotion in the way he'd spoken. She didn't know exactly what to say, and the time it took for her to gather her thoughts gave her time to wonder about the steely control that he'd used to keep his feelings from showing through.

It still hurt, she thought. Her heart ached a little for him. There he was, Mr. Tough, still hurting, and not allowed to let it show.

"I'm sorry," she said softly. "How long ago?"

"Five years."

"That's not long," she said gently.

"No." No. To Raider it still felt as if it had all happened yesterday. He reached for the coffee and took a deep swallow.

A small branch burst into embers. The fire crackled in the silence that fell between them.

"Was he all the family you had?" Carolyn ventured carefully.

Raider hesitated, as if not quite sure how to answer that. He sipped his coffee and thought about it.

"No," he answered at last. His face had hardened again, and his eyes grew cold. "My grandfather's still alive."

Carolyn was surprised to hear it. Raider had all the earmarks of a man with no ties. From the bitterness in his voice, she doubted that he and his grandfather were on very good terms.

He stood up abruptly and retrieved a pair of large steel bowls and some soap from one of the packs.

"Now you know the story of my life," he muttered, shoot-

ing her a faintly hostile glance. "In return, why don't you do
the dishes?"

Carolyn scrambled to her feet and piled the dishes into one
of the large bowls, then reached for her jacket.

"That doesn't sound like an even trade," she retorted good-
naturedly. She gave him a sly look. "If I tell you a little about
mine, will you do the dishes?"

He was already stretched out on top of his sleeping bag,
crossing his legs contentedly at the ankle. "Nope."

Carolyn laughed. "Tomorrow, why don't we toss for it?"

"Okay."

He'd agreed a little too easily, she thought on the way outside. There was a catch there somewhere. She brought out the
kettle and poured hot water into both bowls, which she had
set on the workbench behind the cabin. By the time the dishes
were finished, she'd stopped wondering what trick he would
use to manipulate the coin toss tomorrow.

First she had to get through tonight.

His eyes were on her as she put the utensils back into the
packs. The steady regard made her uneasy.

"Is something the matter?" she asked defensively. "My
slip showing, or something?"

He grinned slightly. The man had the most annoying grin
she'd ever seen. And the way he let his gaze roam slowly
down to her knees…it made her feel as if he could see
through her jeans. That only put her even less at ease.

"I was just wondering if this was the first time you ever
washed dishes in the woods."

She laughed, partly in surprise and partly as a release of
tension. "No, but it *is* the first time I've done them in my
coat in the dark," she admitted. Her eyes narrowed accus-
ingly. "You're not trying to pick a fight with me, are you,
Raider? Especially after pointing out how important it is to
have harmony on the trail?"

He was watching her with a lazy, measuring look. "No
fights," he assured her. He sighed and shut his eyes as if to
close her out. "It's not helping."

His voice was gritty, making her tremble.

"What's not helping?" she asked, half-afraid to hear the answer.

"You told me you'd be dirty and dusty and I wouldn't want you," he reminded her.

She stared at him and tried to think of something harmless to say. Nothing came to mind. Everything she thought of was dangerous. And staring at him wasn't helping, either. He was handsome and masculine stretched out in front of her like that. The trail dust on his jeans just made him more attractive.

Carolyn sat on her bedroll, drew up her knees and wrapped her arms around them, trying to stop shaking. She reminded herself that she was a poor judge of men, that she was out in the middle of nowhere, that she didn't really know a thing about Raider.

It didn't matter. She wanted to go over and lie down next to him, feel him fold her in his arms, taste his lips on hers.

Carolyn closed her eyes for a moment. She shook her head, trying to free herself of the desire to be close to him. "Maybe I'm just not dusty enough," she said weakly. "By tomorrow night, I'll be getting there."

He snorted his opinion of that statement. "I don't think so."

Carolyn tried to think of things to talk about. That had been her plan, she told herself. Unfortunately, she could only think of questions, and they were all about Raider. Not exactly the way to keep a psychological distance between them, she had to admit. On the other hand, he wasn't acting on their mutual attraction. He was just lying there. Maybe he'd go along with her and talk. Anything would be better than this taut silence, she thought.

"Did you grow up near here, Raider?" she asked, picking up the thread of their earlier conversation. She rested her chin on her knees and watched the rise and fall of his chest beneath his red tartan shirt.

He answered without opening his eyes. "On the other side of the mountains."

That covered a lot of territory. Nevada, Oregon, and maybe even Idaho.

"Does your grandfather still live there?" she asked tentatively.

There was a long pause but finally he answered. "Yes."

"Do you ever go back to see him?"

"No."

It was said with finality. Carolyn wondered what had caused such a permanent rift between Raider and his grandfather.

"Is that why you're living in Cold Heart?" she asked softly.

He opened his eyes and turned his head to look at her. "No. I live in Cold Heart because I like it."

"And that's where you intend to stay for the rest of your life?" she asked, steeling herself against his intent regard.

"Maybe. Why all the personal questions, Carolyn?" He measured her, trying to decide what to make of her interest.

"I'm just making conversation," she protested. Her fingers ached from clutching her knees too hard.

"Talk about something else," he said warningly.

She could have screamed that she couldn't think of anything else and it was driving her bananas, but she was too well-bred to let herself. Instead, she took a deep breath and made a countersuggestion.

"What would you like to talk about?" she asked.

Raider scowled. She'd said that in the perfectly modulated tones of a young woman who'd had the advantages of a very fine education and only the most acceptable friends all her life. It reminded him of the gulf between them.

Raider didn't want to be reminded of that gulf. All day long he'd been wanting to close the physical distance and trying to forget about all the others. Those of culture, time, place.

What did he want to talk about? He didn't want to talk at all. He wanted to feel her mouth against his, run his hands over her silky skin, push his body into hers. The same damn things he'd been wanting to do since she'd walked up to his shack in Cold Heart that first day.

He still wasn't quite sure why he hesitated. There was something about Carolyn Andrews... His instincts all told him to steer clear of her. She was the kind of woman who would stay with a man forever, even if it was only the memory of her. He was haunted by enough memories. He didn't want to have to deal with those of her, too. So he tried to think of something to talk about.

"How did you meet Lord?" His question was terse.

Carolyn blinked at the sudden shift to such an unwelcome topic. "He was a friend of one of our big investors. I used to see him at the stables, looking over some of the horses. We...started dating. The usual kind of thing."

"Did you sleep with him?" he asked.

Carolyn's eyes flashed. "Now who's being personal?" she retorted.

"I'll take that as a yes," he said, clipping the last word.

Carolyn stood up and went over to the fire. Absently she poked the dying flames with the twisted branding iron. She didn't really want to leave it at that. Mainly because she didn't like Gary anymore and hated to think of Raider believing she'd been intimate with such a louse.

"No. I didn't sleep with him."

Raider sat up and stared at her, as if trying to decide whether to believe her or not. "Why not?"

She rested the tip of the iron on the stone floor in front of the fireplace.

"It never...felt right," she admitted. "We...we were part of the business group. We were known to everybody. There was no way we could have become lovers without it becoming common knowledge."

"You were ashamed that people would know?" he asked in surprise. Then, in consternation, he added, "But you weren't ashamed to be publicly engaged to him?" He shook his head in disbelief.

Carolyn sighed and tried to explain.

"After we'd been engaged for a month, he seemed to change. It was as if a mask were slipping, and I began to see the man beneath. He wasn't as easygoing and confident as he'd made himself out to be. He was too ambitious. Ambitious for himself. And then, when he gave me that ultimatum about abandoning helping Abel…well, it was the last straw."

She glanced at Raider. "If we'd met under different circumstances I don't know what would have happened," she admitted. "At first, he really swept me off my feet. He knew all the right things to say, to do. But…" She shrugged it off. "It just never happened."

Raider decided to believe her, outlandish as what she'd said sounded. If he'd been in Lord's shoes, engaged to her, he couldn't have kept his hands off her. But then, he wasn't Lord. The stiffness in his shoulder pained him, and he flexed his shoulder blade, trying to ease the discomfort.

"From leading the mules?" Carolyn guessed, watching him.

"Yeah." He grimaced. "Tomorrow I'm going to put them on a line to my saddle."

She came to him, kneeling at his side, and pressed her fingertips into the sore muscles. She felt him tense.

"I don't want to get stuck out here with a disabled guide," she teased him, trying not to sound as uncertain as she felt about doing this.

He knew he should tell her to leave him alone, that it didn't hurt. But it did hurt, and her hands felt so good that he didn't have the will to tell her to stop. He shut his eyes and let his head hang forward as she massaged his tired muscles.

"Don't worry," he murmured. "It takes more than a few stiff muscles to disable me."

She worked on his neck and the knots along his spine. He groaned softly, and she stopped, lifting her fingers.

"Did I hurt you?" she asked apologetically.

He turned to look at her. As she crouched next to him, their faces were a foot apart. Suddenly the distance seemed to be disappearing. Then his lips touched hers, and she closed her eyes.

The sweetness flowed into her, then the fire and the longing.

"You're hurting me, all right," he muttered against her lips. "But the pain's all over." Not to mention one sensitive spot in particular.

"I'm sorry," she whispered shakily. "Oh, Raider, what are we going to do?"

He came to his knees, facing her, and draped his arms over her shoulders. It was as if they'd done it before, as if it were the most natural thing in the world for them to do.

"Are you on the pill?" he asked. His eyes were dark and steady. There was an intimacy in the way he was looking at her that made her heart swell with longing and tenderness.

"No."

He touched her lips gently with his. "Then I'll take care of it."

He pulled her into his arms and kissed her the way he'd been wanting to kiss her all day.

Chapter 8

She wanted to cry.

Being held by him felt so right. She wanted to sob and laugh at the same time. His hard, muscled arms around her made her feel safe, and yet a little afraid. She couldn't figure out what made it so. There was a special spark she felt when she was in Raider's embrace. A spark she knew she would hold dear forever, no matter what happened.

Gradually, he eased the sweet pressure of his kiss.

"You smell like pine needles and mountain flowers in the spring," he murmured against her mouth. "Like the dew in the meadows in the morning, like the cedar of the cabin in the fall." He caressed her cheek with his lips. She was intoxicating in every way a woman could be, he thought. The more he drank of her, the more he wanted.

Carolyn rubbed her lips provocatively against his. He knew just how to touch, just what to say. Every touch, every word, made her tingle, left her yearning for more.

He pulled her blouse free of her jeans and slid his hands up her bare back. His palms, warm and calloused, touched her with a gentling sureness that made her relax. Carolyn leaned into him and put her arms around his waist, holding him tightly, wanting him to keep touching her, to never let her go.

He eased her back onto the bedroll, going down with her so they were on their sides, facing each other, cradling her shoulders in his arms, sinking one hand into her pale hair and kissing her, kissing her everywhere.

"Unbutton my shirt," he murmured huskily, speaking against her jaw as he placed teasing kisses one after the other across her soft skin.

Her fingers shook slightly as she pulled one small white button free of the heavy cotton shirting. She spread the fabric and released another, then another, until his shirt hung open and she could feel the contours of his chest, firm and warm beneath his T-shirt. She pulled it out of his jeans and slid her hand under it, touching hot, bare skin. He grazed her shoulder lightly with his teeth, and she shuddered, sinking her nails gently into his well-muscled ribs. How could a man feel so good to touch? she wondered hazily. But the soft way he was kissing her collarbone made her temporarily forget what a pleasure it was to touch his body and concentrate on what a pleasure it was to be touched by him.

Coolness passed over her back and her breasts as he tossed aside her blouse, then her bra. When he pulled her to him again, his shirt and T-shirt were gone, and he warmed her with his body. Her breath caught in her throat at the wonderful shock of his bare skin against hers. Her breasts flattened against him. He held her fast for a long, tender moment, then gently eased her a little away.

"You're as soft as silk," he murmured, running one hand lovingly over her breasts, her waist.

Carolyn barely heard him. The sensations he left on her skin made it hard to hear at all. All she could do was feel…the soft rasp of his thumb running along her ribs, the tips of his fingers finding the sensitive curve of her waist, the tenderly rough palm of his hand as he slowly explored the vulnerable small of her back.

"Soft, soft," she thought he whispered, as he lowered his head and slowly kissed first one breast, then the other, teasing, teasing, teasing, until she sank her hands into his dark hair and moaned in painful delight. It felt so good, but it wasn't enough.

His tongue was damp, rough, warm, going round and round the dark skin of her nipples. First one, over and over, until it was so hard and peaked that it wouldn't give against his insistent pressure. Then the other, circling, circling, puckering the tender flesh. Her taut nipples were connected to another part of her, deep inside, a part that was tightening and aching at his exquisite touch.

She opened her legs, drawing him to the ache by hooking her leg over his hip and pulling him near. She sensed his smile against her breast. Then he slid one hand down to unsnap her jeans, lower her zipper, unbuckle his Levis, unzip the closure with a quick yank. Then he was rolling her pants over her hips, his too, kicking them away....

There was nothing left between them. There was a quick, crackling sound as he deftly opened a small package, crumpled it, tossed it away. Then the brief snapping sound as he kept his word to her.

He reached down and pulled her leg back up over his hip, slowly running his hand up and down her calf. They were pressed bare thigh to bare thigh, belly to belly, entwined and holding each other tight.

Raider sighed and leaned his forehead against hers. She was made to be in his arms. Every curve, every bend of her body, fit him perfectly. Perfect breasts, perfect legs, perfect hips. Perfect fit.

He ran his fingertips slowly up the nape of her neck and tangled his fingers in her silky hair. He felt her shiver a little, could even feel the tiny bumps on her skin that communicated her pleasure at his touch. He wondered if she knew what a turn-on it was to him, for her to react like that. So quickly, so naturally. Not that he needed any more arousing.

He thought it would be one for the record books if he could last more than thirty seconds once he drove himself into her. As a matter of fact, it was a miracle he wasn't losing control already, just holding her in his arms and fondling her like this. If she touched him or moved against him, he knew he would go off like a firecracker, he was so hot for her.

So he caressed her, kissed her, trying to cool himself down a little before taking them the rest of the way. He wanted this to last all night. Longer.

Carolyn felt the ache of frustration deepen with every move of his hands. He was bringing her to such a peak of wanting that she could hardly stand to have him touch her, at least, not so lightly. She needed him to be hard, now, touch hard, kiss hard, fill her with his rigid manhood. She wrapped her arms around his neck, captured his mouth with hers, and kissed him with a growing sense of urgency. She begged him with her lips as they met his. More, more…now…now. Pleeeeeeease…

Her thigh tightened against him, and she pressed herself close to the hard shaft that was teasing her, teasing her, that firm, round pressure that was caressing her swollen flesh.

Still he held himself back. Carolyn swallowed a cry of near agony. She couldn't stand it. Inside her. She needed him inside.

"Jonathan," she pleaded in a strangled whisper.

It was more than he could withstand. All his determination evaporated, and he gripped her hips, turning her onto her back. He was caught in the throes of an instinct too strong to resist. In one hard, gratifying thrust he was filling her silken, eager body. That thrust was followed immediately by another, and another, and another. They couldn't stop; they were caught in the rhythm, driven by a fiercely urgent need to release the tautly coiled pressure inside, building, building, more, more, harder, harder, faster, faster, until, until…

Raider gave a strangled cry, but it was muffled by Carolyn's mouth. He was kissing her fiercely, and the agonized sound drowned in her, mingling with her own. She was grimacing, but in sweet release, not in pain. They were convulsing, writhing, twisting against one another. Wracked with the tremendous eruption of release. In him. In her. In the one being they had for that millisecond in eternity become.

The great waves subsided into ripples, washing over them, calming, soothing, finishing. Binding them together.

Raider lay on her, deadweight, his breathing still labored, a damp sheen on his hot skin. Carolyn, limp and satiated, held him snugly in her arms, matching her breathing to his, wanting to cling to the wonderful feeling of intimacy with him. She could feel his heartbeat thud against her chest, and she willed her own to match his. To breathe when he did, for her heart to beat in time with his. Yes. She wanted them to stay as one. In as many ways as possible.

After a while he rolled away. His absence chilled her skin, but it chilled her mind and heart, as well. She wanted him to stay close. For a little while, at least. To keep reality away for as long as possible. Was that so bad, to want that? she wondered.

He got up and walked over to the corner of the room, disappearing behind a manty they'd hung like a drape from two big hooks screwed into the ceiling. He'd said it cut down the size of the room the fireplace had to heat, but Carolyn had had the impression he'd wanted to let her have some privacy, if she wanted it. Now she smiled, although it looked more like a grimace. She doubted there was much use for it now. The big tarpaulin could just as well have stayed wrapped around their camping equipment.

He returned carrying a wooden bucket, a couple of towels and a bar of plain soap. Carolyn turned onto her side and watched as he silently filled the bucket with warm water left from earlier.

"Come here," he said, straightening. He held the soap in one hand and an old cloth in the other. The firelight played across his naked body, bathing it in rich, golden tones.

Carolyn scrambled awkwardly to her feet and shyly joined him. His eyes roamed over her, taking pleasure in discovering her beauty at a less hurried pace. Her skin warmed everywhere he looked.

"Closer," he ordered huskily. When she stepped up to him, he reached out and touched her nose lightly with the tip of his finger. "My cabin has all the comforts of home," he explained, amusement softening his eyes.

"Are you the shower?" she guessed as he dipped the cloth into the warm water, lathered it with soap and proceeded to bathe her from head to toe.

"I'm it."

He wasn't trying to be erotic. She was sure of that. But she closed her eyes in pleasure anyway. The warm, cleansing massage felt wonderful. When he was through with her, she offered to return the favor. He finished buffing her dry with one of the towels and shook his head.

"No," he said.

Carolyn was a little hurt, though she told herself it was silly to feel that way. So what if he wanted to be businesslike? Or didn't want her touching him. Her face reflected her loss of confidence.

Raider glanced up at her and caught a glimpse of her worry before she managed to bury it from view. He was lathering and rinsing himself much faster than he had her. Of course, it wasn't at all the same thing, as far as he was concerned. If it hadn't been for the chill in the cabin air, he would have taken all night washing Carolyn. And all the next day rinsing her. Under other circumstances he would have been happy to have her return the favor.

He grinned liked a satyr, envisioning the sexual possibilities they could explore if they spent enough time bathing together.

"I want to get cleaned up as fast as possible. If you do the scrubbing—" he let the sentence dangle threateningly and gave a rough chuckle "—I'll probably forget what we were supposed to be doing, shove you right back down on my bedroll and see whether it's as good the second time."

He sluiced water down between his legs, dropped the wash-cloth into the bucket, picked up the other towel and began briskly drying himself off. It pleased him that she'd been bothered by his refusal. And as soon as he was dry, he intended to make it up to her. He felt himself stir just thinking about it.

Carolyn felt a lot better, having heard the explanation, although it was awkward hearing it from such a distance. She would have preferred to have it whispered in her ear while he held her in his arms. She felt herself go warm and damp.

"Oh. I see," she said, rather lamely.

She smiled softly and twisted the damp towel around her like a sarong. I wouldn't mind being shoved down on your bedroll again, she wanted to say. I wouldn't mind finding out if it could be that good a second time, either. Or a third. Or a fourth. Her cheeks warmed, and she knew she was blushing. With her thoughts galloping off into such lustful directions, she was grateful that he couldn't read her mind. She wasn't sure how he'd take an admission like that right now. And it mattered to her what he thought. She was reluctant to let him know just how much she wanted him, how eagerly she would come to him, if he called.

Deep in her heart, she was afraid that he would turn away from her, if he knew. Perhaps not tonight. He'd probably be more than willing to accommodate her tonight, she thought with a grimace. But by the end of the week…

She tightened the knotted towel.

At the end of the week? What did it matter? She wasn't going to be here forever. When they found the stallion, she would have to leave. She had responsibilities to return to.…

And Raider? He would be here, doing as he pleased. He'd made that perfectly clear. He was a loner. A rogue male. A man who wanted to be on his own.

Depression closed in around her. This was a love affair that had no future. She tightened the knot until it hurt. Love affair? Could you call a few weeks and a series of one-night stands a love affair? Oh, God. Her heart twisted, and she wished she could make the world be as she wanted it. Make time stand still. Make this cabin, this feeling she had with Jonathan Raider, last forever.

Raider got rid of his towel and turned his attention to Carolyn. He was startled at the change that had come over her.

She wasn't the same woman she'd been just moments before. A shadow had fallen across her. It was there in the subtle stiffness in her shoulders, the awkwardness in her stance. She was giving off all the signals of someone who had suddenly realized they were in the wrong place. And that melancholy look in her beautiful eyes... He could see it in the dying firelight, shining like a teardrop of sorrow. What the hell had brought that on? Was she already regretting making love? He'd half expected to have to deal with that, but not this soon.

Grimly, he circled her and put his arms around her from behind.

Carolyn closed her eyes and leaned back against him as he wrapped his arms around her and hugged her close. His breath was warm and tickled her ear, making her smile a little. It was comforting to be in his arms again. Safe. Or, at least, she had the illusion of safety, she told herself cynically. Remember your track record, Carolyn. Men are never what they seem.

"Raider?" she asked tentatively.

He pressed his lips against her bare neck, sending a shimmer of tingles racing down her shoulder and hips.

"Hmm?" he murmured.

Vividly, he remembered her calling his name in the heat of passion. "Jonathan," she'd cried out to him, her voice so choked with desire that he'd nearly gone crazy trying to enter her. Now she was calling him Raider again. He wondered if that meant he was back to being the local man for hire in her eyes.

Anger flared in him. That was one of the things he'd always disliked about the rich. They thought they could buy whatever, whomever, they wanted. But the feel of her sensuous curves neatly fitted against him made it impossible to be angry

with her. He couldn't really blame Carolyn for thinking of
him like that. That was more or less what he'd been for the
past five years. For the most part, anyway.

His anger subsided. The question remained. Why was she
calling him Raider?

"The day we met…" she was saying, talking slowly.

He cupped her breasts, enjoying the feel of them against
his palms, even through the damp towel.

"What about it?" he replied.

"You seemed to dislike me on sight." It was hard to recall
that as his thumbs skillfully rubbed her pebble-hard nipples,
and his mouth, warm against her neck, sent sparkles up and
down and all around her.

"I wasn't interested in working for you," he conceded,
lifting his mouth just long enough to reply.

Right now he would have to admit he was fast losing interest in *talking* to her, too.

"It was more than that," she persisted, holding his eyes
with hers.

He stared into their soft brown depths and debated how
much to tell her. He ran his hand over her breast in a teasing
caress.

"Yes," he conceded. "You reminded me of a way of life
I…dislike."

She tried to ignore the feel of his hand on her skin and
concentrate on what she wanted to know.

"And when you thought I was a magazine writer, why were
you so angry about that?" she asked.

He pressed his mouth against the bumps of her spine, kissing his way up a little, then running his tongue provocatively
over the tender nape of her neck. He felt her shiver and bend
her head to give him better access.

"A flashy magazine writer did a first-rate job of destroying
the lives of two of the people I cared about most in this
world," he admitted reluctantly. He tightened his arms around
her and breathed softly on her back. "Can we talk about this
tomorrow?" he demanded in a passion-roughened voice.

She turned and kissed the corner of his mouth, the fine sandpapery rasp of his jaw, the heavily beating pulse in his neck. She cupped his face in her hands and pressed her lips fully against his, kissing him hungrily. Raider responded instantly.

"Okay. Tomorrow…" she agreed in a whisper.

"Now…where were we?" he murmured.

He caressed the sensitive skin of her thigh, and his blood surged in his veins as she twisted, and her breathing caught and became more ragged. Her skin felt feathery soft and salt-sweet on his tongue; the scent of her, intoxicatingly female, filled his nostrils like an ancient aphrodisiac. Had he ever noticed it before with other women? He couldn't remember. Maybe it was something about Carolyn. She had what he wanted. And he wanted it violently. He could feel the primitive male urge to conquer her, to leave his mark on her. It surged up in him like blood-lust in the heat of battle.

But there was something else, too. He wanted to feel her mark on him, on his skin, on his soul.

Carolyn felt the surge of heat and tension in him and arched against him, to comfort and to fall completely into the well of passion. She touched her lips to his, and sweet fire burst out where they met. He moved softly, shifting the pressure of his mouth from one corner of her lips to the other, expertly coaxing wave upon wave of pleasure. The ecstasy grew and spread until Carolyn began to moan softly.

Raider lifted his head and stared down into her soft, doe-like eyes. "What magic do you use on me?" he muttered fiercely.

She stared at him wide-eyed, surprised at his admission. "Does it feel like magic to you, too?" she asked in an unsteady whisper. She ran her hand over his rough cheek, a tender light in her eyes.

He nodded twice. "I want to feel the magic again, beautiful," he told her, lying on his back and pulling her astride him.

He was hard and pulsing as she moved onto him, and she

gasped softly as they joined together in that perfect, magical fit.

He gripped her hips and pulled her hard against him as she clung to his neck, sobbing as the first waves crashed outward, sweeping over both of them at the same time.

When Raider finally stirred again, he touched her tear-dampened cheek. "Why the tears?" he asked huskily. "Regretting this already?"

She was curled half on his chest, half at his side, and shook her head. She nestled her head against his shoulder and tried to explain.

"I wanted it to last forever."

Raider reached over and pulled the other sleeping bag on top of them, then curled Carolyn tightly against his body.

She had wanted it to last forever. Well, so had he, but he wasn't going to tell her that. It would be better for them both if he didn't. Easier to say goodbye, when the time came.

Because he was sure it would.

Only now, it was going to be one hell of a lot harder to do.

The cabin was cold when Carolyn awoke the following morning. The fire had long since turned into a pile of dead, gray ashes. The damp chill of the early morning air seemed to permeate the very walls and seep in around them. She snuggled closer to Raider, who obligingly tightened his arm around her, warming her with the heat of his big, strong body.

But not for long.

"Time to get up," he announced, tossing the sleeping bag off them without warning and bounding to his feet.

Carolyn shrieked and doubled up into a ball, struggling in vain to warm herself.

Raider, already stepping into his pants, grinned and shook his head. "Lady, I gave all I had last night. No showing off is going to get me back down there, so you can just get up and put on your clothes."

Carolyn gave him an indignant look and crawled over to her things, searching for underwear.

"You arrogant devil," she shot back. "This isn't showing off, this is freezing my derriere!"

Raider grinned and looked at her sideways as she hurriedly pulled on her clothes. "You could have fooled me."

She gave him a threatening look, but she shouldn't have bothered. He had already turned his back and was taking down the manty and beginning to lay out the items to be wrapped in it.

They dumped the fireplace ashes, packed, ate a cold breakfast of cereal and juice, and loaded up the pack animals. When the last hitch had been taken and the pack line was firmly tied to Raider's horse, they mounted and rode out of camp.

"Did you build any more cabins, Raider?" she asked.

She was addressing his back, since he was leading the way and she was bringing up the rear, the mules strung between them. He didn't turn around to answer.

"Nope. That was it."

Carolyn tried to be philosophical. She took one long last look, though, before the cabin disappeared behind them in the woods.

"Well, it was one more cabin than I was expecting," she told herself.

She turned her attention to her surroundings and began keeping her eyes open for signs of horses. After four hours she began to wonder if they were ever going to see any.

"Raider, where are all the mustangs?" she finally blurted out, unable to contain the question any longer.

The only ones she had sighted had been miles to the west, on the other side of some hills she could occasionally glimpse.

"We ought to begin running across some of them later on today," he said. He turned back to her, looking much the way he had that first day. He was staring at her from beneath the brim of his stockman's hat, as if daring her to ask another question. "Don't worry. You'll see them. You'll see them all, if you want."

They were just coming down from a twist in the trail when Raider halted his mount and motioned for Carolyn to keep quiet. She turned her head in the direction he was looking, pulling out her binoculars and carefully lifting them to her eyes.

She scanned the valley below them repeatedly, then, suddenly, something moved and she could see them.

There, among the new spring grasses and hardy lowland trees, stood a stallion and his small band of mares and their foals. He had a *manada* of nine. Five mares and four foals. The fifth mare looked as if she would drop a foal any day now.

Scenting the air, the stallion was alert and constantly surveying their surroundings, searching for danger. Since Raider and Carolyn were upwind, quite a distance away and partially hidden by the mountain trees, he hadn't seen them yet. When he did, he'd probably bolt, sending his *manada* off at full speed ahead of him.

Raider, who'd also lifted his binoculars, settled them back onto his chest, letting them dangle from his neck. He eased his horse back into a walk and continued to pick his way down the rock-strewn mountain trail. The stallion caught sight of them when they reached the bottom. With a vicious scream, he whirled on the mares and sent them off at full gallop across the valley floor, never looking back.

Carolyn watched in admiration as they tore off, finally vanishing like ghosts. They were thrilling to watch. It was a small consolation, though, for the prize she sought and hadn't found.

The stallion hadn't been a Thoroughbred.

"How do you know where to find them?" she called out.

Raider twisted in his saddle and turned his head a little to reply. "I've spent a lot of years out here," he said with a shrug. "I know most of their hiding places, their tricks, how they think."

She saw him in her mind's eye, wandering out here alone in the wilds. He would have the dogged determination to pursue the stallions that piqued his interest, studying their habits until he was satisfied that he knew everything there was to know about them. That would suit Raider, she thought, having the upper hand like that.

"So where do you think the next ones will be?" she asked curiously. She didn't have any doubt that his prediction would be accurate. Raider would know, all right.

He pointed to the rise slightly to the northwest of them. "Over that hillock."

"Let's go," she said, eager to get on with it.

Raider grinned at her and pulled down the front of his hat brim in a mock gesture of respect. "Yes, ma'am," he said, then touched his heels to his gelding's flank. The horse started forward. The mules and Kettle instantly followed suit.

They trotted across the plain where the mustangs had been grazing so peacefully a short time earlier. Carolyn began to feel her enthusiasm rise again. Now they were getting somewhere.

If she could only find Firefight...

Chapter 9

Raider knew how to find mustangs, all right.

Over the next three hours they found band after band. Each was jealously guarded by an alert stallion who was not about to let anyone or anything near his mares. As soon as the stallion got wind of them, he charged toward his grazing band, and the *manada* sprang instantly into a gallop. The young foals were expected to keep up, and, amazingly enough, they did. Even the wobbliest-looking youngsters managed it.

Carolyn watched with a mixture of admiration and relief as one especially spindly-legged foal disappeared in the distance. As far as she was concerned, it was nothing short of a miracle that he could keep up with his long-legged elders. They were running like the wind.

Raider reined his horse to a halt and stood in his stirrups, searching some nearby gullies for signs of any horses hiding from view.

"What happens to the foals if they can't keep up?" Carolyn asked, as the herd's fleet-footed gray stallion vanished among the trees with a last defiant flash of his tail.

"His dam usually slows down with him and stays at his side until the stallion comes after them."

She frowned worriedly. "Then what happens?" she asked.

Raider was still scanning the shadows, not looking at her. "The stud comes at the mare with his head low, teeth bared, warning her to keep up with the others or suffer the consequences."

"What if the foal can't keep up?"

He let the binoculars dangle around his neck and sat back down in his saddle. Resting a hand on the saddle horn, he turned to look at her.

"Usually they can," he told her. "The mare brings them back to the *manada* within a few days of foaling. By then, they can run like deer. The stallion usually runs his band a lot, so they build up their endurance pretty fast." He was staring at her curiously.

"And...if they can't?"

He shrugged, as if the answer ought to be pretty obvious. He didn't appear too surprised that she'd asked, though. "The stallion will drive the mare on."

"And leave the foal?" Carolyn asked, dismayed. "The poor little thing."

Raider gave her a long, unblinking look. "If the foal's lucky, he'll be left, and the mare can round him up later. If he's not so lucky...I've seen a stallion kill a foal that couldn't keep up. From the stud's point of view, that one member of the herd was endangering all their lives. The dam wouldn't leave her young, so he eliminated the problem at the source."

Carolyn fell silent, shocked.

Raider shrugged, as if it couldn't be helped. She knew it was hardly something he could control, but it was difficult to see him acting so unmoved by the tragedy.

"Out here, if you can't keep up, you're on your own," he pointed out succinctly.

She looked at him uncertainly. There was a hardness in his voice that reminded her of that first day they'd met. Where was the tenderness, the sensitivity, that she'd sensed in him the night before? Was it still there, beneath the tough exterior? Or had it been her wishful thinking?

"You think the stallion made the right choice?" she asked tightly.

He tilted his head to one side, considering what was really behind her question. From the look on her face, he had the feeling they weren't talking about wild horses anymore.

"I understand why he did what he did," Raider replied. "It was just one of life's tragedies." His voice hardened. "This is reality out here, Carolyn. There isn't any insulation from the things that can go wrong. They fall apart right in front of your eyes. If you want the world to be polite, pleasant, courteous, don't look for it here."

Her eyes flashed angrily. "I don't expect animals in the wild to be that way," she argued vehemently. "And stop trying to see me as some kind of a citified ninny! It's..." She bit her lip.

He didn't let it go.

"It's what?" he prompted her grimly.

"It's the way you react to it that bothers me," she admitted. "You seem to accept it. If they can't keep up, to hell with them." She leaned across the saddle horn toward him. "Did you try to save that foal?" she asked, though she was afraid to hear the answer.

His face went blank, his eyes cool. "No."

Carolyn's heart fell. She didn't quite know why this was so important, but it was. She told herself it was ridiculous to identify with a dead foal, but it didn't help at all. If he'd stood by and watched the stallion murder a helpless little colt, he wasn't a man she could trust. No doubt he'd be just as coolly philosophical, just as pragmatic and tough, about her.

Raider saw the deep disappointment in her eyes and clenched his teeth in anger. She was willing enough to see him as a heartless bastard, it seemed. That infuriated him. It also hurt, but he didn't want to admit that to himself. It was a lot easier just to get angry at her for her lack of faith in him. Perversely, he withheld the rest of the information about the incident with the colt. Let her think what she liked, he told himself. That proud thought gave him cold comfort, though, as he nursed the hurt inside.

He gathered the reins and kneed his mount hard. The horse, startled by Raider's uncharacteristically rough handling, leaped into an effortless lope. The astonished mules brayed in protest, but jumped forward and easily kept pace.

Carolyn bounced hard on the saddle as Kettle took off in an effort to keep up with the others.

She watched Raider's ramrod back and unbending shoulders and told herself she was behaving like an idiot. But she couldn't help it. She knew what the problem was, and that only made it worse.

She was falling in love with him. She was falling hard and fast, and he wasn't going to be there to catch her in the end. He was going to shrug and say it had been a pleasure and ride off into the sunset. She wanted to cry. Of all the cowboys in Nevada, why did she have to run across Jonathan Raider? she wondered mournfully.

"The stallion ought to turn and fight for his foal," she shouted at him stubbornly. "What kind of a male is he, anyway?"

Raider tossed her a look of pure exasperation. "Tell *him* that," he shouted back over the hoofbeats.

"I will. Just point him out to me."

Raider muttered something about the incomprehensibility of the female of the species and glowered at everything in general. Why the hell did he have to find her now? Here? He swore silently, using every curse he could remember.

He was tempted to pull his horse to a stop, drag Carolyn down from her horse and pick up where they'd left off the night before. Then maybe they could have a sensible conversation again. That cooled his temper a little. It was an interesting idea, the more he considered it. Maybe that *was* the problem.

Well, he'd see to that tonight, he vowed.

* * *

They camped at sunset near a gently gurgling stream on a hillside with the most beautiful view Carolyn had ever seen.

They hadn't spoken much since their unhappy exchange earlier. Their comments had been limited to the business at hand. *Did she see that mare? Was that the colt she'd seen? No? Well, time to move on. They could make the next valley before nightfall.*

The stock were grazing contentedly nearby. The fire had been started. The packs were stacked on the ground. The saddles, too. Carolyn sat by the fire, tending the pot filled with tonight's supper, while Raider finished stringing a hammock between two pine trees. He came over and squatted down next to her, taking a cup of coffee from her and drinking it down.

"We could be out here looking forever and not find that horse," she said in discouragement, preferring to talk about *that* disappointment. It was easier than the other one that was bothering her.

"If he's still here, I'll find him. It may take longer than you like, but he can be found, all right."

Carolyn lifted her eyes and looked at him. He was watching her with a steady, thoughtful expression that made her even more wary. She scrambled to her feet and dusted off her jeans in a fit of nervous energy. It was hard to remember that she shouldn't let her guard down with him when he was looking at her like that.

She located the spoons and gingerly filled the bowls with hot, spicy chili. In spite of the warmth from the food, her fingers felt cold and stiff as Raider took his bowl from her.

"Thanks," he said, his eyes still on her.

"You're welcome." She kept her attention on her food and ate.

The nearby branches rustled with the sound of some birds nesting for the night. A soft breeze bent the nearby grass with a subdued whistling sound. Somewhere an owl began to hoot.

Raider watched as she efficiently cleared away the equipment and settled down on the hammock a short time later.

"You've camped before, haven't you?" he asked finally.

That idea had been plaguing him for over a day now. He stretched out by the fire, crossing his long legs comfortably at the ankles, lacing his hands behind his head.

Carolyn turned on her side and stared at him through the hammock mesh. "Lots of times. When I was a little girl, my father took me to a friend's in Colorado to spend the summers. They lived in the mountains, on a ranch. We backpacked, packed-in on horses, hunted...."

He heard the wistfulness in her voice. It wasn't exactly the kind of childhood reminiscence he would have expected from her. He'd half expected to hear that she'd gone on a hunting trip in Idaho with a guide and a half a dozen rich friends one week. As a lark. Or for the experience.

He had the impression that she'd enjoyed those summers in Colorado, too. It was another oddly disconcerting idea. It made her more...accessible. He couldn't tell himself that she didn't belong. That she wouldn't fit. That she couldn't be happy here.

"What kind of a ranch was it?" he said, curiosity overcoming his reluctance to ask. The urge to know her was too strong now to hold back. He wanted to know her the way he knew the back of his hand.

"They ran cattle," she replied. "It was small. A family operation." She was smiling affectionately now, remembering her childhood friends. "They were a real family. A mother. A father. Three boys and two girls." She laughed. "The girls were always the happiest to see me come. They figured I sort of evened up the odds among the kids. They weren't outnumbered by the boys anymore."

He watched her in the darkness, listening between the lines as she talked. She'd been lonely, he thought. Hungry for companionship. Probably so hungry for it that she would have taken whatever was given and tried to make the best of it. Maybe that was what had happened with Gary Lord, he thought. Contemplating that ruined his temper again, and he tried to think of something else.

"They taught you well." It was a frank compliment.

He'd been surprised to see how easily she'd unlashed the ropes from the D rings when they unpacked the mules. He wouldn't be surprised if she could barrel hitch the packs tomorrow morning when they loaded up again. She could probably even balance the manties.

Carolyn turned onto her back and tried to ignore the ache that was tormenting her heart. It was hard talking to Raider like this, sharing her life a little more. She felt as if she were becoming more and more connected to him. And the more they were entangled, the harder it would be when it was over. She wouldn't want it to end then. She tried to stop thinking about it, tried to think of something else to talk about.

She was startled to see Raider suddenly standing over her a moment later. She hadn't heard him move. The heat of desire rushed through her body.

"You move like a cat!" she exclaimed in exasperation.

He pulled off his boots and calmly dropped them on the ground. Then his hand went to his belt, and he began to unbuckle it.

She was tempted to ask him what he was doing, but it was obvious, so she just watched, wide-eyed. He pulled down the zipper and stepped out of his jeans, draping them on top of their piled saddles. Then he loosened the buttons on his shirt.

His naked shoulders were broad and manly, his waist lean and muscled and tapering to straight, strong hips and legs. The dark hair that lightly shadowed his chest narrowed into a slim line at his belly, then burst out in a cloud lower down. She dragged her eyes away from his growing arousal and caught the ripple of his shoulder muscles as he leaned over her. Her breath caught in her throat. The sight of his naked body, so close, so ready, had spread the ache in her chest all through her.

He silently removed her boots, then pulled her to her feet and methodically began removing her clothing—jacket, shirt, jeans. One by one, he dropped them on top of his. The night air was cool against her skin, in sharp contrast to the warmth of his hands as he touched her. Each time he brushed against her, she tingled a little more.

Then he stood straight in front of her, sinking his hands into her soft hair, tilting her face back so she had to look up at him.

His eyes were dark with desire, but she saw a shadow of something else, too. Something that looked like pain. She couldn't bear to think of him suffering, suddenly, and she threw herself against him, wrapping her arms around him tightly, pressing herself close as if that would soothe and comfort him.

He sucked in his breath and lowered his head, capturing her mouth with his and kissing her with a primitive urgency that sent fire through her innermost being. He slid one hand hard down her back and pulled her hips close to him. His fingers bit into her rounded flesh, and she moaned in pleasure.

"Carolyn," he whispered raggedly. "Forget about the rest of the world while we're here." His lips branded the soft skin of her throat and shoulders, over and over, sending sparks of passion racing across her skin. "You're mine," he muttered, grazing her skin with his teeth as if he would mark her as his. "Mine."

Carolyn shivered in response to his possessiveness. When he pulled her thighs up around his hips, she instinctively closed over the hard evidence of his desire for her. She was shaking all over, clutching him, kissing him frantically as he crushed her to him and thrust, withdrew, thrust again, and again, faster, until they were frantic, caught on the edge, had to get over it....

She cried out as one great thrust exploded the tight knot of passion in her and sent it bursting outward, a great fireball that incinerated everything in its wake. She shook as if wracked with a fever that went on and on. Then she wasn't sure anymore if it was just she who was shaking, for Raider's whole body convulsed against her. Her senses cleared, and she heard his strangled cry, felt the gradual easing of tension as his own violent climax eventually came to an end. She clung to him, praying he wouldn't let go of her just yet.

She wanted so desperately to say the words, to say, "I love you." And it was so tempting to say it now. Naked in his arms, in the afterglow of such intense satisfaction, she wanted to tell him how she felt. But she didn't. Fear held her back. He'd said that she was his. He'd said, "Forget about the rest of the world while we're here." But he hadn't invited any confessions of undying love. She told herself to face it and accept it. That was what she would do.

Gradually she relaxed her death grip on his shoulders and hips, and she felt his arms ease their pressure on her ribs. As her senses returned to normal again, she became aware that her ribs hurt. If he'd held her any tighter, he could have cracked them, she thought with a shock. But he hadn't. He'd held back.

She looked into his slate-blue eyes and gently pushed back a lock of dark hair that had fallen damply across his forehead.

He'd wanted her very badly. She took comfort in that. To be wanted that badly by him was really something. She smiled gently and touched her lips tenderly to his. He kissed her gently in response.

"I didn't know you could do it like that," she murmured shyly against his lips. "I mean…standing up…."

She felt the rumble in his chest, heard his rough chuckle as he rubbed his cheek affectionately against hers. They were still joined, to her amazement, and, holding her, he walked the few feet to the fire where one of the bedrolls was spread.

"I didn't, either," he admitted. "Hold on."

She did, and by some miracle he lowered them both to their forest bed, still intimately connected. He had her on her back and raised himself over her, supporting himself on his hands on either side of her head.

"I didn't think…" she whispered in astonishment as she felt him, hard and pulsing inside her.

He grinned like a bandit and threw his head back, laughing

with abandon. He shoved his hips forward, and Carolyn gasped. Instinctively, she tightened her legs around his hips.

"Then this is another first for both of us," he chuckled.

He lowered himself fully onto her and gathered her into his arms. Carolyn tightened her embrace and felt him push into her, that velvet hardness bringing them both instantly back to life, thrust after exquisitely arousing thrust.

He was breathing raggedly, his muscles bunched and taut with the effort to hold back the tide of his own release. He wanted to bring her to ecstasy, no matter what the cost to himself. But she was soft and silky and eager and touching him just right, just right. He gritted his teeth and murmured her name in a hoarse plea. Just when he thought he couldn't last another stroke, he felt her tighten and convulse against him. The first waves of release broke over him a second later. He was saying things he didn't want her to hear, strangling them in his throat, so she wouldn't know....

Carolyn cried out as, once more, the exquisite pleasure overtook her, wringing her with delight after delight. And when he bucked hard against her, sobbing, her happiness doubled. He was chocking back words. She didn't know what they were, but it didn't take a genius to realize that they were endearments. She kissed his damp cheek as he slumped against her in exhaustion, telling him, "I love you," in her silent heart.

"I'm freezing my tail!"

The words were growled against her ear. Drowsily, she struggled to open her eyes. Raider rolled off her and stood up. The loss of her warm human blanket made Carolyn's eyes snap open. She was instantly wide-awake.

Carolyn struggled to her feet, hugging her naked breasts and crouching a little for warmth as she hurried after Raider.

He was already arranging the other sleeping bag in the hammock. He grinned at her over his shoulder as she scampered up to him and hugged him like an oversize hot water bottle.

"Much as I hate to hear myself say it," he told her regretfully, "I think you'd better put on your clothes."

Carolyn nodded and reached for her jeans. It was a pleasure to snuggle against Raider, but it wouldn't be much fun if they came down with pneumonia from exposure, she had to admit. She tossed him his shirt; he'd already put on his pants, although he hadn't bothered to zip them up, she noticed with interest.

Carolyn gratefully crawled into the sleeping bag as Raider zipped the other one onto it, making it king-sized. Then he climbed in beside her. The hammock sagged, and the tree bough creaked. Carolyn stiffened anxiously and looked at the branches.

"Are we going to fall, Jonathan?" she asked, a little testily. Much as she enjoyed sleeping with him, she wasn't eager to collapse on the hard ground. She eyed him closely.

He was looking mildly astonished that she'd asked.

"Do I look like a man who wants to fall on the ground in the middle of his sleep?" A distinctly roguish gleam came into his eyes, and he reached out and fondled one of her breasts teasingly. "Let me amend that," he said huskily. "Do I look like a man who wants to fall on his back while making love in a hammock?"

The creaking had stopped. Everything felt secure again. Carolyn breathed a sigh of relief and snuggled closer. Their shirts hung open, and Raider was making the most of that. She could feel the delightful sensations of his fingers cupping her breasts, gently exploring the puckering nipples.

"You can't make love in a hammock," she protested in sleepy amusement.

He nuzzled her throat and ran his hands down across her belly, then lower. Carolyn stopped breathing as he found the sensitive nub and teased her into readiness for him.

"No?" He pulled down her jeans and lowered his head, taking one eager nipple into his mouth and rubbing his tongue over it, while continuing the excruciatingly delightful massage of her sensitive, feminine flesh. Carolyn wriggled one leg out of her jeans. She was damp and growing hot again in anticipation as he yanked his pants down just beneath his buttocks, just far enough to find out for sure if it was possible to make love in a hammock. "How much would you like to bet on that?" he growled provocatively.

He rolled onto his side and pulled her leg firmly over his hip.

"Hmm?" she murmured, having difficulty remembering the question. She wanted to feel his hands on her again, expertly fondling, caressing, arousing her.

Carolyn moaned as his tongue entered her mouth and deftly caressed its sensitive surfaces.

He pulled her hand down, closed her fingers over him, made her guide him inside her. He moaned his satisfaction at her touch, and Carolyn went liquid with desire. The trees were creaking again in no time, but Carolyn didn't hear them. She was lost in Raider's passionate embrace. And he was lost in hers. She couldn't hear anything but their labored breathing, their groans of pleasure, their mingled cry of satisfaction when release came at last.

The last thing she murmured, before falling asleep in his arms not long afterward, was, "I didn't know you could…" as Raider grinned contentedly at her side.

"…do it in a hammock?" he supplied, tousling her hair affectionately.

"…or…do   it…three…times…in…one…night," she barely managed to add.

He kissed her on the lips and smiled. In the space of those few words, she'd drifted off to sleep. He would have to wait until tomorrow to suggest that they see whether they could do it four times in a night. He would have laughed, but he already knew the answer to that.

He shut his eyes, content in the starlight, with Carolyn in his arms. He wasn't going to think beyond that for now. He'd worry about the rest later.

The following morning Raider was standing on the bank of the stream, stark naked, dripping wet and laughing at Carolyn's efforts to pretend the water wasn't freezing cold. He was rubbing himself dry with a towel while she hastily stumbled over the rocks, her teeth chattering. She gave him an infuriated glare and struggled to dry herself off with the towel he'd thrown into her half-frozen hands.

"How could you stand there and tell me *'It's fine'*?" she demanded indignantly, imitating his drawl with remarkable accuracy.

She stalked across the grassy bank and jerkily pulled on fresh underclothes. She felt a lot cleaner, though, and as she warmed up, her irritation faded. Besides, Raider looked so relaxed and content this morning that she couldn't resist feeling the same.

He saw the softening of her eyes and walked over to her, bending to kiss her softly on the lips.

"Sorry," he said unrepentantly, his eyes still gleaming as dangerously as they had when he'd gotten up earlier. "Since you're a genuine outdoorswoman, do you want to pack the manties today?" he asked with interest.

Carolyn stared at him in surprise. She wasn't sure exactly how he'd meant it, but she decided she'd enjoy showing him that she could do it.

"Sure," she said confidently. "Just stand back and give me some room," she ordered, whipping out one big tarpaulin and shaking it onto the ground. She put her hands on her hips and studied the things to pack. "Let's put this over here," she muttered to herself.

An hour later, they were on the trail. Even the mules seemed pleased with Carolyn's packing.

"Jonathan!" Carolyn exclaimed.

He was already looking in the direction she was pointing.

"Look!" she said excitedly. "Look at them all!"

In the lush green valley below, five *manadas* of mustangs were racing at breakneck speed, the lead mares flying across the ground, the stallions nipping and urging the stragglers on without regard for the other studs.

"Looks like they're kicking up their heels," Raider observed, resting his hands on the saddle horn. He pulled out his binoculars and studied them carefully.

"That blood-bay stallion in the center is the king of the hills around here," he told her. "The buckskin stallion to his left was a friend of his in their bachelor days. The other two stallions—the black and the paint—were the blood-bay's colts. He drove them off a couple of years ago. Last year they finally got old enough and strong enough to catch and keep their own mares."

Carolyn watched in rapt fascination as the horses thundered exuberantly across the wide expanse, tossing their manes, kicking up their hooves, whinnying and snorting like youngsters. She spotted the fifth stallion, whose small band of mares was a little apart from the others.

"What about that one?" she asked.

"I think I saw that stallion last spring about fifty miles from here. And two of his mares. He was just getting started then. Maybe he's passing through, looking for better range for his group. They're just letting him in on the fun, I guess."

"Why aren't the stallions fighting for control of each other's mares?" she asked curiously.

"If they settle down to grazing, that'll eventually come up," Raider allowed with a laugh. "Even the stallions are occasionally willing to have some fun, take a break from expanding their empires."

Carolyn grabbed her own binoculars and peered intently at one mare and colt running with the small band of the fifth stallion.

"That's the colt!" she told Raider triumphantly.

He looked in the same direction.

"A year ago, I think I saw that mare about ten miles from the ledge in that photo you showed me." He returned his binoculars to their case and turned to Carolyn. "I'd say we're headed in the right direction. It looks like Firefight was there a year ago, at least.''

Carolyn leaned back as they descended the narrow trail that would lead them eastward into a neighboring valley.

"How long will it take to get to that ledge?" she asked.

"We should be there tomorrow evening."

For both their sakes, he hoped they didn't have to stay there long. He'd recognized the ledge in the photo the instant he'd seen it. He'd played on it as a kid. And if he was seen in that area now, he might end up with a bullet in him.

The owner of that property was nursing a deep and passionate grudge against him. And he wasn't interested in hearing Raider's side of the story, either.

They were just beginning to think about looking for a campsite when the horses cocked their ears and raised their heads.

"What do they hear?" Carolyn asked, perplexed. "I never saw horses with such acute hearing," she added in a mutter.

Raider grinned at her in amusement. "Old habits die hard," he said.

"Don't be vague, Raider. Just give it to me straight, will you?"

He shrugged and chuckled. "They're mustangs. Even after living in a barn for a couple of years, they still can hear better than most horses. But it's probably the smell they're reacting to."

Carolyn wrinkled her nose. She didn't smell anything. Other than the usual woodland and meadow scents, of course.

"Why didn't you tell me I've been riding a mustang!"

"I didn't think it mattered."

"Raider!"

He held up his hand for silence and reined his gelding to a quiet halt. He cocked his head to one side, listening intently.

"So that's what's got their attention," he said.

Carolyn listened hard. Just as she was about to accuse him

of pulling another practical joke on her, she heard the faint tinkling sound of metal on metal.

"What kind of a bell is that?" she asked. "And what's it doing out here in the middle of nowhere?"

"It's a bell on a nanny goat named Begi Beltza."

Carolyn stared at him in disbelief. Kettle followed behind the mules as Raider proceeded down the narrow trail. The mules wouldn't be hurried, though, so they went slowly.

"Begi Beltza?" she repeated with a definite question in her tone of voice.

"It means Black Eye in Basque."

She decided that he was telling her the truth. Not even Jonathan Raider would make something like that up. At least, she didn't think he would.

"And you know this goat so well that you can identify the sound of her bell at a distance of…" Since they hadn't even seen the goat, she had no idea what to call the distance, so she left it hanging.

Raider was laughing again. "Yep. I know that goat well."

Just then they heard the sound of bleating and barking. They rounded a rocky corner and saw the small valley stretching out to the east. The mountain cast a long shadow over it now. The eastern horizon was purple and rapidly turning the dark gray-blue that preceded nightfall. Flowing across the valley were two hundred white-faced rambouillet sheep. And in the lead was a nanny goat, bell tinkling away as she proudly stepped toward home.

Two mixed-breed Border collies were energetically herding the stragglers. Behind the band walked a tall man with a long walking stick in his hand. His white hair was visible even at a distance.

"Do you know him?" Carolyn inquired. Since Raider seemed to know everything and everyone around here, she would only have been surprised if he'd said no.

"Yes. I know him. That's Uncle Maness."

"Uncle Maness?" He'd managed to surprise her anyway. Since they'd reached the valley floor, they rapidly began closing the distance between them and the sheep and their shepherd. They proceeded at a fast walk, carefully trying to avoid stampeding the flock.

Raider made it clear that he had no more to say for the time being, and Carolyn decided to bide her time. She would have more than enough opportunities to find out about Uncle Maness later, it seemed. The way they were going, they were apparently going to be spending the night with him.

Chapter 10

Maness Biscari greeted them with exuberance.

"Juaness!" he called out genially, raising his walking stick high in the air and grinning from ear to ear. "You've come to visit me, *hein*?"

Raider dismounted and led his horse and the mules toward his uncle as Maness came toward them. The white-haired, rangily built Maness enclosed Raider in a huge bear hug, rocking him from one side to the other for a long moment.

"You look the same," the old man said with satisfaction, taking Raider's measure and holding him at arm's length. Then Biscari looked over Raider's shoulder to take a closer look at Carolyn. He was filled with polite surprise. "Who is this with you?"

Raider turned as Carolyn dismounted and joined them.

"Uncle Maness, meet Carolyn Andrews. Carolyn, my uncle, Maness Biscari." Raider's mouth twisted in a thin smile. "Watch out for him. He has a terrible reputation with the ladies."

Maness, who'd been looking his most charming, switched

to mild outrage and glared indignantly at Raider. "How can you say that about your own blood, *hein*? What kind of a disrespectful whelp have you turned out to be in your old age, Juaness?" he demanded.

Soon his angular, weathered face was wreathed again in smiles, and he was guiding them toward the disappearing flock. The soft tinkling of Begi Beltza's bell was joined by two others, each with its own distinct pitch and tone, as two castrated bellwether rams lumbered along with the group.

Carolyn felt a little like an outsider, walking silently beside the two men, leading the ever-patient Kettle. Or maybe she had just become used to having Raider all to herself; she wasn't really sure. Maness had his arm around Raider's shoulders and was laughing and talking, apparently sharing old familiar stories or updating Raider on happenings of mutual interest. She couldn't follow all of what they were saying. Half of what Biscari said was unintelligible to her, since he freely mixed English and Basque. Every once in a while there was a word that sounded French or Spanish, which she understood, but it only whetted her curiosity. Jonathan obviously had no trouble understanding. He laughed at all the right places and responded in the mixture of languages as if he'd been born to it, which she presumed he had.

The men's talk faded into the background as Carolyn eventually stopped trying to follow the conversation. She watched the flock, spread out ahead of them, leading them to Biscari's camp. The sheep were plodding and bleating and trying to keep out of the way of the ever-circling sheepdogs. Above everything came the song of the bells. Carolyn listened with new interest, realizing that she could tell one from the other. She could pick out the tinkling, sweet sounding tones of Begi Beltza's bell up at the front. But now she also heard the deeper pitch of a second bell and the singsong contralto of a third. Each had its own distinct rhythm, too, as it rang to the gait of its wearer. She scanned the sea of fluffy white backs and finally located the two bellwethers plodding along at their chosen corners of the flock.

The sound of the bells was comforting, she thought. She glanced at Maness as he gave an animated account of something, although of what, she had no idea. It must be lonely out here, with just the sheep and dogs for company for days, weeks at a time or even longer. She could imagine why Maness was so talkative, and she didn't mind not understanding half of what was going on anymore. She understood the most crucial part. He was delighted to see them.

The sheep knew just what they were supposed to do and politely did it, scampering into a very large, partially fenced enclosure that served as their nighttime resting place. The older ewes faced east and lay down on their knees, settling in for the night. The rest of the flock followed suit, as if they were all of one mind. The dogs, seeing that everything was under control, trotted over to Maness, tongues wagging and teeth bared in canine smiles.

Upon seeing Jonathan, they ran to greet him, leaping and playing at his feet, licking his hand in affection.

"The *txakurrak* have missed you," Maness said with a warm smile. He turned toward Carolyn and explained. "The dogs—*txakurrak* in Basque." He looked a little embarrassed then. "I hope you forgive an old man for his bad manners. You don't understand Basque, do you?"

"No." She smiled at him reassuringly. "But I have the feeling I might be about to learn some."

Maness threw back his head and laughed heartily. "Good! Good!" he exclaimed. He gave Jonathan a look of mock disregard, then turned toward Carolyn respectfully. "And what exactly are you doing with such a disreputable character as my nephew, *hein*, Carolyn Andrews?"

"I'm searching for a horse. Jonathan offered to help me."

Maness appeared quite surprised. He looked long and speculatively at Raider, who was beginning to frown beneath his uncle's piercing regard.

"Come," Maness declared firmly. "You are just in time to join me for supper. I'll hear all about it then."

* * *

Maness Biscari's sheep camp consisted of a very large canvas tent the size of a small cabin, two log-cabin-style buildings, and a shed for livestock. He had a wooden outhouse, a well, and a rudely built outdoor shower. It looked as though it had been used for many years as a base camp. There were corrals, water troughs, loading shoots and a winding dirt road that led northeast, down into a lower valley and the ranchlands that adjoined it.

When they sat down to eat at Maness' table, Carolyn felt as if she were stepping into the life that Basque shepherds had lived for decades in the west. The smells were of sheep and stew and the mountain air. Inside the tent, it was cozy and plain. The walking stick rested against the wall by the entrance, near a shepherd's crook.

"Once the sheep are in the *makada*, the bedding down place," Maness was explaining to Carolyn, "I feed the *txakurrak*, and then I feed myself."

He reached for a wineskin and poured homemade wine into thick, clear glasses that were scratched from years of use. He held one out to Carolyn with a smile.

"Drink," he told her. "It's *arnua*. Red Basque tea." He laughed. They raised their glasses in a toast and drank the "tea" down. "It's good, no?" he asked her eagerly.

It was. She smiled and nodded and held out her glass for more.

"Yes. The best tea I've ever had," she agreed.

Maness chuckled and poured. He eyed Raider askance from beneath his bushy white eyebrows. "How did you come to meet my good-for-nothing nephew, *hein*?" he asked. From the affection in his voice, it was obvious that Maness held Jonathan in high regard, in spite of his deprecatory description.

Carolyn looked at Raider, but he wasn't helping her. He seemed to be waiting to hear what she would say with almost as much interest as his uncle.

"I went to Cold Heart to look for a Thoroughbred that I thought might be running with the mustangs there. I was told that Jonathan knew everything there was to know about them. And…he agreed to help me look.''

Raider's eyes were gleaming, and she was pleased that she was able to stare right back at him without losing her aplomb. They both knew she'd left out quite a bit. All the good parts.

"That doesn't sound like Jonathan," Maness said, looking from Carolyn to Raider and back again. He chuckled and poured some more *arnua* into their glasses. "You must be special."

Raider leaned back in the rickety, handmade chair and downed his "tea" in one long swallow. He slapped the glass down on the weatherworn table with finality and looked pointedly at the two great dutch ovens sitting on the camp stove in the middle of the room.

"What's for dinner, Uncle Maness?"

"You don't like our subject?" Maness guessed with a chuckle. He shrugged philosophically and ambled over to his stove.

The scent of lamb, garlic, spices and wine permeated the room as he lifted the lid of one simmering kettle. They feasted on lamb stew, sourdough bread and goat cheese, wiling away the hours of early evening eating and drinking and talking. Maness did most of the talking.

Carolyn began to be able to follow along, though, and now it became fascinating, because Maness was reminiscing. And much of the time he was reminiscing about Raider.

"…and Juaness…do you remember the first summer your father sent you to me in the mountains, to learn to be an *artzaina*?" He leaned toward Carolyn, explaining, "A shepherd."

Raider looked resigned to the fact that his Uncle Maness, his *otio*, as Carolyn had learned, was determined to talk about what he pleased and there wasn't anything that was going to deter him.

"I remember, *Otio*."

"You were so proud to finally be able to come with me. All those summers before, you'd watched your older brother,

Sauveur, have the honor. Then, when he wanted to stay on the ranch with your father to chase cattle, you finally had a turn. Such a fine time we all had, you and I and the other *artzainak*. Remember how Bertrand Menduri taught you how to call the sheep for their honey cakes? How Louis Irola showed you how to throw the *makhila* so hard you could kill a quail for breakfast with it?'' Maness laughed affectionately. ''Oh, the good times we had. It's too bad you and your brother couldn't both come together.'' Maness seemed sad then. ''Your mother never could bear to have both her sons gone at once, she said. Always she feared some accident would befall you, and then you'd both be gone.''

Maness fell silent and looked as if he were regretting the directions his thoughts had taken. ''They were all such good people,'' he said at last, a great sadness in him.

''They're dead,'' Raider said bitterly. ''And it turned out that my mother was right, in the end. Talk about something else, Maness.''

Raider shoved back his chair and strode angrily across the room. He grabbed a bell-shaped glass and filled it with Amer Picon, grenadine, ice, soda and lemon, floating brandy on the top. He glanced at his uncle and Carolyn.

''Shall I make some for you?'' he asked them tersely.

Maness said yes and insisted that Carolyn try it, too.

They sipped their Picons in a somber silence until Raider broke it with a question.

''Tell me, Uncle, have you seen a Thoroughbred stallion running loose around here in the past two years? He'd be about five years old now. He's the color of copper shining in a fire.''

Maness shook his head. ''No. And I would have remembered if I had,'' he assured them. He grew thoughtful. ''I have seen a stranger, though.''

Raider was interested in that. ''Where?''

''He moved onto the old Echeverry ranchlands, the open land with no buildings, about two years ago.'' Maness rubbed his chin thoughtfully. ''He must live in the center of the property, because I never see him when I pass by with the *ardiak*, the sheep." He added the translation for Carolyn. "He isn't very friendly. One day the ewes decided to walk onto his land, and the *txakurrak* and I had to trespass to get them back. Stupid *ardiak*!" His bushy eyebrows arched as he recalled his amazement at the nasty reception they'd received. "He came out waving a gun! A gun!" Maness could still hardly believe it. "I thought for a minute I'd have to down him with my *makhila*." He pointed toward the sturdy walking stick that could be thrown like a weapon if necessary. "But he let us leave. Of course, we made sure never to go near his land again."

"Were there buildings there, Uncle?" Raider asked with interest.

Maness nodded.

"Yes. A small cabin and a large, one-story barn. It's very deserted out there. He probably never sees anybody unless they're coming to visit him. The nearest road is miles away. The nearest town..." Maness shrugged as if it weren't worth mentioning, it was so distant.

Carolyn looked at Raider. "You think they might have hidden Firefight there." She wasn't asking. It was a statement.

"We can find out."

Maness frowned fiercely. "You two be careful! I don't like that man there. He's bad. You can see it the moment you look in his ugly face." Maness wagged a finger at Jonathan warningly. "You are the last of your family. You owe it to yourself, and to all of us, to remain in one piece." He glanced at Carolyn with paternal concern. "And a man does not endanger a lady!" he pontificated.

Carolyn laughed. "I don't think you can blame Jonathan for that," she said. "I told him I was going to look for my horse, even if I had to do it all by myself."

Maness shook his head. "Just be very, very careful." He pressed his lips together thoughtfully. "Would you like to take one of the *txakurrak*? A dog might help." He glowered at the absent stranger. "Especially with coyotes like that one!"

Raider shook his head and got up from the table. He'd had enough conversation for one night. And it had been a long day, to boot.

"Even sheepdogs can't move faster than bullets," he observed in a hard voice.

He looked at Carolyn, as if turning over a possibility in his mind.

She wondered what he was considering, and as soon as they walked out of the tent she asked him.

"Nothing," he said, that annoying tone of finality back in his voice.

She was sure he was keeping something from her, and *that* was something she did *not* appreciate. Since there wasn't much she could do about it, however, she let it go for the time being. Eventually he'd tell her. She hoped.

She followed Raider to the cabin nearest the tent. It was cold and dark inside. He took a long match from the box above the fireplace and dragged it once across the side, drawing it into flame. Within a few minutes the tinder had caught, and the logs that had been laid were licked by the growing flames. She rubbed her arms for warmth as they waited for the fire to begin providing some heat.

"Is this where I should stay?" she asked neutrally.

She wasn't sure what their sleeping arrangements were going to be. She didn't want to upset Raider's uncle. She hardly knew the man, and wasn't certain how he'd feel about her sleeping with Raider in his camp. Much as she hated to admit it, she felt a little awkward about it herself. She caught her lower lip pensively between her teeth.

Raider put his arms around her and drew her close. He gazed down at her with a strange look in his eyes. It was a mixture of seriousness, exasperation and faint amusement.

"Uncle Maness is from the old school. They knew all about sex and passion, but they didn't admit it too much." He sighed. "You're a lady. That means I can't sleep with you while we're his guests."

"I understand." But, oh, how she was going to miss being held in his arms, she thought despondently, snuggling a little closer to him. She'd enjoy him while she could.

His arms tightened, and he lowered his mouth to hers. Carolyn felt the silvery kiss of desire as their lips met. His mouth was firm and hard, but infinitely tender. She opened hers and closed her eyes as he slid his tongue provocatively over the inner surface of her lips. The sweet, spicy sensation tingled right down to her core.

"Jonathan," she moaned, pleading. "It would be easier not to even start...."

He buried his face in her neck and held her tightly. "If you think I'm going to sleep alone, you're crazy," he muttered.

"But I thought you just said..." She leaned back and cupped his face in her hands, trying to see him.

He lifted one dark eyebrow and grinned slightly. "I'll come back," he promised.

And he did. After the camp lay in darkness and the sheep were still, after Uncle Maness was no doubt snoring deeply and loudly, he came back.

She felt him lift the edge of the bedroll spread over the hard wooden frame, felt him lie down next to her, take her in his arms, caress her with the knowledge of how she liked to be touched, kiss her with the sweet mastery that she was thoroughly addicted to now.

And it was as good as it had been the night before. No, she thought sleepily, as she lay tangled in his arms just before unconsciousness claimed her sated body. It was four times as good.

"I ... didn't ... know ... you ... could ... do ... it ... four ... times ..." she murmured.

Was he chuckling, or was he saying that nothing could surprise him anymore? Carolyn didn't know. She fell asleep.

* * *

The next morning Carolyn awoke feeling like the cat that had gotten the cream. *All* the cream. She stretched languorously, remembering the feel of Raider's body on hers the night before. She forced her eyes open and, with an effort, got out of bed. It was hard, since it was so much more delightful remembering the touch of his skin on hers, his mouth on hers, his...

"Carolyn! Think of something else!" she ordered herself as she rummaged for clean clothes in the pack by the bed.

She was alone, but she'd been expecting that. Raider had returned to his uncle's tent, in the interest of propriety. She was surprised, in a way, that he would bow to his uncle's sensibilities. Raider wasn't quite as brusque and independent and devil-may-care as he chose to appear, it seemed. Carolyn found that comforting and very endearing.

By the time she'd dressed, the sheep had been milling about for an hour, bleating and generally stamping their hooves as if itching to hike up to the valley to eat some more succulent spring grass. Maness was standing outside, *makhila* in hand, looking trim and fit for a man of his age.

"Good morning, Carolyn!" he boomed. He led her into his canvas tent and urged her to try some of his sourdough bread and cheese while he cooked some eggs for breakfast. "You'll like this," he assured her, handing her a mug full of coffee mixed with hot goat's milk and sugar. "We call it *kafeznia*."

It was all very good, but by the time she'd finished eating, she began to wonder where Raider was. She'd seen the bleating *ardiak*, the energetic *txakurrak*, and *Otio* Maness. But she hadn't seen Jonathan.

Maness seemed determined to keep her mind occupied. He was showing her his handmade shepherd's flute and playing a few bars of some sweetly sad Basque songs.

"And I can teach you to play *mus* today, too," he was saying.

"*Mus?*" Carolyn inquired politely as she washed the last dish in the washtub and dried it off.

"Basque poker," Maness explained.

"Mr. Biscari..."

"Uncle Maness," he insisted.

"Uncle Maness...where is Jonathan?"

Maness looked away from her, and Carolyn felt the first pang of real worry. He obviously didn't want to tell her, and he didn't want to lie. She went to the door of the tent and looked toward the shed where their horses and mules had been.

Raider's horse was gone.

She turned toward Maness in alarm. An awful thought had struck her. "He went on alone, didn't he? After all that talk about how it was too dangerous for me, he went alone! Didn't he?"

Maness, very sober and a little worried, nodded. "Yes."

Carolyn ran to the shed and saddled Kettle. She pulled her revolver from the saddlebag and strapped it to her hip, checking to make sure that it was loaded and there was extra ammunition in all the belt loops. She mounted and gathered up the reins.

Maness, who had followed her and was looking very upset, grabbed Kettle's bridle.

"He wants you to stay, Carolyn," he said, pleading and persuading in every way he could. "Don't go after him. It will be easier for him if you don't."

She considered that for a long moment. Then she remembered Maness' description of the stranger. A vicious man. A coyote. She pulled Kettle back, and the horse broke free of Maness' grasp.

"I can't let him get hurt, Uncle Maness," she said, a note of desperation in her voice. "It would be worse than if *I* were hurt. I'm sorry. I hope you understand."

She wheeled Kettle around and rode out of camp in the direction Raider had taken hours earlier.

"But you will get lost! You don't know where he has gone!" Maness shouted after her in consternation.

"Don't worry about that. I learned to track when I was fifteen. If his horse's hooves touched the ground, I can find him."

The old Echeverry ranchlands stretched over a lot of countryside, some of it flat and grassy, some of it craggy and studded with rocky hills. The last time Raider had been out there, he had been with his brother. They had been trying to decide whether to make the Echeverry heirs an offer for the southern half of the ranch's holdings.

In the end, they'd decided against it, but not before they'd ridden over what had seemed at the time like every square inch of the place. As Raider reined his gelding to a halt behind the sheltering walls of an outcropping of rock, he could remember how they'd shaken their heads, wondering how the Echeverrys could think they'd ever get their asking price. By some miracle, they had. It had sold, and he recalled hearing that two or three years ago the place had been sold again at an even higher asking price. And not a building on it safe to stand under, either!

Somebody had really put out a lot of money for this expanse of isolated land out in the middle of nowhere. He scanned the landscape, seeing no evidence that the property was earning its keep…not as a working ranch, anyway. There were only a few head of cattle wandering around. They sure as hell weren't paying the taxes on this spread.

Raider slung his leg over the saddle horn and tried to remember precisely where there were places a man could hide around here if he needed to.

Not many came to mind.

He dismounted and loosened the gelding's cinch, then settled down to rest. He didn't have a lot of choice. He was going to have to ride straight in. There was only one cloak he could use to hide his approach from the stranger Maness had seen, and that was the cloak of darkness.

He would wait until night.

As he dozed in the shade of the rock, his hat pulled down low across his brow, the hint of a grin tugged at the corners of his mouth. Carolyn would have figured out what had happened by now. He could just imagine how hopping mad she'd be to find she'd been left behind.

Let her hop. At least she was safe and sound and not around here.

Carolyn stared at the dry, grassy lands, looking for a sign that Raider had passed by. She hadn't seen a hoofprint in longer than she liked. She was beginning to wonder if she'd drifted off his track. Kettle was taking the opportunity to nibble the grass nearest his mouth, content to do whatever she wanted.

Carolyn patted his neck affectionately. He was a good horse. Sound and surefooted and willing.

"Where do you think they went, Kettle?" she asked him.

The horse twitched his ears; he recognized his name. Then he stretched his neck out and stepped closer to a particularly tasty-looking green stem and lipped it hungrily.

It was midafternoon. She couldn't track in the dark. If she lost him, she'd be stuck on her own. Reluctantly, she turned back, searching for the gelding's familiar tracks.

"There!" she said softly to herself. She patted Kettle, who was startled at her sudden excitement and threw up his head sharply. "That way, Kettle."

She just hoped that when she caught up with Raider he would be all right. That had been worrying her ever since she'd realized he'd gone ahead of her.

"Blasted, chauvinistic, uncooperative..." she muttered under her breath. Kettle's ears tilted back, the better to hear her. Carolyn patted the crest of his neck apologetically. "Not you, Kettle. It's Raider I'm calling names."

Kettle's ears twisted forward again.

Raider pushed himself up and rotated his arms experimentally. Either he was getting too old to lie down on the rocky ground, or the earth was harder than it used to be, he thought.

He crawled onto the peak of the jagged rock formation where he'd been hiding out and looked through his binoculars. He could just make out the top of some buildings. Smoke was curling out of the chimney at the corner of one.

Someone was home and cooking. He scrambled back down and put the binoculars into his saddlebag, pulling out some mutton jerky and drinking from his canteen.

That damned horse had better be there, Raider thought. He wondered just how disgusted he would feel if it turned out he was spending an afternoon hiding behind a rock for a rich girl from California only to find that the man living on the old Echeverry ranch had absolutely nothing to do with Carolyn's horse.

He took another swallow of his water and thought about it. He could think of stupider things he'd done in his lifetime.

Then he thought of Carolyn, safe and sound and no doubt madder than a ram in a herd of hermaphrodites. At least he wasn't worrying about her, he thought.

His horse raised his head, lifting his nose as if to test the scents in the air.

"What is it?" Raider asked him softly.

He scrambled to take a look around, but discovered nothing. Just the whispering of the grass and the fast fading light. It made Raider uneasy, though, not finding a cause for the horse's unrest.

When Raider was uneasy, his reflexes became hair-trigger fast. If something was stalking him, it would live to regret it.

Chapter 11

Carolyn studied the barren, rocky hillock. Here and there a hardy pine tree clung to the inhospitable surface. She wondered if, by any good fortune, Raider had decided to hole up there. She could see the thin wisp of smoke on the horizon and guessed that was the location of the buildings that Maness had mentioned.

Kettle had picked up his head, pointed his ears sharply forward and tensed his ribs to whicker. Carolyn leaned forward and slapped him softly on the shoulder to distract him.

"Shhh! I thought you knew better," she admonished him in a severe whisper. "We don't want the bad guy to know we're here yet."

Kettle's ears tilted back and forth, and he turned his head to look at her with one great brown eye. Carolyn was patting his neck and murmuring soothingly when she heard the distant sound of a rotor beating against the air. She touched her heels to Kettle's sides and raced him to the rocky hill.

They disappeared beneath an overhanging boulder just as the helicopter appeared above the eastern horizon.

Carolyn slid off Kettle's back and rubbed his nose to keep him calm. He kept flicking his ears and tossing his head. He'd scented something. She just hoped it was Raider and not the stranger, or a wild animal looking for a meal.

Hidden beneath the rocks as she was, she couldn't see exactly what the helicopter was doing, but she could imagine well enough from the sounds. He'd landed. And probably near the buildings.

"Great!" she muttered to herself. "Of all the days for company to come, they had to pick this one!"

There wasn't much she could do about it. She'd just have to be sure she wasn't seen. She led Kettle around to another slab of overhanging rock and coaxed him into the deepest recess, tying him to the tough roots of a tree that was stubbornly trying to grow on the rock overhead. She had rarely seen a less likely spot.

Just like Jonathan, she thought with a grimace. The tougher it was to succeed, the more determined they were to do it. Maybe it came with being born out here.

"You stay put," she ordered Kettle.

He shifted his weight and rested the toe of his left rear hoof on the ground. He'd gotten the message.

Carolyn crept outside and crawled halfway up the rocky hill. She was low enough not to be seen from the distance, and high enough to see what was below her.

Come on, Jonathan, she prayed silently. *Be here.*

Raider heard the soft scrape and crouched into readiness.

It didn't sound like a wild animal, or something foraging for food or burrowing in a nest. No. It sounded like a leather boot grating softly on rock. He reached down and slid the knife out of its sheath. His fingers tightened. It never hurt to be prepared, he thought.

There it was again. Scrape… Scrape…

Whoever it was would be coming around the corner just about now.…

* * *

Carolyn saw the figure coming at her in a blur. Instinctively she tried to dodge, but there wasn't any place to go. When she jumped away, her right foot was stepping on nothing but air. She felt hard, strong fingers biting into her arm, and then she was slamming against the solid body of her attacker.

She was futilely shoving as hard as she could, but she froze the moment she heard a very familiar male voice swearing viciously in at least three different languages at once. After a solid minute of invective, he began to run out of steam, at least as far as profane comments were concerned.

"Damn it to hell!" Raider seethed.

He was clenching her arms so tightly that he knew she'd have marks for days, even though there had to be three layers of clothes between her arms and his fingers. The idea that he was hurting her only made him madder. He didn't want to hurt her. He wanted to protect her, for crying out loud.

"What the hell are you doing here!"

He was shaking all over, furious and horrified and scared at what could have happened to her—and by his own hand, no less. He leaned against the rock face, then slumped down to sit with his knees jackknifed. He pulled Carolyn down with him without paying the slightest attention to the fact that she was almost falling over trying to keep her balance along the way.

Carolyn was trembling all over and didn't mind sitting down in the least. It was a lot better than collapsing.

"Why did you grab me like that?" she retorted in a furious whisper. "We're supposed to be on the same side. Remember?"

He was looking at her as if nothing would have given him more pleasure at the moment than to drop her over a cliff somewhere. And there was one quite handy.

"On the same side? Over my dead body! You're supposed to be in Maness' sheep camp." He leaned toward her threateningly. "Damn it, Carolyn, I could have killed you!"

He held out the knife. His hand was still shaking a little.

Carolyn paled and looked at him in shock. Maybe he didn't need her help, she thought faintly.

He'd closed his eyes, and she noticed the sweat beaded on his forehead and upper lip, the slight shaking of his hand, and her anger eased somewhat. He was scared to death, she thought. That was why he was so furious with her.

She reached out and closed her hand over his; he was still clutching the knife in a death grip.

"I couldn't let you come alone," she said, pleading with him to understand. He was still looking gray, and he hadn't reopened his eyes. She put her arms around him and laid her cheek on his chest. She could hear the painfully hard thudding of his heart. "I don't want any harm to come to you," she murmured unsteadily.

He rolled his head from side to side and blindly slid the knife back into the sheath strapped to his boot.

"Why do you think I left without you this morning?"

"For the same reason, I guess."

"You guess right."

"But I can help you," she pleaded.

His eyes flashed open, and he glared at her. "By shortening my life by ten years like you did just now?" he snapped sarcastically.

Carolyn stiffened. "No, by being your partner, your backup, in case this guy turns out to be as nasty as Maness thinks." She loosened her arms and wriggled away from him angrily. "I got you into this," she pointed out defensively. "This isn't your problem. It's mine."

Raider smashed his fist against the palm of his hand. "*You're* my problem! And that means your problems are my problems!"

He sounded and looked as if he was thoroughly disgusted by that fact. Carolyn felt the pain in her chest and then in her eyes. She was not going to cry, of all things, she told herself in desperation. That would be the last straw. She jumped to her feet, only to be yanked back down by Raider, who was once again swearing like a Basque sailor.

"Don't push me around!" she told him furiously. "You don't have to sound so put upon, Raider. And *don't* call me your problem!"

He pulled her down onto the rock and half covered her with his body, pinning her with his shoulders and hips and one strong thigh flung possessively across hers.

"But you *are* my problem," he growled, only this time he was searching her face as if to reassure himself that she was really all right.

Carolyn stared at him. Much as he might grouse about it, he *wanted* her to be his problem, she thought in astonishment. He took a very deep and jealous pleasure in that role.

"I lost a woman I loved once," he told her in a harsh whisper. "I lost her because I let her run free. I didn't protect her. I believed her when she said she could take care of herself, when she said she wasn't really in any danger."

Carolyn's heart stopped. His face was twisted with pain, the kind of pain that eats away inside a man and never lets go. The pain of remorse, remorse for actions not taken, things not done that could have made a difference. And it was the pain of a man who was in love.

He loves me, she thought in amazement. Her heart swelled, and a joyous, giddy sensation made her face soften into a tender smile. He loves me.

She raised her hand to his cheek, and he closed his eyes as if in pain, turned his mouth to her palm and kissed her hand, sank against her and buried his face against her cheek, scenting her hair, her skin, reassuring himself that she was whole and safe and his.

"Jonathan," she whispered shakily. Her heart was full of love for him, and she wanted it all to spill out. The words jammed together in her chest, and she couldn't find the ones to say first, so she just caressed his shoulders and hugged him close, saying his name softly, lovingly. "Jonathan…"

He pulled himself together and rolled off her, pulling her up with him as he got to his feet.

"Come on," he said abruptly, drawing her by the hand.

"Let's find someplace where we can keep an eye on what's going on." He glanced at her. "And talk." He looked around. "Where's Kettle?"

"Beneath that rocky overhang," she said, pointing in the direction she'd come from.

Raider found Kettle and led him to the sheltered spot where he'd hidden his gelding. The two horses seemed pleased as they companionably draped their heads over one another's withers and dozed, standing.

Carolyn took a drink from her canteen and followed Raider back up into the rocks. They huddled behind a solid gray boulder as darkness swallowed the land. A small light glimmered brightly in the blackness. The stranger's. And his helicopter-flying guest.

Carolyn was sitting with her knees drawn up to her chest, her back against solid rock. Raider was a foot away, watching the buildings through his binoculars.

"It's too dark to see anything with these," he said at length.

"When are we going to take a closer look?" she ventured.

"*I* am going to have a closer look whenever that light goes out."

She decided not to argue about who was going to be where just yet.

She caught her lip between her teeth. She wanted to ask him about the girl he'd loved, the one he felt he could have saved, but hadn't. And yet she was a little reluctant to find out exactly what had happened. It wasn't always easy to hear about people's old loves. She wasn't sure she wanted to hear about his. Especially a love that had died. Sometimes an old love was transformed into a model of perfection in the memory of the one who had been left behind. Perfection was awfully hard to compete with.

An uncharacteristic stab of jealousy struck Carolyn, which only made her apprehension worse. She didn't want to be jealous of a dead woman. She wanted to feel sympathy and sadness for her.

Maybe the truth would be easier to deal with than her imagination, she decided. *So ask him.*

"Jonathan?"

"What?"

"Tell me about her...the girl who died...."

He sighed and leaned his shoulder against the boulder. He didn't want to have to drag it all up again, and yet, in a way, he wanted her to know. He would prefer that she heard the story from him before she heard it anywhere else. And if she stuck around much longer, she'd hear. He wanted to be the one to tell her about Kimra...and his dead brother, Sauveur.

"Her name was Kimra Barnetche. She came from an old Basque family in California, cousins of cousins of my mother's. She was a beautiful girl. The kind of girl boys blush and stammer around when you're young, the kind they'd give their right arm to walk down the street with when they're adolescents."

He paused.

"When she was twenty-three, she met my brother. She'd taken a job teaching school on one of the neighboring ranches. He was ten years older and already running our ranch. She liked him. He...fell in love with her."

Carolyn had an awful feeling then. She could do nothing but let him tell her, though. She clasped her hands tightly in front of her knees and listened as he recounted the family tragedy.

"They got engaged. But...Kimra wasn't really happy here. Her family had money. She'd come here, taken that job, as a fling. She'd wanted to see something different in the world. She'd seen Europe. She'd gone to school in the East. But a ranch in Nevada...for her, that was something different."

"They broke the engagement?" Carolyn asked cautiously when he didn't continue.

"Oh, yeah," he said. He gave a short, bitter laugh. "Kimra was a very gentle, soft-hearted young woman. She told me she wanted to break up with Sam...Sauveur was his Basque name. But she wanted to let him off easy, she wanted him to fall out of love with her.'' Raider shook his head. ''I told her she might as well expect him to stop breathing, but she was determined.''

''So she talked you into helping her?'' Carolyn guessed.

''Right. We'd met a few times…when my brother was around. So it was easy for us just to build on that. I would take her into town, drop her off at her friends', be the means of her escape. She spent less and less time with my brother, and more and more time with everyone else.''

''Including you,'' Carolyn said sympathetically.

''Including me.'' He grew angry then. ''Her plan might have worked, too, except a flashy female journalist who wanted to study some Basque families who'd made it big decided to interview people around here. She made a big reputation for herself by writing a series of articles that bent the truth without actually lying.''

''That's why I got such a nasty reception when you thought I was a magazine writer?''

He nodded. ''By the time she'd finished, my brother felt his honor had been damaged. Basque men take their family honor very seriously.''

''He thought she'd been unfaithful.…''

''Yes. But he couldn't be sure. Kimra gave him back his ring and moved into town. But…I…I couldn't stay away from her. And Sauveur…found out.''

Carolyn crept over to him and put her hand gently on his arm. ''What happened then?'' she asked him softly. Better to hear it all. Then she would never ask again.

''Sauveur wanted to kill me. He didn't believe me when I told him I'd never touched her. He knew my reputation.'' Raider laughed cynically. ''He'd been the good son. I was the wild one in the family. Drove them all crazy with my tearing around. And then I'd gone off and studied mining instead of ranching, and they'd thrown up their hands for good. He couldn't imagine that I'd be seeing so much of her, especially as beautiful as she was, and not bedding her.'' Raider shook his head. ''Hell, if we'd been anywhere out of the county, I probably would have. But I...I couldn't do that to my brother. Anyway, he took a punch at me. More than one. I'd never in my life let anyone hit me without flattening him. But he was my brother. And I felt guilty. I loved him. I couldn't stay. So I left. On my way out of town, I asked Kimra to come with me. I told her that I had some money. I even had a job. She laughed and said she was fine. She could take care of herself. She told me she'd come to me in six months...after everyone had calmed down. Neither of us wanted the family to be destroyed by this. I didn't like it, but...I couldn't do much about it. That was the biggest mistake I ever made in my life.''

He paused.

''We get some bad electrical storms here in the summer, and one that year was a killer. It started a fire. At first they thought they could handle it, but the winds came up, and within a day it was destroying everything in sight. It rolled across the grasslands and ate through the trees like they were tinder in its mouth. Sauveur rode out to the school to help get Kimra and the kids out. The kids were already gone. So was Kimra. He followed her Jeep tracks and found her in the rocks, where she should have been safe. But she wasn't. And neither was he. The wind had turned. They were trapped. The fire boiled for days, and they were surrounded on all sides. They...died...suffocated in the smoke.''

She tightened her hand on his forearm. ''I'm so sorry.''

They were silent for a long time.

''By the time I got back, things were in bad shape. Money...was something the banks didn't want to talk about. There had been more damage than anybody's insurance could begin to cover. And my grandfather...he was heartbroken. My parents have been gone quite a while now. My brother and I were my grandfather's whole world.''

''Surely he didn't blame you?'' Carolyn asked, aghast.

Raider nodded. ''He blamed me. If I hadn't been a thief and stolen Sauveur's woman, he said, Sauveur and Kimra would have been at the ranch house that day. And still alive.

He disowned me. Told me to get out. Said if he ever saw me again, he'd shoot me on sight.''

"Oh, Jonathan, how awful!" she said, shocked. How could a man say that to his own grandson? How could he believe that of Jonathan? She knelt beside him and put her arms around him, rubbing her soft cheek against his in a gesture of comfort. "Where is your grandfather now?"

"At the ranch," he replied unemotionally. "With a foreman and a few hired hands that come in when he has some stock to run."

"Surely he can't run the ranch alone?"

"No. He can't. But he's too damned stubborn to admit it."

Raider slid his arm around Carolyn and lifted her onto his lap. He wasn't going to tell her the rest, the fact that he had taken care of all the financing and refinancing to keep the ranch going, without his grandfather's knowledge. Besides, he wanted to hold her in his arms. Just hold her, for a while.

Carolyn rested her head next to his, nuzzling his soft, dark hair and pressing her lips softly against his temple.

"Thanks for telling me, Jonathan." She kissed him gently on the cheek.

He looked into her eyes. "I wanted you to know."

He slid his hand behind her head and drew her mouth toward his. Their lips met, and he felt her softness opening to him. Fire darted through him. Fire of longing for her, for her spirit, for her kindness, for her passion as she unfolded in desire for him. He searched a path through her clothes and found the warm, silky skin of her belly.

Then they were sliding down, lying prone together so he could touch her, caress her, have access to her the way he wanted, the way she wanted him to. He wanted to lose himself in her, close out the world and lose himself in her soft fires. His heart began to pound, and the hot pulse of wanting sent heat pouring through him like a fire storm. He felt himself stir and grow hard, and when he pressed against her and moaned in satisfaction, he grew harder still. The scent of her filled him with an eagerness that astounded him. The taste of her on his tongue left him instantly aching for more.

He was muttering against her mouth, dark, secret words, pouring his soul out to her, but in words she wouldn't understand. He wanted to protect her from him, from his passion for her. It could never work. And yet, he couldn't let her go. He wanted her here in his arms. He wanted to have her in his dreams.

He didn't have to ask her; she sensed his need and was already fumbling with buttons and zippers. He smiled at her eagerness, the trembling in her hands. She drew herself closer to him, their clothes hanging loose and open, like teenagers in their haste. The cold night breeze was easy to ignore. Her hands were like liquid fire on his skin. Everywhere she touched him, he burned for her.... His belly, his thighs. She caressed him as if...

He grabbed her hands just in time, and, laughing, she settled on him, swinging her breasts tantalizingly over his chest, her mouth on his, her tongue on his, and she squeezed tight against him, riding slowly, slowly, until he writhed in frustration and forced the pace. She was kissing him, breathing in his mouth, he in hers, and they were one person. He drove sharply upward into her, convulsing as she cried out against him. His seed poured into her quaking body, and she was sobbing against his mouth, "I love you. I love you."

He moved his mouth against hers lovingly, holding her head still, finally letting her relax against him.

He could still hear her words in his mind. A sigh of defeat left him. He'd known what would happen to them the moment she'd walked into Cold Heart. The hell of it was, he hadn't listened to his own sterling advice. No matter how hard he'd told himself not to let her get under his skin, she'd managed to entrap him anyway.

"I hope you don't regret doing that," he murmured. He lifted a strand of damp blond hair and tucked it behind her ear. "I didn't use anything." As she was only too well aware.

She smiled against his shoulder. "I won't regret anything, Jonathan Raider. And don't you, either."

He held her tight. Then he gave her one last squeeze and slapped her on the bottom before pushing her over into a crumpled sitting position next to him.

Carolyn looked up at him, standing spread legged, pulling up his zipper, thrusting his shirttails in his pants, fastening his belt. He looked like a man with a purpose. She wondered how he could recover his strength so quickly. Enviously, she slowly untangled herself from her chaotic array of clothes and began gradually getting everything back into place.

They were back to reality again, she thought, trying to toughen herself to the fact that their time alone with each other was almost gone.

Raider pulled her to her feet and peered intently in the direction of the hill. The lights were out.

"Time to go," he said, leading her back down the rocks.

It was slower going in the pitch dark. Even the blanket of stars didn't help a lot. And she couldn't regret the moonless sky. The less light, the better, when they got to the buildings.

The dual-toned yelping of a lone coyote sent a shiver down Carolyn's spine. She hoped it wasn't a premonition of disaster.

Raider stood by the opening of the rock shelter, legs spread slightly, hands on his hips. It looked like the pose of a pirate captain just before barking an order to his crew, she thought.

"I want you to stay here."

It didn't come as a surprise.

"Would you say that if I were a man?" she asked, trying to be as reasonable as possible.

"You're *not* a man," he pointed out.

"No. But I'd probably be more help to you if I could see what was happening than if I couldn't."

"Forget about helping me. If anything happens, take Kettle due east as fast as you can. There are some woods running along the river there. The helicopter would have trouble spotting you. In two or three hours you'll be at the edge of town."

She put her hands on her own hips and shook her head.

He raised his eyes heavenward as if searching for help from the Almighty. "Do I have to tie you to that tree like the horses?" he demanded.

Raider wasn't sure which was greater, his anger or his frustration. Carolyn—passionate, beautiful Carolyn—was once again demonstrating her capacity to infuriate him, and he was helpless to do much of anything about it. If there was anything he hated, it was the feeling of helplessness!

"Tie me to a tree?" Carolyn echoed in disbelief.

At first she was speechless, then she burst out laughing, covering her mouth in an effort to keep quiet.

"And what happens to me if that coyote comes hunting around here later on? Or if that man discovers you and then comes looking for me? Or you don't come back and no one is here to let me go?"

He held up his hands in defeat. He'd been hoping she'd be too rattled to think of those little details. As usual, she'd dashed his hopes to the ground without a thought, so he would have to protect them both. At least if she needed to run, he'd be there to order her to do it. Although considering the way she resisted his advice, he wasn't so sure she'd pay the slightest attention.

"Then come!" he barked. "But keep behind me!" He shot her a final look of pure frustration. "You can be a royal pain in the *ipurdia*, did you know that?"

He turned on his heel and headed toward their quarry at a dogtrot. Maybe he'd outrun her, just for the pure satisfaction of it.

"A pain in the where?" she asked in an indignant whisper as she ran along breathlessly behind.

He patted his backside and signaled for her to cut the chatter.

A pain in the *ipurdia*, she thought. She'd have to remember that one.

The buildings stood like great black hulls in a landlocked seascape of grass. Except for a large corral, the helicopter parked a few hundred feet from the main house and the barn, there was nothing.

It was, therefore, a little difficult to creep up on the place without feeling exposed. The closer they got, the lower to the ground they ran, ending up nearly on all fours and slowing to a walk.

Raider headed for the barn first. When they reached it, they rested and listened for a moment, half kneeling, half crouching.

The coyote howled again.

He sounded closer.

Raider motioned for her to stay behind him and proceeded along the back wall of the barn, bent low. The windows were shuttered, and the shutters were closed. They continued stealthily around the other end and checked the front of the building.

The door was padlocked. Raider sat back on his heels and stared at it in consternation. "Know how to pick a lock?" he whispered into her ear.

She shook her head regretfully. "Do you?" she mouthed.

He nodded. "But not this kind. It's for pros."

They cautiously felt their way around the barn, slumping against the back wall, out of sight of the house. Getting a look inside wasn't going to be simple.

Raider took out his knife and carefully slid the blade along the sill of one of the windows. Not liking the results, he tried another. On the third try, he smiled slightly. The shutter moved. He jimmied the frame with the knife until it squeaked softly. One more twist and the shutter popped free.

Raider looked inside, opening the shutter a little at a time. Finally, opening it all the way, he lifted the grating inside and pushing his head and shoulders through, balanced for a moment, then dropped soundlessly back to Carolyn's side.

"This opens onto an empty stall. I can hear a horse, maybe two, in there, probably wondering what we're doing. I'm going in for a closer look," he whispered into her ear.

Carolyn opened her mouth, but he put his finger on it.

She kissed his finger and pressed his hand to her cheek, then nodded in agreement. As he lifted himself through the opening and into the unknown, she prayed.

She heart the soft, nervous snorting of a horse, and the low, soothing murmurs of Raider's voice. Then he was back. He reached out to her and whispered, "I think we found your horse. You'd better take a look."

Chapter 12

It was even darker inside than it was outside. When Carolyn slid through the window into Raider's waiting arms, she couldn't see a thing. Gradually her eyes became accustomed to the interior, and she followed him farther inside, feeling her way along the stalls as they went.

Then she saw the horse.

He was a tall, elegant shadow, standing in the center of his box stall, head up, ears alert, a muscle twitching nervously in his shoulder as he watched them approach.

"Easy, boy," Carolyn murmured soothingly.

She stepped slowly onto the lower slat of the stall door, trying to get a better view.

Carolyn peered hard, but it was difficult to see enough detail. He was a Thoroughbred. She was sure of that. Even in the dark, his clean legs, height and graceful carriage were easy to spot. But he was a few feet away, and she couldn't see enough to know if it was Firefight or not.

She reached out her hand a little, palm flat, and called softly to him.

The horse jerked his head back, unsure of the strange approach, disliking being called to in the dark. His eyes were big as he strained to make out the creatures who had ventured into his domain. He let out a soft snort of anger, and he laid back his ears in a show of warning.

"Here, boy, come to me," Carolyn murmured, cajoling him with her voice. No sudden moves. Nothing to startle or alarm a hot-blooded horse. "I'm Carolyn. Who are you? Easy, fella…easy."

She heard Raider move across the hard-packed floor and return to her side a moment later. He was carrying a canvas feed bag and scooped out a fistful of oats, which he proceeded to dribble onto the palm of Carolyn's outstretched hand.

"Maybe he's waiting for you to sweeten the offer," Raider whispered. "That ought to raise the ante enough to get him into the game."

Carolyn made soft murmuring sounds, talking to the suspicious animal standing just beyond her reach. Just when she was beginning to think she'd have to climb into the stall, something she wasn't eager to do until she knew exactly what to expect, the Thoroughbred's ears twitched forward. He stretched out his neck. He took one tentative step toward her. And then he took another.

She felt him blow air out of his nostrils onto the tips of her fingers; then his firm lips cautiously tasted the oats in her hand. And then the ice broke. He moved over to the door, hungrily eating from her open palm.

Carolyn leaned forward and touched his neck. She would recognize that head, those markings, in her sleep.

"Firefight!" she whispered. After all these months, she could hardly believe it. He *was* alive. She turned toward Raider exuberantly. "It's him. It's *him*!"

She swung her leg over the stall door and put her arms around the stallion's neck. Raider, who'd been fully prepared to yank her back if the stallion suddenly became aggressive, breathed a sigh of relief. Firefight was rubbing his face against Carolyn's shoulder like a long-lost friend.

Of course, that was what he was.

"Aren't you glad you didn't tie me to that tree?" Carolyn asked with an elfin laugh of delight.

"Yes and no."

"Just think, if you'd left me behind you'd be sitting here now wondering if this was Firefight or not."

"True," he conceded. "But at least I'd only be trying to figure out how to get the horse and me out of here without getting caught. Keep him quiet. I'm going to take a look out-side."

Carolyn cradled Firefight's velvety nose in her arm and crooned to him.

Raider went to the windows that faced the house and was disturbed to note that a light had gone on. He glimpsed two men walking through the room that was lit and standing in front of the porch door. Apparently they hadn't turned in for the night after all.

He swore under his breath and gave the interior of the barn a quick once-over. Then he grabbed Carolyn's hand and dragged her away from the stall.

"Someone's coming! We've got to hide."

He would have preferred to get out of there, but he didn't know if there was enough time for both of them to climb back out through the window. Not to mention to get away from the buildings without being noticed. Forget kidnapping the stal-lion altogether. Who knew what these guys were going to do? Maybe they always did an evening check of the premises.

Carolyn felt cold all over. Hide? Where? The slats of the stalls wouldn't conceal the figure of a man, or a woman. And there wasn't much of anything else around to crouch behind.

"This way," Raider whispered harshly.

He shoved her to the far end of the small barn and propelled her up the ladder into the low-lying hayloft overhead. She burrowed under the hay while Raider pulled the musty-smelling feed on top of them like a disintegrating blanket.

"Keep still," he whispered.

The straw poking into her side made it difficult, but Carolyn focused on trying. She held on to Raider's waist as tight as she could. If only she didn't sneeze from the dust...

The door to the barn was pushed open, and a light flicked on.

"...I don't care what you think. As a matter of fact, Amory, it would probably be best if you just didn't think at all."

Carolyn recognized the sarcastic male voice of the speaker as belonging to Rance Gagan. So he *was* involved in this, she thought in dismay. But who was Amory? That was a name she didn't know. She held her breath and strained to hear every word.

Gagan stood by a fireproof filing cabinet at the opposite end of the barn from the hayloft ladder. He opened the top drawer and pulled out a folder, riffling through its contents until he found the page he was seeking.

"I need three more vials of the stallion's semen. I'll take them with me when I fly out of here later tonight." He looked from beneath his brows at Amory, who was standing by the stallion's stall. "Amory? Are you listening to me?"

Amory grunted. "Yeah."

"What's the matter?" Gagan sounded suspicious.

"Aw...I been out here too long." Amory was shaking his head slightly, as if to clear it. "I left the feed bag close enough for him to gorge himself on grain." He lifted the bag off the post next to the stall door.

Up in the loft, Carolyn's fingers flattened against Raider's stomach. The feed bag. What else had they left? The window... Her heart froze. Her ears ached with the effort to catch every hint of sound, every syllable uttered below. If they were uncovered, they'd have to act fast if they wanted even the slimmest chance of escape. She felt Raider's long, hard fingers close over hers.

Below, Gagan snapped the file folder shut and put it back into the drawer. He leaned on the gray metal and watched Amory assessingly.

"Tell me, Amory, how long have you been out here horse-sitting?"

"Two years." Amory, a thin, rat-faced man who looked as if he didn't bother to wash more than once a week or so, stared dumbly. "Why you askin' me that? You know the answer."

Gagan nodded. "Yeah. And I remember telling you that all you had to do was stay away from everyone and everything for a few years and we'd all be rich. Remember that?"

Amory never found it easy to follow Gagan, but he'd learned to bide his time. If he just let Gagan talk long enough, sooner or later he would get to the point. It almost always seemed to be some form of reminding Amory that he had to do what Rance said. Amory, his mouth hanging open a little on one side, waited for Gagan to get to the point.

"I'm very disappointed in you, Amory."

"Yeah? How come?" This time a wariness had crept into Amory's voice. He had a sinking suspicion of what was on the way.

"Because you haven't kept your end of the bargain, Amory." Gagan's voice was as smooth and silky as a rattlesnake's nose. "You let us down."

There was a cold, fearful silence. "N-no, I haven't let you down, Rance," Amory stuttered nervously. "I did what you told me."

"Oh, no, you didn't," Gagan said, his voice a cool thread of fury. "You were told to keep this stallion here. Not to let *anyone* see him. *No one.*"

Amory was mumbling his innocence of all charges, but Gagan steamrolled over the other man's protests without hesitation. "People have seen that stallion running loose!" Gagan hit the top of the filing cabinet. The sudden violence spooked Firefight, who tossed his head and stood ready to take flight.

"No…" Amory denied fearfully, shaking his head.

"I can't stand to be lied to," Gagan swore. The sound of

his fist connecting with Amory's cheek made a horrible crunch. "They're looking for him now, Amory."

"It weren't my fault, Rance," Amory sniffled pathetically as he cowered against the stall door. He was furious at being treated this way. But he was more scared of Rance Gagan than he was infuriated at being pushed around. Rance Gagan was not a man to take on in a fight. "That horse is too damned smart. He got the latch up and took off before I knew he could do it. And that old nag over there," Amory nodded in the direction of one of the other three stalls, "he can't keep up with a racehorse! It took me six months to catch him. He was running with the wild horses in the mountains yonder. Nobody saw him. Anytime anyone come near, those mustangs disappeared like smoke in the sky, and this here stud with 'em."

Amory let out a squealy yelp as Gagan gave his elbow a vicious twist. "Horses don't let themselves out, Amory!"

"This one here did!" Amory was grimacing in pain. Gagan still hadn't let go. "Look at the lock I put on the stall door. Why d'ya think I did that?"

Gagan gradually eased the pressure, but he didn't let go. "You know who I work for," Gagan said coldly. "They don't usually give people like you a second chance. If they get wind of what a lousy job you did for them, you're not going to have to worry about keeping track of this horse, or anything else, for much longer."

"It won't happen again," Amory gasped, shaking with fear.

"It had better not. If someone finds this horse, discovers what we're doing…what you're doing…the people I work for aren't going to be making the millions they've been expecting to on this deal. Some of them may even have to have their lawyers earn their retainers by bailing them out of jail, defending them in court. They wouldn't like that, Amory. They wouldn't like that at all."

"No." Amory was staring at Gagan with the horrified, hypnotized fascination of a mouse staring at a cobra.

"And Amory…"

"Yeah?"

"If they end up in trouble, or lose money on this little gamble because some chicken-brain couldn't keep this horse in one place, they're going to take the man who blew it for them and roast him like a pig on a spit."

There was a near sob of relief as Gagan loosened his hold on the trembling Amory, then calmly brushed his hands together, as if dusting the feel of the other man's dirty clothes from him.

"Don't worry, Rance," Amory said shakily. "I know his tricks now. He's not goin' nowhere."

Gagan grunted. The sound of his footsteps fell dully on the hard floor, followed by the clink of the metal door of a laboratory refrigeration unit being opened.

Gagan checked the frozen samples and closed the door again.

"The backup equipment will be ready for delivery in a month. I'll fly it in for you. In the meantime, keep the horse inside the barn. Don't let him see the light of day for the next few weeks."

"Is something going on?" Amory was rubbing his sore arm as surreptitiously as he could.

"Yeah. There's a blonde out here looking for him. And she's talked a local man into helping her out. Jonathan Raider."

Carolyn was surprised to hear the epithet that Amory emitted upon hearing Raider's name. Apparently Jonathan's reputation had preceded him.

"If he comes around, I'll take care of him," Amory assured him.

Carolyn pressed closer to Raider's back. Over her dead body he would, she thought protectively. Apparently Raider had similar thoughts, because his other hand tightened over hers.

Downstairs, the two men were packing a few items for

Gagan to take with him in a heavy, insulated, metal carrying case.

The tickling sensation that had been teasing Carolyn's nose grew more and more intense. She buried herself hard against Raider's back, but the dust tortured her until she couldn't hold back the urge to sneeze any longer.

There was a faint whishing sound, and Gagan, whose life had at times depended on his animallike survival instincts, fell silent, listening.

"What was that?" Gagan asked sharply.

Amory looked at Firefight, who was blowing air through his nostrils in short puffs.

"It's him." Amory gestured toward the stallion.

Gagan concentrated hard, looking in the direction of the ladder. He could have sworn it had come from that direction. But...nothing seemed amiss. He'd been so exhausted when he arrived that he'd had to sack out for a few hours before getting down to work. He shook his head. Maybe he needed to get some more rest. He was beginning to hear things.

"Let's get this stuff back into the house. I'm going to take off in a couple of hours, and I want to catch some more sleep before then."

Otherwise, he'd be falling asleep at the controls.

Carolyn held her nose, forestalling another sneeze, and sagged with relief against Raider when she saw the light go off and heard the door to the barn close and lock.

"*Now* ask me if I'm glad I didn't tie you up," Raider growled warningly as he tossed hay off them and surged to his feet.

"I couldn't help it," she protested. She stumbled to her feet, plucking straw from her hair and quite a few other places.

"It sounds like your racehorse is being used to secretly beef up the bloodlines of somebody's racing stables."

Carolyn was perplexed. "I can understand the insurance fraud," she said. "Somebody wanted to collect the insurance money, preferring it to a live and racing Thoroughbred. But how are they going to be able to use Firefight as a sperm donor? The breeding of Thoroughbred racehorses is very carefully monitored. People are very touchy about that. Bloodlines are crucial in planning breeding programs, in estimating the asking prices of yearlings, and just about everything else."

Carolyn followed Raider down the ladder.

"How about this?" Raider suggested. "The owner of a high-earning filly decides to breed her. He surreptitiously has her artificially inseminated with Firefight's sperm. Then the owner has the mare covered by a respectable but not sensational Thoroughbred." Raider thought a moment, and the possibility of an even more grandiose deception occurred to him. "Better still, he takes the egg from a great mare, inseminates it with Firefight's sperm and implants the embryo in a mediocre mare. They do it with cattle, use surrogate mothers to produce top quality young. Only in this case, the insemination is done in secret, with a public covering by another stallion to hide what they're doing."

"Why go to all that trouble?" Carolyn asked in amazement.

"As far as the public record of the conception is concerned, the foal should be a decent but not sensational Thoroughbred. The colt or filly would be expected to do well, perhaps, but not to be a great winner at the track. But the foal isn't what he seems. He's Firefight's get. And if he's also got the bloodline of a great dam, he's got the possibility of being a stakes winner, a great stud after his racing days are gone. They figure that the foal will be a top winner, but he won't be expected to win because of the lackluster appearance of his publicly recorded pedigree."

Carolyn saw the possibilities unfolding.

"So they win big in the beginning by placing big money at the track on what looks like a complete dark horse. Then, later, when it's obvious the horse is great, they make big bucks on his stud service, maybe even add syndication shares and rake in cash from people wanting to buy in for a piece of the breeding action.''

Raider nodded. He was already looking through the files, searching for something that would help put Gagan behind bars and identify the ringleaders. It was especially slow going since he had to do it in the dark. He studied one sheet carefully, a frown on his face. Then he crouched down behind the cabinets and pulled a match from his pocket, lit it and held it up to the paper.

''This ought to help,'' he muttered. He blew out the match and folded the paper, cramming it into his pocket for safekeeping.

''What is it?''

''Looks like some coded information. The format would fit a list of names, amounts of money, and dates…maybe when a delivery has been promised.''

Carolyn wasn't certain how happy to be. It didn't sound too definitive, but it was better than nothing. She'd been looking over Raider's shoulder and realized that Gagan was being careful to cover his tracks. He wasn't leaving information around that could be easily used against him. Or against anyone else. She shivered at the realization that a group, perhaps a rather large one, was involved in this dangerous deception. Perhaps even people she knew…

''I guess that will have to do,'' she agreed. She moved back to Firefight's stall. He was hanging his head over the top slat, watching with interest. ''Firefight here ought to be pretty solid evidence that something's been going on.''

Raider agreed with her, but he thought it might be kinder not to point out that her father wouldn't be off the hook until they could provide some evidence that led directly to someone else. He wondered how much Amory knew. Somewhere, there had to be a weak link in Gagan's plan. He figured that Amory was pretty weak, but he doubted that Gagan had allowed the man to have much information. And to be useful to Carolyn, the link had to know something.

Raider didn't have time to think about that anymore. They

needed to get out of here. The quicker the better. They'd have to ferret out a talking, knowledgeable link later.

"Let's get out of here," he whispered.

Carolyn was already slipping a bridle onto Firefight. "I don't think he's going to fit through the window," she murmured.

"Very funny," Raider muttered, unamused.

"Just trying to be helpful," she said innocently.

Firefight walked out of his stall peacefully enough, but he stretched out his neck to touch noses with his placid companion in the neighboring stall.

"This is not the time for long goodbyes," Carolyn hissed warningly to the horse. He swung his head around to look at her curiously. "Come on," she ordered firmly, giving him a comforting pat on the neck for encouragement.

He followed, beginning to tense and prance a little as he sensed that they were going to leave the confinement of the barn.

"Easy...easy, boy," she murmured. Carolyn's efforts to calm him were only marginally effective. His ears were pricked sharply, and he was stepping lightly, eager to be free.

Raider was cautiously opening the barn door. They were going to have to leave that way, and it faced the house. If anyone were looking toward the barn, they'd be sure to see them.

"He hasn't been exercised enough," Carolyn complained worriedly. "The minute he's outside, he's going to want to run like wildfire."

Raider lifted his eyebrows as if wondering why she sounded upset about that.

"He's going to be at the right place at the right time, then."

Some clouds had drifted across the starry night sky, settling an additional shroud of darkness over the landscape.

"We can't race him across the countryside in the middle of the night," Carolyn objected fiercely. "If he steps in a hole and breaks his leg, we've lost everything. We'll be lucky if we can see well enough to walk him back to the rocks without finding any animal burrows.''

"Beggars can't be choosers.''

Great. Now he's a philosopher, Carolyn thought darkly.

He swung open the door and motioned for her to lead Firefight out. While she led him around to the back of the barn, Raider closed the door firmly behind them. He couldn't lock it, though, without a key. As soon as someone opened it, they'd realize that something was wrong. With luck, that wouldn't happen until morning.

He found Carolyn wrestling with Firefight. He took the reins from her and gave her a leg up.

"Have you ever ridden a racehorse before?'' he asked as he swung up behind her.

"Not one at his peak,'' she admitted in a whisper.

Raider had his hands full controlling the headstrong stallion, but he managed to hold Firefight down to a quickstep for nearly half a mile. Then, finding the old dirt road still barely visible against the dark matting of underbrush and grass, he let the stallion leap forward into a full gallop.

Carolyn clung to Firefight's back like a burr, her hands buried in his mane. The wind whipped across her face and tousled her hair. It was exhilarating to feel the stallion's power, tremendously relieving to be speeding away from the men they'd left behind. As they drew near the rocks, Raider pulled the stallion in. By then Firefight didn't seem to mind quite so much, and he settled down to a slow trot without much argument.

"He can run, all right,'' Raider said admiringly as they walked toward the rocks where the mustangs were hidden. He patted the stallion's sweat-darkened shoulder. "I can see why they wanted you, old boy.''

Raider slid off Firefight's back and held the horse's head while Carolyn did the same.

"Let's get the other horses and get the hell out of here,'' Raider said tersely, leading the way to the rock shelter.

The clouds boiled and slithered across the sky. By the time

they emerged from the rocks, half the stars were once again twinkling brilliantly, shining their eerie white light down onto the darkened land. They would be visible, if someone chose to follow, Carolyn thought. She glanced back toward the rise that hid the buildings from view. It was hard not to give in to the chilling, insistent tug of fear.

"You said there was a town not too far from here," she murmured uncertainly.

Raider, sitting astride his big gelding, slid his leg forward and leaned down to tighten the cinch on his mount with his left hand.

"Yeah. But Gagan flew in from that direction. If he's flying out in an hour or so, he might be going back that way. Even in the dark, he might spot our movement." He didn't add that if someone noticed that the barn had been broken into, the nearest town might be the first place they'd search. "The town isn't much. If Gagan is connected with big-time racketeers, they'd be able to get their people in there faster than the local law-enforcement official could get us out." Raider slid his leg back down and stared at Carolyn. "And that's assuming that the lawman believed us in less than a few hours and then had any interest in getting us out."

Carolyn caught her lip between her teeth. They were in a very difficult situation. Who could be trusted? Who couldn't?

"All right," she said staunchly. "If the closest town's out, what's the second choice?"

Raider had hitched a tether between Firefight and his horse. He gave the two animals a last few moments to get accustomed to one another before setting out.

"Through the edge of the forest," he said, pointing toward the mountains they'd come from. "We'll stay down in the valley. It's faster than picking our way through the trail. But we'll hug the trees for cover."

Carolyn hiked up the collar of her jacket and settled the heels of her boots downward, the ball of her foot balanced snugly on the heavy wooden stirrup.

They set off at a gentle lope, and Carolyn prayed that the

mustangs hadn't forgotten how to find good footing in the dark.

She tried to stop wondering whether Gagan or Amory was stirring yet, whether they'd gone to the barn and discovered Firefight was missing. She concentrated on the ground ahead, trying to keep alert for rabbit holes, gopher holes, or any other kind of hole a horse could step into, but something was still niggling at her, bothering her. Something from Gagan and Amory's conversation.

"Jonathan..." she called out. It wasn't easy being loud enough to be heard, yet not a bit louder than absolutely necessary.

"What?"

"When Gagan told Amory that you were with me, he seemed to recognize your name."

Raider didn't reply.

"How would they know you?" she asked doubtfully.

He looked over at her; they were riding abreast, with the stallion running along outside. She couldn't make out his expression clearly in the silvery darkness. The impression she had, though, was of a man withholding his answer.

"Do you know why they'd recognize your name?" she pushed him.

"I think I can guess."

"Well?"

The horses shied to the right as one, avoiding the startling shape of a manzanita branch that had suddenly blown across the trail.

"Gagan probably had to do some research on the landowners around here when they were buying this ranch."

"Go on."

"They probably found out how I managed to fight off the wolves and keep my grandfather's lands after my brother died."

Carolyn was confused. "But I thought you were working someplace else...." She'd envisioned some kind of vague, rough, engineering-type job in one of the many mines that dotted the Nevada countryside, opening in good times, closing in bad.

"I was. I was working a mine that I'd bought a few years earlier. And I'd patented a process for extracting ore that was doing in my competitors at quite a clip. I sold the patent, and the mine to put up the capital the ranch needed."

"But why would they know, or care?"

"Probably because they were among the scavengers trying to snap up the property. We pressured a couple of buyers where they felt it the most, threatening to take over some of their more lucrative businesses through stock acquisitions."

"Good heavens, Jonathan!" The fight for his land sounded like a vicious, no-holds-barred quasi-corporate battle. No wonder they would remember.

"Surprise was on my side," he pointed out. "Until their accountants told them what was going on, they didn't know who I was or what I was doing to them. They thought I was the black sheep of the family. They weren't worried at all."

"But how can your grandfather still bear you such ill will?" she asked sadly. Jonathan had saved his home, yet he was treated like a pariah.

"He doesn't know." His profile was hard and unyielding. "He thinks the banks had faith." Raider snorted cynically. "They had faith, all right. In my cash, my assets, and my collateral."

He could have added that the mining company that he'd sold out to had had their pound of flesh. They'd forced him to sign an agreement not to start up a new company in less than five years after selling out. They'd given him a sizable settlement, but they weren't foolish enough to want to wake up the next morning and have to compete against him again.

"Why didn't you tell him?" she asked in amazement.

He gave her a look of pure astonishment.

"As much as he's come to hate me, he might just be stubborn enough to sell the ranch rather than keep it if he knew I'd financed it. He's as stubborn as a jackass sometimes. And his pride isn't much of a help, either."

Carolyn couldn't believe it. "It sounds to me as though stubbornness runs in your family," she told him. "You could at least try!"

He laughed cynically and shook his head. "If I were you, I wouldn't give lectures on stubbornness," he warned. Stubborn woman. She could write the book on the subject.

"What was that?" Carolyn turned to look over her shoulder. "Oh no!"

The helicopter was whirling up into the sky. It tilted and began to fly parallel to the ground. But it wasn't flying toward the small town on the other side of the ranch.

It was flying toward them.

Raider dug his knees into the gelding and gave him his head. "Ride, damn it!" he shouted at her.

He didn't have to bother. They were all flying over the ground like the wind, racing for the trees in the distance. But could they make it before the helicopter reached them?

Chapter 13

They raced toward the trees that sprouted in shadowy clusters over the sprawling foothills. The forest's rough form spilled across the countryside in inky waves, vanishing along the horizon where the darkened land met the stygian night sky.

The leather reins bit into Carolyn's fingers. They had to make it to those trees, their only hope of cover. She leaned low over Kettle's neck, urging him on, flowing with him, rocking him faster, faster....

The sound of the pursuing helicopter spurred them on. Even the horses seemed to sense the desperation of this race; they were accelerating with every stride. Carolyn couldn't feel Kettle's hooves touch the ground anymore. She felt as if they were flying over it, he was so light-footed, so sure.

They broke under the sinuous branches of some box elders and hurtled beneath their sheltering arms. Carolyn sucked the air into her lungs with a heartfelt shudder of thanksgiving. The horses slowed sharply, continuing into the light forest of alders and birch at a nervous, prancing walk.

Raider looked back at Carolyn. "You okay?" he asked sharply.

"Yes." Just a little breathless from fear, she thought, hoping he wouldn't notice.

They halted beneath a pair of thirty-foot trees and strained to locate the helicopter. From the sound, they decided he was hovering about a half a mile ahead of them, then turning, combing the barren, lower ridges of the mountainside.

"Maybe he's not after us," Carolyn suggested, wishing it had some faint chance of being true. "Maybe he's doing something else...."

"Like what?" Raider asked skeptically.

"I don't know...." Carolyn wished forlornly that she could think of something.

Raider backed the horses farther under a thicket of wild vines that were just beginning to grow back from their winter rest.

"Listen," he said sharply. "It sounds like he's doubling back...."

It certainly did. The copter overflew them without hesitating, kept on, heading straight back toward the ranch. Carolyn was tempted to cheer.

"Maybe he ran out of gas," she crowed as her euphoria spilled out in the form of giddy laughter.

"If he did, it won't take him long to fix that," Raider pointed out. Her relief died down. "Watch your step," he warned her. "Let's see how much ground we can cover in the dark. We need as big a lead as we can get."

They urged the horses out into the open and headed south across the gently rolling flatlands.

Carolyn had no idea how far they traveled. By the time Raider called a halt and dismounted, she was practically falling out of the saddle in exhaustion. Lack of sleep and hours of brutal physical effort had sapped her strength. It took almost her last ounce of strength to slide off Kettle, unsaddle him and tie him to the stock line that Jonathan had rigged.

She staggered to a sheltered spot with her sleeping bag,

fumbling badly as she tried to open it. She was beginning to feel like a woman working in a sea of molasses. Nothing moved quickly or accurately anymore. Everything seemed to require ten times more energy than it had in the past. Things didn't get any better when she sank down on her hands and knees in the dark, somehow unable to grasp the zipper, trying to pull it down.

As if from a great distance, through a sound-muffling fog, Carolyn heard Raider's voice by her shoulder. "I'll do that..." he was saying.

She was only vaguely aware of his hand touching hers as he unzipped the sleeping bag. And then she was rolling down onto it, into it, his hands pushing firmly at her shoulders, at her waist, her legs...lifting her...he was lying down beside her...pulling the flap over them, putting his arms around her....

"Jonathan..." she murmured, reaching out. She should have helped, shouldn't have let him put her to bed like a ninny.

"I'm here."

His lips touched her cheek. He didn't seem to mind, she thought fuzzily. Her eyes had sagged shut, too heavy to stay open any longer, but she knew he was close, and she snuggled against him.

His warmth seeped into her, and she began to relax as darkness slowly swallowed her up. As she lost consciousness, nestled in the shelter of his arms, her ear against his chest, she heard him rumble soothingly, "I've got you...." Felt him caress her back in a long, slow, sweeping gesture of possession and tenderness.

"Never let me go," she whispered, thinking it in her sleep.

But he heard the mumbled words and tightened his hold on her.

"Never," he whispered soothingly. Let her believe that, for tonight, anyway. It was true enough.

Carolyn didn't want to wake up.

She was wrapped in Raider's strong arms, feeling infinitely safe and secure. She had no desire to move, to disturb that wonderful sensation. Her eyes were closed, but she sensed the lightening of the sky. The warmth of sunlight filtered through the trees, playing across her face.

She snuggled closer to Raider, trying to keep out the rustling, chirping noises that kept demanding her attention. Birds. She usually liked the little devils, but not today. Their incessant twittering as they roused themselves from a wary night's sleep was making it impossible to slide back into that deep, slumbrous cocoon in which she'd blissfully spent the past few hours.

The touch of Raider's hand on her cheek made her smile wanly, and she buried her face in his neck with a sigh of contentment. The birds whistled and sang, flapped their wings and scattered into the sky. Gradually, she felt her senses beginning to turn on for the day.

"That's our alarm clock," Raider murmured against her throat as he nuzzled her affectionately.

"Too early," Carolyn objected. "Especially after the late hours my date kept last night," she teased.

She stretched, catlike, and curled back against him.

As soon as the word had been said aloud, she'd known it didn't fit him. She couldn't conceive of Jonathan as a date. She lifted her hand to his cheek, blindly, feeling the fine rasp of his unshaven skin, the warmth of his breath as his lips touched her palm. Fire speared her, shooting down from her hand straight to her heart, and drifting insistently lower. No. Jonathan would never be a date. He was a man, her man. Nothing less.

"You shouldn't keep company with a man like that," Raider muttered. He raised his head slightly to speak, then bent to press another tender kiss on her wrist, the crook of her elbow....

"He kept me from harm," she argued gently. She wrapped her arms around his neck and forced her eyes to open and focus. "Thank you for that, Jonathan."

She spoke to him with a softness that was reflected in her eyes.

He sighed and rolled onto his back, pulling her half on top of him. Their clothes were wrinkled, but firmly in place. He made no move to change that, just held her bone-crushingly close for a long, silent moment. Reluctantly he eased his hold on her, expelling a sigh of frustration as he did so.

He couldn't let her look at him like that, with the softness of love so clear, so tempting. He felt a stab of longing for her, not just sexual, although there was that, too. He longed for her in other ways. In every way. He forced the feeling down. There wasn't time for that. Not now.

"Don't thank me yet," he warned her. He ran a hand gently over her tangled hair, slowly down across her shoulders, as if he were committing her every curve to memory. "We're not out of the woods yet."

Carolyn groaned at the pun, and Raider laughed softly to break the tension.

He glanced upward at the overhanging trees and grimaced. They couldn't afford to lie around like young lovers. The sun was up. They needed to make tracks. There was no telling when the hunters would be back, searching for them. He had no doubt they'd have rifles, probably with high-powered telephoto sights.

"Let's get up before I start babbling like an idiot," he grunted.

Raider pushed himself up onto his elbows, but Carolyn pressed him down, splaying herself over him like a wrestler. For a moment he let her. It was hard to resist. The feel of her spread over him was too tempting. Just for a moment, he promised himself.

"Babbling like an idiot, Raider?" she prodded, giving him a curious look.

His eyes were dark and serious. It was like falling into his soul to stare into their naked depths. Carolyn let herself fall, reveling in the sensation of intimacy with him. Gliding, sliding, spilling into his thoughts.

''What would you say?'' she whispered, mesmerized, as she clung to him.

He sighed and closed his eyes. He couldn't bear to let her see any more. When she saw into his heart like that, it was as if she'd taken it, captured it from him. But he'd seen the look in her own eyes, the eager, yearning look of one who loved and needed to know her love was returned, needed to hear the words.

Saying the words would be a death knell. He had to resist the temptation to give her what she wanted, even though he would have given his right arm to tell her just that.

''What would you say?'' she repeated.

This time there was a tremor of doubt in her voice that hadn't been there before. He knew that she'd sensed his love, had been hoping he'd admit it. Now, since he had hesitated, she was beginning to wonder if she had been wrong. Maybe it hadn't been love, after all. Just lust. The light faded from her eyes a little. A small line of worry appeared on her brow.

He found he couldn't look at her and say what he knew he had to. So he pushed her firmly off him and got up, turning his attention to shaking out the sleeping bag and tightly rolling it up.

''I'd probably be stripping your clothes off and telling you I'd never had the hots for a woman like I've had them for you.'' He permitted himself a masculine chuckle of relish. ''You're a hell of a good roll in the hay, Carolyn Andrews.''

He tied the bedding, giving a sharp yank on the cords. Carolyn flinched as if he'd struck her.

''Good roll in the hay?'' she echoed in quiet disbelief.

She was completely stunned at the sudden absence of any hint of tenderness on his part. Gradually the shock wore off, and she thought about it. It was simply too sharp a transition. She couldn't believe it. The memory of his tender caresses still burned on her skin. She recalled the worry in his voice, in his face, as they'd struggled through the past few days.

His words might be cool and distant, but his body had certainly been quite the opposite.

"You find me a good roll in the hay, is that it, Raider?"

Humiliation and the awful tearing of rejection assailed her, hurting bitterly. Her mind might know he was lying to her, but her heart suffered all the same.

"I wouldn't put it quite like that," he conceded with soul-chilling neutrality. He turned his attention to checking the horses' hooves and legs for any injuries sustained in their race through the night. He wasn't looking at her at all.

Carolyn tried to shake off the hurt and joined him.

He was briskly going about the business of saddling his horse, appearing uninterested in further conversation. Carolyn mechanically lifted Kettle's bridle and slid the bit between his teeth. She saddled her horse, finishing just as Raider mounted his. Anger and the pain of needing him burned inside her. She ran to him, holding his horse's head, grasping his knee with her hand. She stared up at him defiantly.

"Don't try to make believe that this has just been some kind of exercise in the slaking of lust," she told him angrily. "I don't know why you won't admit it, but it doesn't change anything. You wouldn't be out here with me, wouldn't have behaved with me the way you have, if you didn't care, Jonathan Raider."

He stared down at her with a face carved in stone. "Don't make this into more than it is," he told her.

The cool, hard edge of his voice was intended to cut her off. He felt it stab at his own heart as he saw the hurt in her eyes. It didn't help that he was doing it for her own good. He didn't want to hurt her at all, for any reason. Silently, he swore.

Carolyn blinked back the pain that his words had inflicted. She wasn't some Victorian maiden, a spineless girl who would swoon if her lover turned away. Besides that, she didn't believe he was being honest with her. She clung to that small consoling thought.

"Don't you try to deny what happened between us," she countered.

He gathered the reins and looked away. He wasn't going to deal with this now. He couldn't.

She let go of the horse, let her hand slip away from Raider's hard knee. There wasn't time for the conversation she wanted to have with him. They had to get out of here. Fast. Stiff-legged, Carolyn marched back to Kettle and swung up onto his back.

Raider was already riding out into the less densely treed area, leading Firefight as before. Carolyn urged Kettle into a lope, quickly catching up. She swore that after they'd gotten out of this, she was going to confront evasive, pigheaded Jonathan Raider.

She wasn't sure why he was denying that he cared for her. Maybe it had to do with the mess his life had become since his brother's death. Maybe he was just one of those stubborn males who couldn't see themselves taking on a woman who had more money than they did. At the rate her finances were evaporating, he hardly had much to worry about on that score, she thought in a burst of dark humor. Maybe it was something else. She rejected the possibility of another woman. Not for any particular reason. She just couldn't stand to think about it.

Carolyn didn't care *what* it was. When they got out of their current predicament, somehow she'd make him tell her. Then she'd find a way to get him to ignore it. She'd gotten investors to ignore plenty of things over the years. Her powers of persuasion weren't exactly untried. And she'd always had a stubborn streak of optimism in her. Where Jonathan was concerned, she wasn't going to admit defeat without putting up a fight worthy of an Olympic gold medal. She was willing to pull out all the stops.

She watched him ride a little ahead of her, a lone, determined figure of a man. In that instant she knew in her heart that there would never be another man for her. There was only one man on this earth with whom she could be truly happy. And his name was Jonathan Raider.

* * *

They'd been riding hard for an hour and a half, Carolyn estimated, when Raider pulled up to a walk and motioned her to come up abreast. He pointed to a twisting streamlet gushing down over some rocks and into a small river overhung by willows on both sides.

"I want you to follow that stream into the mountains. Keep taking the forks to the left. You'll find my cabin about five hundred feet off to the side in a couple of hours. Can you remember the way back to Cold Heart from there?"

"Yes, but—"

"Don't go into town. They may have someone waiting for you. Go west. Follow the cattle trail to the Longsworth ranch. They'll help you. You can phone for help from every police authority you can think of. These guys are probably on everyone's list of lawbreakers, or soon will be."

Raider tossed her the oilskin-wrapped container of food from his backpack. She caught it awkwardly. It was all they had left to eat.

"This ought to keep you from starving. You still got that pistol?"

"Yes, but—"

"Good. Keep it handy." He didn't look too thrilled. "I hope you know how to shoot it."

"Yes. I can hit a bull's-eye as far as I can see, but—"

"Hitting a target isn't the same thing as being willing to shoot at a man," he pointed out in the same hard, businesslike voice he used when he didn't want her to remind him that they'd been sleeping together, sharing more than just sexual intimacy.

Carolyn was getting very frustrated at being cut off every time she replied. Since he obviously wasn't interested in letting her have any say in their plans, she simply sat in the saddle, oilskin-covered pack in hand, and stared at him rebelliously.

He pointed toward some buildings about a mile to the southeast.

"I'm going to see if the phone is still working down there." He didn't look at her. "I want to take the stallion with me."

"Why?"

He shrugged. "If the helicopter comes this way in the next half hour, they're going to spot us for sure. There's nothing but open land around those ranch buildings for a couple of miles. The few shade trees won't hide anything. If they come back and see me alone, they'll start looking for you, probably guessing that you're somewhere in the mountains. But they're probably more interested in getting the horse than you. If they've got the horse, they've still got time to silence you."

"You're drawing them after you?" she suggested. It was amazing how cool she could feel when she had to, she thought. Must be all those years of fighting corporate snakes.

"Not quite that noble." He laughed harshly. "I can run faster alone, if I have to, without you tagging along."

She didn't believe him for a second. She shaded her eyes and stared down at the ranch. She didn't ask him whose it was. She already knew.

Carolyn touched Kettle's sides and sent them hurtling down into the valley at breakneck speed. She heard Raider bellowing behind her in outrage. When he caught up with her, they were traveling at a full, flying gallop.

"What the hell do you think you're doing?" he shouted. "I told you to go up through the mountains!"

"You have no rights over me, Jonathan Raider!" she shouted back at him. "I'll do what I please."

And what pleased her was sticking to him like a burr. He couldn't shake her out of danger so easily. And she wasn't fooled by his arguments, either. He wanted to protect her. Well, she wanted to protect *him*, too.

He was swearing again. At least, she was fairly confident it was swearing, but since it was in several languages, and she hadn't learned those words in the two that she recognized, she could only guess that they were profanities he was yelling with such violent frustration.

* * *

The ranch appeared to be nearly deserted. A few head of cattle could be seen in the distance, grazing and slowly moving away. The corral was in need of a new fence, the mending that had been done looked second-rate, as if it had been carried out by someone who'd never done that kind of work before.

They entered the open area between the barn and the old ranch house at a trot, then walked the horses the last quarter mile. Raider reined in his gelding at the partially opened barn door and pulled the door wide. Firefight pranced and snorted, rearing slightly on his hindquarters.

"Easy, boy," Raider commanded firmly. Firefight rolled his eyes.

They rode into the barn, the horses' hooves clopping dully. They put the horses in three empty stalls. Carolyn had just finished latching the last stall door when she noticed that Raider was already sprinting toward the barn door.

"Hey!" she called after him as loudly as she dared. "Wait for me!"

He had one boot on the bottom step of the front porch to the ranch house when Carolyn heard the pistol shot. She froze and looked toward the open ground in front of the house, where the gunfire had come from. There was a tall, ramrod straight old man standing there, pistol held out in front of him as if he were aiming to fire again. His hair was light gray, curling around the temples and ears. His face was a portrait of agonizing fury.

She heard a sound from the porch and turned back to see Raider crumpling, facedown, onto the steps.

Carolyn opened her mouth to scream, but no sound came. She ran to his side, dropping down beside him, calling his name, heedless of the old man with the pistol still standing there looking down the barrel at her.

"Jonathan," she pleaded, gently pulling his shoulder and trying to turn him over. "Jonathan!" Oh, God, please let him be alive. Let him be all right.

He moaned and helped somewhat as she heaved him back

against her arm, across her lap. Blood was trickling down from his scalp, streaming past his ear and onto his clothing. Carolyn grasped her shirt and violently ripped a strip of fabric from along the bottom hem. Gently she pressed the wound.

Raider flinched and grimaced.

"I'm sorry, darling," she murmured comfortingly. "We've got to stop the bleeding."

He moved his head slightly, then thought better of it. Everything had swirled the moment he'd moved.

"Forget it," he murmured faintly, then, with more strength, he added, "Go inside. See if the phone still works. Call for help."

A shadow fell across them. Carolyn had been trying to ignore the sound of the man's boots as he approached. Now she turned and glared up at him. She didn't need any further introduction. She had no doubt who this man was.

"You're Jonathan's grandfather, I presume?" she challenged furiously.

The old man's eyes blazed down at her, but she noticed that the pistol was hanging from his hand, limp now at his side. Some of the white-hot fury appeared to have drained out of him.

"Mr. Biscari, to you," he spat contemptuously. "Get off my land! And take this cur with you." From the motion of his leg, she guessed he would have kicked Raider if he'd had the opportunity.

Carolyn felt Raider stiffen and struggle to rise. She held him down, still pressing the pad of cloth to his bleeding wound. He didn't have the strength to get up yet, even if he didn't want to admit it.

"Mr. Biscari." She gazed at him without flinching, speaking in her most withering tone. "I can't say that I approve of your method of welcoming people who come to call. You could take lessons from your brother."

"You know Maness?" he asked, startled. He was so dumbfounded on hearing her refer to his brother that he temporarily forgot to take offense at her criticism of his manners. It didn't take him long to remember, however. "Who are you?" he demanded. "And what is that worthless get of my daughter doing on my land?" he added arrogantly, indicating Raider with a contemptuous wave of his pistol.

"He wouldn't have come here on his own, I can assure you," Carolyn snapped in defense. "I don't know which of you is more pigheaded! How can you treat one another like this?"

Raider was turning onto his side, trying to get a grip on his swimming senses. She tried to talk fast, to get to the most pressing concern.

"The men who bought the Echeverry ranch to the north of you stole a horse that belonged to my father and several other people. Your grandson helped me track him down. He's helping me get the stallion out of here and back where he belongs."

Biscari seemed grudgingly surprised. He scowled ferociously. "I told him never to set foot on my land! I told him if he did, I would kill him."

Raider brushed Carolyn's arm away and staggered to his feet. He swayed a little, and Carolyn leaped to his side, putting her arm around him in spite of his weak effort to push her away.

"I didn't know you were such a bad shot, Grandfather," Raider said tautly, pushing himself a little ahead of Carolyn. He tried to shove her up the stairs, but she wouldn't budge, and he was still too groggy to force her. He hissed at her, "Go inside and call for help, damn it."

Carolyn saw Biscari raise the pistol slowly to eye level and once again stare down the barrel at Jonathan. His eyes looked glazed, mechanical, as if he were going through the motions in a dream. Her throat constricted, and her heart stopped. Without thinking, she wriggled in front of Raider, blocking Biscari's line of fire with her body. Raider twisted her around in his arms, turning her away with a violent effort.

"Don't you ever do anything like that again," he warned

her furiously. His strength had certainly come back, too, she noticed in frustration. She couldn't move a muscle.

Raider looked over her shoulder at his grandfather. The old man looked stunned. He stared at the pistol in his hand and then at Jonathan. He shook his head slowly, as if trying to clear it.

"We're going inside," Jonathan said tersely. "If you still want to shoot me, I'll be back in about fifteen minutes. Leave her out of this."

Carolyn felt Jonathan's hand on her back, propelling her up the steps and through the wooden front door. Apparently he was feeling a lot stronger, she thought with relief.

"In there," he said, pointing toward the study to her right, where an ancient telephone sat on a dusty old desk.

He sank down into a lumpy, overstuffed chair, slumping against its rounded back and closing his eyes. The fabric she'd used as a bandage had been dropped in the retreat from the front step, and blood was once again flowing down his face, though much more slowly than before. Carolyn ripped off more of her shirt and held it gently to the wound. She dialed the phone with her other hand, fingers shaking, missing the numbers the first time through. She swore and dialed again.

She felt Raider's hand close over hers. Their eyes met.

She thought he was going to say something, but someone picked up the phone at the other end and she had to speak.

"This is Carolyn Andrews. I'm at the Raider-Biscari ranch and need help right away...."

When she hung up the phone, she could have heard a pin drop in the room. Raider sat, unmoving, staring at her. She gently lifted the pad from his head. The bleeding had almost stopped, she noted with relief.

"Where's the medicine cabinet?" she asked as matter-of-factly as she could. Her hands were shaking, but the rest of her was holding up well, under the circumstances.

Raider's grandfather stood in the doorway, the pistol still in his hand, dangling at his side.

"I want you to get out of here," Raider said. "Kettle could run all day and all night, if he had to. He's a mustang. Take him and keep riding until you reach Longsworth's."

She knelt beside him and laid her head on his arm. "No."

Raider hadn't really been expecting her to agree, but it was hard hearing her say it. He gripped her shoulder and pulled her up onto his lap. The effort cost him, and sweat broke out on his upper lip.

"Will you go if I tell you what you want to hear?" he whispered, pressing his lips to her cheek, to her hair. It was as close to pleading with her as he could come.

She smiled and shook her head gently, lacing her fingers through his and holding his hand with all the strength in her heart. She leaned forward and kissed the dampness from his lip.

"You can't get rid of me so easily," she told him softly. She kissed his cheek. "Show me where the bathroom is. Let's get you patched up."

He held her for a moment longer. "You're a pain in the *ipurdia*, Carolyn Andrews," he swore mournfully.

She laughed and got off his lap; he followed. They stopped to stare uncertainly at Jonathan's grandfather, who was still blocking the doorway.

"He doesn't deserve this, you know, Mr. Biscari," Carolyn said cautiously. "Don't you think you've punished him, and yourself, more than *anyone* ever deserved?"

The old man stiffened, but he didn't lash back. He looked like someone whose one purpose in life had been met, and who had now found that there was nothing left to cling to— only a great emptiness. He looked at Jonathan in anguish; the hollow vestiges of anger darkened his eyes.

"If only…" Biscari moaned.

Raider's jaw tightened. "If only what, Grandfather?" he demanded acidly. "If only my father hadn't ridden in here all those years ago, my mother would have married a Basque instead of an independent man with no place to call home? If only he'd broken his neck on the ranch before I was conceived, you would have had a perfect grandson, Sauveur? If only I hadn't been like my old man—a lady-killer, crook my little finger and watch the girls beg for it—Sauveur would have been married and safely producing a crop of grandchildren for your Biscari lands to go to?''

The old man stepped forward and struck Raider across the face with a hard blow that knocked Jonathan back a step. Biscari's face crumpled, and he raised his fists as if he would curse the heavens.

''Yes! Yes! I've wished all those things,'' he wailed loudly. He fixed his tortured gaze on Raider. ''And do you think I have not hated myself for feeling that way?'' His shoulders sagged. His hands spread in a gesture of pleading. ''I...as soon as I saw you fall, I knew I could not go on living if I killed you, Jonathan.'' He closed his anguished eyes. ''I love you. Though I hated you. And you're right. It was easy to heap the blame on you when Sauveur died, because you are the spitting image of your father, and he took the love of the one great treasure of my life: my daughter. Your mother. When she went with him on that trip, to her death, I wanted to kill him. But he was already dead. And he was a hardworking, faithful husband, so I knew it was wrong of me to nurse such jealousy, such anger. Your mother adored him. But...I could not. God forgive me, I could not.''

Old Biscari sagged into the chair near the door. He let his face fall forward into his hands, and his shoulders shook with sobs.

Carolyn turned to Raider. He looked as if he'd been whipped. All those years, she thought, hurting for him. All those years he'd had to live around the edges, in the shadow of a disapproval he hadn't deserved. Oh, Jonathan...my love...

She pressed his hand. He stood stiffly at her side, his cheeks dark with emotion. She moved a step forward and reached out to Raider's grandfather.

''Mr. Biscari,'' she said, gently touching the old man's

shoulders, "bury the past. Please. Now. Jonathan and I need your help. If we don't get it, we may all be killed."

The old man raised his head and nodded tiredly. "Come. I'll fix him up. Then...we'll work on the other...."

Carolyn held Raider's hand while his grandfather washed the wound, applied the stinging antiseptic and held a bandage to it to stanch the renewed flow of blood.

"You must need glasses, Grandfather," Raider said, raising a dark brow in sardonic amusement.

The old man looked offended. "Why?" he demanded.

"You used to be able to shoot the brass tacks off my pants pockets at a hundred paces without leaving a scratch."

The old man gave a dismissive snort. "I hit what I aimed at," he declared.

Raider nodded, a hint of affection behind the hardness in his eyes. "That's what I thought," he said.

The sound of a rotor beating the air brought an abrupt end to the conversation. Biscari frowned and turned to them. "What's that?" he asked.

"More guests, I'm afraid, Mr. Biscari," Carolyn supplied. She looked at Raider. "They're sure to find Firefight," she said worriedly. "Is there someplace all of us could hide? Maybe they'll decide we left the horses and took off in a ranch truck."

Raider gave her a skeptical look. "Would *you* think that?" he asked bluntly.

"No," she admitted. "But that doesn't mean they wouldn't."

Biscari snapped his fingers and hit his head with his palm. "That boy I hired two weeks ago to mend the fence. He's been gone all morning. Always he's out wandering. If he comes back..."

Raider shook his head. "There's not a lot we can do about that." He was shoving them ahead of him down the stairs and toward the old-fashioned kitchen in the back.

"Yes," Biscari said urgently. "The old winter tunnel..."

"The what?" Carolyn asked.

Neither man explained. They were busy pulling a table away from the wall, opening a cellar door.

"Go," Raider ordered her. He snatched a flashlight from the hook on the wall and flicked it on, pushing it into his grandfather's hand. Biscari led the way, descending a rickety, handmade wooden staircase, with Carolyn creeping along behind. Jonathan maneuvered the table close to the wall, slid through the door and pulled it closed.

"They may notice it, but maybe we'll buy enough time to escape," Jonathan whispered. His voice sounded harsh, reverberating in the dark, musty tunnel.

"What is this place?" she asked.

"It's the way we get back and forth to the barn when there is a blizzard," Grandfather Biscari explained in a whisper. "Shh! What's that I hear?"

Chapter 14

Carolyn held on to Raider's arm. They'd left their jackets in the house, and she could feel his muscular warmth through the brushed cotton shirting. Touching him was reassuring, holding at bay the sudden rush of fear that had shot through her as they stood in the cool, damp darkness. The yellow beam from the flashlight illuminated straight, plank-covered walls and a floor of hand-cut, hand-fitted stone.

The sound they had heard became clearer and much, much louder.

"Gagan's helicopter," Raider muttered. He pulled Carolyn along, holding her hand firmly in his. "I don't want to be trapped in here."

They covered the short distance underground to the barn at a stumbling run. When they'd almost reached the end, Raider pushed Carolyn against the wall and held her there with his body.

"I want you to stay here," he whispered against her mouth. His firm, warm lips touched hers, and she slid her arms around his neck as a potent mixture of ecstasy and fear swirled within her. "For once, will you do what I ask?"

She felt the tension in him, heard it in his voice. Much as she hated being left behind, she hated to argue with him about this. She had faith in his judgment, she realized. Enough faith that she was willing to gamble her life on it.

She kissed him on the lips, as if she would give him her soul. He kissed her back as if he would gladly take it.

"Whatever you say," she whispered, shaken by the near desperation she sensed in him, and in herself.

He rested his face against hers and pressed his lips to her jaw. He recognized the gift of trust she'd just given him, and he couldn't find the words to tell her just how much that gesture of faith and confidence meant to him. In the end, the words came out without his thinking about them. It was the right time, the right place.

"I love you," he murmured huskily against her ear, so only she could hear. He felt her hold back a sob and held her more tightly. "Never forget that I love you...."

Then he hugged her hard and tore himself away.

"Keep that peashooter handy," he whispered. The tenderness was gone now. He was all business.

"You're welcome to it," she quickly offered, unsnapping the holster cover.

"No," he said firmly.

Carolyn could barely make out the half smile on his lean features. Unerringly, his hand found hers in the darkness and closed over it comfortingly.

"It'll be easier knowing you've got it. Just grit your teeth and squeeze the trigger, if you have to." He added, more softly, "Remember, they can't afford witnesses, Carolyn. And they've already shot at you." The hard sound of anger returned to his voice as he recalled that.

"Right," she said, striving for calm and confidence.

Raider laughed softly, easing the tension for a moment. "You're beginning to sound like me," he observed, ruffling her hair in tender amusement.

They heard the sound of the helicopter landing on the west side of the buildings. Raider sobered and made his way toward the end of the connecting tunnel. He handed the flashlight to his grandfather, who'd been standing there, listening for any identifying sounds overhead.

There was a wooden ladder at the tunnel's end, rising from the stone floor and stopping at the ceiling just inches above Raider's head. It opened into the barn floor above. Exactly where in the barn, Carolyn couldn't tell. They probably wouldn't have put it in the middle of the entrance, she reasoned. More likely it was along one wall, perhaps in the section reserved for saddlery and small equipment. She held her breath and hoped no one would see Raider.

He cautiously pressed the trapdoor upward and crawled out onto the floor, shutting the door quietly behind him. He was gone.

Old Mr. Biscari put a hand on her shoulder and doused the beam of the flashlight.

"My grandson has hunted since he was very little," he told her softly. To Carolyn's surprise, for the first time she heard the unmistakable ring of pride in Biscari's voice. "He's as light-footed as a cat, as shrewd as an eagle, and he's as strong as those mustang stallions. Two men are no match for him, Carolyn...."

"But what if there are more than two?" she whispered anxiously.

Carolyn fingered her revolver and prayed she wouldn't have to find out if she could actually use it in self-defense.

Biscari patted her shoulder comfortingly. "Jonathan held off four men in a bar once when he was nineteen. And they were men who knew how to fight. I don't think he's forgotten much since then."

Carolyn had the feeling the old man was trying to reassure himself as much as her. She hoped he was right. Most of all, she hoped they managed to avoid fighting altogether. That seemed highly unlikely at the moment, she thought unhappily.

There was no way to escape from the ranch without being seen.

Her hand closed over the butt of the revolver, just in case....

Raider crawled along the floor on all fours, skimming over it quickly, his belly brushing the ground from time to time. He was in the storeroom at the end of the barn nearest the ranch house. Within seconds he was crouched beneath the storeroom window, cocking his head to listen.

The helicopter engine had been turned off; the long, heavy blades were silent and still. The doors opened. Slammed shut.

Raider cautiously raised his head and peered over the sill through the weather-stained glass. He could see Gagan approaching the front porch, and Amory sneaking around to the back.

They were both carrying rifles. Grimly, Raider sank back down and quickly made his way into the barn in a crouch. His family's rifles were locked in a cabinet in the ranch house. The closest things to weapons in the barn were pitchforks and shovels.

He wasn't wild about throwing one of those at a man pointing a gun at him. Bullets traveled faster than he could throw, although when he thought of Carolyn and his grandfather trapped in hiding below him, he was willing to give almost anything a try.

He promised himself that when they got out of this mess, he was going to lock Carolyn up in a room somewhere for a month and neither of them was leaving it. Which brought him back to his original problem. He had to find a way to get them out of this.

He looked over the rafters, the stalls, the horses staring at him curiously as they roused themselves from their brief rest.

Perhaps he could trap the bastards....

Carolyn leaned her head against the cold, hard planking that shored up the tunnel and served as its walls. She had lost all sense of time since Jonathan had vanished through the trap-door. It seemed as if an eternity had passed, yet she knew it probably hadn't been more than ten or fifteen minutes.

Old Mr. Biscari was rubbing his hands together, pacing a little, mumbling to himself in his impatience and worry.

"Jonathan said you had a foreman and sometimes hired hands," she whispered hopefully as she recalled Raider's comment. "When are they coming back?"

Biscari's shoulders sagged a little and he shook his head mournfully. "No hired hands. Just that boy I told you about. There hasn't been enough work to keep many men busy. Even my last foreman quit. I could only pay him part-time wages."

Carolyn was astounded. "You and this boy have been run-ning the ranch by yourselves?" she asked.

Biscari sighed. Sometimes it took a disaster for a man to realize how stubborn and blind he had become. It looked like this was one of those times.

"The bank has been willing to back me," he said, proudly defensive.

He stubbornly refused to admit the full breadth of the di-saster to Carolyn. She was a stranger. More importantly, she was obviously very close, and very dear, to his grandson. He couldn't bear to have Jonathan, whom he had tried so hard to hate, see the horrible extent of his failure. It was bitter enough having to endure it himself day after day. He clung to the idea that at least the bank was with him, although for the life of him, he couldn't really understand why. They'd never seemed so willing to back so little before, as far as he knew.

"The bank," Carolyn said in a whisper.

She bit her lip. She had no right to tell Biscari otherwise. Jonathan had confided in her in a moment of weakness. She had to honor his wish that his grandfather not know the true source of his financial backing. But she couldn't keep the sadness, the frustration, completely out of her response. Bis-cari's head lifted suspiciously.

"Why not? Banks extend credit to businesses...."

"Yes..." She didn't want to talk about it anymore.

She listened for the telltale sounds of someone approaching, but heard nothing. She didn't know whether to be relieved or frustrated. Waiting, not knowing, was awful.

Carolyn moved closer to the ladder and gripped it, pressing her fingers against the wooden slats where Jonathan had stepped before disappearing through the trapdoor. Where was he now? What was happening?

Biscari made no effort to continue their conversation. He'd been assailed by a mind-numbing thought when Carolyn had so distractedly replied to his last comment. What if it hadn't been the bank? What if, these past five years, it had been someone else?

He stood in frozen horror as the last five years of self-deception unraveled under the stress of the past hour and a half. Tears welled in his eyes. Jonathan, he thought. It was Jonathan all along.

Gagan was standing in the upstairs hallway of the ranch house, staring at the bathroom. The door was open, and he could see into the small trash container. Someone had been injured. Bloody bandages were visible, and an applicator stained with antiseptic.

Amory slithered up the stairs, his eyes darting furtively from side to side. "No one up here?" he asked, having already concluded that that was the case.

Gagan nodded and shifted his rifle to a more comfortable position. "But they can't have gone far. That's fresh blood." He went back down the stairs and into the study, then the front parlor. "They must be around here somewhere." He paced like a caged beast. "This girl has taken up enough of my time," he growled. "Shoot her on sight. The cowboy, too. And anyone else you see around here."

Amory nodded, following nervously at Gagan's heels. "But won't there be an investigation? What if they come out to our place and start asking questions?"

Gagan had already thought of that. "We'll burn the place to the ground. We'll leave one of the rifles with the cowboy, the other with the old man. Make it look like they finally shot it out and the girl just got in the way.''

Amory was grinning. That sounded brilliant to him. Gagan was wandering into the kitchen, searching the walls, looking behind the door.

Amory trailed along behind. ''What are you lookin' for?'' he asked, his mouth beginning to sag open in mystification.

Gagan was tempted to put a bullet into Amory along with everyone else. The man had the intelligence of a field mouse.

''I'm looking for the cellar door,'' he growled. ''A storm cellar… Something underground…'' A cold, feral grin spread across his twisted lips. He pointed toward a table that wasn't quite flush against the wall behind it. He could see the clear markings of a door, complete with a rope-pull handle. ''Something like that,'' he said.

Raider figured he'd done what he could with what he had. He heard a small scratching sound and looked around, alert to the possibility of imminent danger. The sound, whatever it was, stopped. It must have been something from the house, he supposed. He looked at the horses. Their ears were up. The mustangs relaxed first, going back to grinding their teeth in boredom. Firefight was different, though. He was as tense as a horse in the chute before a race. He was looking anxiously at one of the barn windows. Raider looked there, too. There was nothing.

Whatever it was, he couldn't stick around to investigate, Raider thought uneasily. Maybe it was just the nerves of a hot-blooded horse. He hoped so. He didn't need any more twists in his day. He was beginning to get nervous about having left Carolyn and his grandfather in the tunnel so long. Sooner or later, Gagan was bound to discover it. He'd gun them down like animals if he did. Raider felt a cold chill of fury and fear curl in the pit of his stomach.

He'd willingly kill Gagan with his bare hands if that happened. In a running crouch, Raider dashed across the barn toward the storeroom and the trapdoor.

Carolyn heard the sound first. It was the soft, grating noise of the table being dragged across the floor of the kitchen.

Biscari pushed her up onto the first step of the ladder. Carolyn gripped her revolver again. She wouldn't let them shoot down poor old Biscari, who'd had nothing to do with this. Except having a grandson who she'd found irresistible...

"Go," Biscari urged her.

"Jonathan wanted us to wait...."

They heard the sound stop. Light filtered into the far end of the tunnel. They couldn't wait. In a matter of seconds they'd be seen. And caught. Carolyn put her hand up against the trapdoor just as it was flung open.

Raider's face was above her, and he leaned down and hauled her up. Biscari scrambled up after her, and they closed the trapdoor behind them.

"Push these on top," Raider told them, indicating three big, heavy barrels nearby. "I'll trap them from the other end."

He was out of the storeroom and sprinting toward the ranch house before Carolyn could do more than nod.

Biscari and Carolyn put their shoulders to the job, rolling the barrels awkwardly the short distance necessary. As they settled the last barrel in place, they heard men's voices below, followed by creaking and pounding as Gagan and Amory tried in vain to open the door now buried beneath the barrels.

The barrels didn't budge.

But what about the other end? Carolyn swallowed a sob of terror and raced out of the barn, stumbling on the porch steps in her fear-fueled race. She had to get back to the kitchen entrance of the tunnel in time to help Jonathan block it before Gagan and Amory realized what had happened. He would be facing them alone, unarmed.

Jonathan...

Amory was pushing against the trapdoor, growing beet-red in frustration.

"They gotta be up there," he whined angrily. "They sure ain't anywhere else."

Gagan stood back and thought. Then he whirled and raced back toward the thin ray of light filtering down from the other end of the tunnel. He didn't have a flashlight, and he stumbled and went down hard when he was halfway there. He shoved himself to his feet immediately, cursing his stupidity.

"Just one clear shot, Raider," Gagan swore. "That's all I need. Just one clear shot at you."

Carolyn burst into the living room just as Raider put his back against the twenty-year-old refrigerator. Only two or three more feet and he'd be close enough. Then he'd push the door shut with the refrigerator to keep it closed.

He recognized Carolyn's footsteps, but he was too busy trying to close the tunnel to yell at her to stay away.

The refrigerator touched the door and Raider shoved it again, grunting with the effort. Six inches more.

"Stop right there," Gagan snarled.

He had his shoulder and half his chest in the doorway opening, the rifle awkwardly aimed in Raider's direction. Because Gagan couldn't quite fit, the rifle wasn't fully against his shoulder, and he wasn't looking down the gunsight. Raider wasn't tremendously reassured by that. There was a good possibility that someone who'd done as much shooting as Gagan had could hit him even from a ridiculous position like that.

"Come around to this side," Gagan demanded. "And push the refrigerator away from the door."

Carolyn had frozen on hearing Gagan's voice. She stepped carefully toward the kitchen door and pulled her revolver out of its holster.

Raider was estimating his chances of diving behind the refrigerator before Gagan squeezed the trigger. He figured he had about a fifty-fifty chance of catching a bullet. If he opened the door for Gagan, he calculated the odds at more like 100 percent. He was preparing to do a swan dive when he heard the pistol report and saw the rifle bob in Gagan's hand.

Carolyn was standing in the doorway, calmly aiming for a second shot. The rifle lifted, swung toward her. Raider dived on top of it just as Carolyn squeezed the trigger, firing again.

Biscari was walking as fast as he could, but when he heard the shots, he rediscovered the strength of his youth. When he arrived in the kitchen, he saw Raider on the floor, Carolyn kneeling beside him, and Gagan slumped against the door in the wall, bleeding and saying he wanted his lawyer.

"I should think you would want a doctor," Biscari said sourly.

A whining voice from the tunnel called out, "I give up. Don't shoot." Amory's rifle came flying through the open doorway and clattered onto the floor.

"The brains of a field mouse," Gagan muttered before passing out.

Carolyn was down on her knees, holding on to Raider's shoulders as he pushed himself into a sitting position. She was shaking badly from head to toe.

"I thought I'd hit you," she cried, tears welling in her eyes.

Raider looked gray and stared at the rifle on the floor under him.

"No. You didn't hit me." He gave her a slight grin of approval. "You hit him. Nice shot." He took an unsteady breath and put his arms around her, as if reassuring himself that she was really there, whole and well. "I saw him aim at you, and…" He swallowed and closed his eyes, tightening his hold on her painfully. In his mind's eye he'd seen her hit by a bullet from that rifle, and it was worse than anything he'd ever faced in his life. All he wanted to do was hold her forever. Not let her out of his sight.

Carolyn sank against him, tears of relief beginning to roll down her cheeks.

They heard the sound of a single-engine airplane overhead, then the unmistakable changes that signaled descent and landing.

"Who the hell would be landing in the middle of the

ranch?'' Raider asked, wondering what new threat might have arrived. There wasn't a landing strip here. There was barely any smooth, clear ground. The pilot must have had a pretty urgent need.

Biscari was taking reluctant charge of providing emergency medical care to the unconscious Gagan.

"He'll be all right," Biscari assured Carolyn. "It's a little bullet, and he's big. I don't think you hit anything vital." He grimaced at Gagan. "Too bad."

Amory poked his face into the light but quickly withdrew back into the tunnel when Biscari growled at him angrily.

"I'd better take a look out front and see who's joined our little party," Raider said, appearing none too pleased.

Carolyn, still clutching his hand, trotted alongside.

The plane had already landed by the time they got to the porch. Raider frowned at the tall, sandy-haired man jumping out of the plane and running toward the ranch house. A state trooper emerged from the other side and was following on the run, gun drawn.

"The good guys!" Carolyn cried in relief.

"What's a BLM pilot doing with a state trooper in tow and choosing to land here? Now?" Raider demanded suspiciously.

Carolyn squeezed his arm. "It's okay. I know the pilot," she said euphorically. "That's Ted Weston, the friend of a friend who took that photograph. I called him just before we left and asked him to keep an eye out for Firefight if he was flying in this area. I told him we'd be searching on the ground."

Weston took the steps two at a time and stopped dead when he saw Carolyn and Raider. A big grin lit his squarish face, and he heaved a sigh of relief.

"The police said you called for help," Weston said. "Lucky I happened to be flying around, huh?"

Carolyn crossed the room and gave him a hug. "Lucky for us," she admitted.

The state trooper proceeded to take charge. "Are you the woman who called for help?" he asked. When Carolyn said yes, he added, "The sheriff is on the way. In the meantime, somebody tell me what's going on here."

Raider had already lifted the phone and was dialing. "There's a man sleeping in my grandfather's kitchen who appears to need a doctor's attention..." he began.

It took three hours to sort things out. The authorities loaded Gagan and Amory into a county fire marshal's observation plane that was hastily drafted to serve as emergency police transportation to the nearest hospital and jail. By then, most of the facts had been sorted out, and the state police had called in some other investigators to join them in a search of the old Echeverry ranch as soon as someone dragged Judge Nolan away from his fishing and obtained a search warrant.

Carolyn saw a small figure dart into the barn, and she decided it might be a good idea to check on the cause of all this excitement. When she reached Firefight's stall, she was startled to see a slightly built, dark-haired youth standing there with his arms thrown around the great stallion's neck.

She was so astonished that Firefight would let him get close that she didn't speak, just stood watching in amazement as Raider quietly joined her.

The boy was sobbing as if his heart would break. His scrawny shoulders shook as if he were in the grip of an invisible giant. She thought there was something familiar about him, though, and she approached the stall as realization slowly dawned.

"He must be the kid my grandfather was talking about," Raider said. He sure didn't know much about mending fences, if he was.

The youth raised his head sharply and turned to face them, his face ravaged with tears of joy. His dark eyes shone triumphantly, in poignant contrast to the dirty wet streaks on his boyish cheeks. And then the light of recognition glowed in them as he saw Carolyn.

She went into the stall and hugged both him and the stallion while Raider watched, a little apart.

Carolyn held out her hand and motioned for Jonathan to join them. "Jonathan Raider, meet Elias...Firefight's truest friend, and my friend, too."

Two hours later, the sheriff was finishing his questioning of Carolyn. She came out of the living room and noticed that the door to the study was slightly ajar. Hoping to find Raider there, she put her hand to it, to push it open so she could enter. She paused, however, when she heard Biscari speaking in an emotional, tear-choked voice, struggling manfully to keep from breaking down openly in front of his grandson.

"...All this time, you were the one who kept the land.... I...I thank you, Juaness."

Raider's back was to her, so she couldn't see his face. From the stiffness in his shoulders, the way he was angrily slapping his hand on his thigh, she could see he was as uncomfortable as his grandfather.

"Look," Raider said tautly, "this doesn't change anything. Keep on as you have. In the next six months I'll be back in business again, and showing a profit within nine. Just hang on a little longer. Next spring you'll have pastures full of cattle again, or sheep, if you want."

Biscari shook his head and stood resolutely by the window, his hands crossed stubbornly over his chest. "The ranch is yours," he said. The anger and fight and fury were no longer there. In their place was a fatalistic calm, an acceptance. He had finally let go of his hatred and was prepared to move on. He turned and held out his hand to Jonathan. "The ranch is *ours*, Juaness," he amended with iron conviction.

Raider seemed taken completely by surprise. It took him a long moment to realize that his grandfather truly meant it. Slowly, he raised his hand and gripped Biscari's. One firm shake, and Biscari stepped forward. Stiffly, he embraced Raider, then awkwardly stepped away.

"Let's talk," Biscari said brusquely, hiding behind the comfort of a business conversation. There had been enough emotion for one day.

"All right," Raider agreed.

Carolyn quietly withdrew. Let them begin the mending, she thought tenderly. It wasn't going to be easy. There was a lot to forgive. The two men walked outside together, deep in conversation, discussing ways to keep the ranch going for one more difficult year. Carolyn slipped back into the study and dialed the Winset Nursing and Convalescent Center. They connected her immediately to Nurse Barnes.

"Frances? This is Carolyn."

"Thank God you've called! Your father was taken into emergency surgery early this morning."

Fear chilled Carolyn to the marrow. Her grip on the receiver tightened painfully. "Is he all right?" She held her breath in agony.

"He made it through the operation, but he's just been taken to the recovery room. If there is *any* way for you to be here…"

"Of course. I'm in North Central Nevada. I'll fly back as fast as I can. If you can, tell him…tell him that everything is going to be all right. I've found what we were looking for…."

There was a mystified pause at the other end, but the nurse was accustomed to delivering private messages, and she once again rose to the occasion. "I'll tell him."

Ted Weston was standing in the doorway when Carolyn turned away from the phone. "Can I help?" he asked. "I've got enough gas to fly you to an airport."

"Oh, Ted, I could hug you!" she exclaimed in relief.

Ted grinned but stepped back, hearing Raider's firm stride approaching through the living room.

"The thought counts," Weston assured her, casting an interested glance at Raider as he crossed the room and swept Carolyn up into his arms. "But I think I'd better pass…." Weston wasn't the least bit interested in arousing the jealousy of a man like Jonathan Raider.

"Jonathan," Carolyn murmured weakly as he covered her face in kisses. "They've just operated on Abel. I've got to go. He needs to know that he's going to be cleared.... I have to be with him.''

Jonathan stilled, then slowly let her slide down his front and settled her on her feet. A frown settled over his hard face. He nodded in agreement.

''I take it Weston offered you a lift?'' he asked, tilting his head in Weston's direction.

''Yes.'' Carolyn nodded.

Everything was so chaotic. She desperately wished that Jonathan could come with her, but someone needed to take charge of the situation here. And someone had to keep an eye on the coppery-colored million-dollar racehorse in Biscari's barn that had been the cause of almost everything.

''Go, then,'' he said. He shot a hard look at Weston. ''Take good care of her.''

Weston nodded and grinned. ''Let's go, Carolyn,'' he said, turning to explain the situation briefly to the lawmen before they left.

The last thing that Carolyn saw as the plane soared up through the clear western sky was the lone figure of a man standing in the open land, away from the ranch buildings. He was looking up at them, watching them go. Not waving.

''Goodbye, Jonathan,'' she whispered tremulously.

She closed her eyes and tried to get a grip on herself. There was still a lot left to do. She couldn't fall apart now. There was an ache for him in her, though, and it was hurting worse the farther away she got. She wished he'd told her that he loved her again. Just once more.

Chapter 15

Carolyn was so exhausted that she was unaware of the stares she got during the next seven hours. She had been out in the woods for a few days, and she most certainly looked it. She catnapped on the two flights it took her to get back to Los Angeles. When she arrived in Long Beach, the news from the hospital was encouraging. Abel was sleeping now. The operation had been a success. Since she was both filthy and flat broke, she decided to get cleaned up and go to the bank before heading for the hospital.

The house was musty and damp, having been closed up for weeks, ever since Carolyn had gone to Nevada. With a growing feeling of relief, she stepped into her shower stall and turned the water on full blast. The scented shampoo standing on one gold filigree-edged tile in the corner felt wonderful. And so did the big fluffy towel she used to dry herself a luxurious half hour later.

Carolyn changed into a stylish silk dress that tied casually at the waist; the soft peach and cream colors made her feel like a woman again, instead of something the cat had dragged in. She was smiling as she put on her makeup.

If only Jonathan were here…

Her smile dimmed. She wondered what he'd think if he *were* here. She remembered the first day he'd seen her, the way he'd rejected her with such contempt. Raider had an aversion to wealthy women and their comfortable life-style. She put the lipstick down and looked at the nails she'd just carefully polished.

He'd loved her when they'd been living in the woods, but would he feel differently when he saw her on her own turf?

She couldn't afford to worry about that now. First, she had to get to the hospital….

Abel lay in the white-sheeted hospital bed, tubes running down into his arm, his face pale. Outside, it was nighttime. Only a small night-light shone in his room, but the light from the hospital corridor provided enough illumination for her to see in the semidarkness.

Carolyn quietly stepped toward his bed and drew up a chair close to it. She slid her hand over his and held it. His eyes gradually opened; he blinked, as if concentrating hard to focus his vision. Then he rolled his head slowly to one side, to see who had come to sit with him. Shock, then happiness, flooded his exhausted face.

"Ca…ro…lyn…" he whispered. His speech was slurred, but it was recognizable.

Tears of joy welled up in Carolyn's eyes. The operation had been a success indeed. He was going to recover. And now he didn't need to worry about what he would face when he finally got out of the hospital, she thought in sweet triumph.

"We found Firefight," she told him, brushing away a lone tear that had stubbornly rolled down her cheek. "And we caught some of the men who'd been holding him."

"Got…Firef…" He couldn't manage the rest of the word.

Tears blurred his old blue eyes, and he sniffed, then cried openly.

Carolyn leaned over him and embraced him as carefully as she could, holding herself back so she didn't hurt him, kissing his cheek tremulously.

"We'll get them all, Abel," she swore. "You just concentrate on getting better. When you're ready...you're coming home."

There was a rustling at the door, and the nurse bustled in.

"Not too much excitement, the doctor said," the nurse informed her kindly. She smiled at them, but there was a no-nonsense gleam to her experienced eyes. "Sit with him, but no more talking."

Carolyn nodded. She sat back down and clung to Abel's hand, as if she would infuse him with her own strength merely by that touch. Abel closed his eyes and took a deep breath.

They sat together like that until the staff chased Carolyn away. She walked across the hospital parking lot, hearing the lonely tap of her stylish heels, and wishing that she wasn't alone right now. The Mercedes leaped forward as she pressed on the accelerator. She was home in half an hour.

A good night's sleep wouldn't hurt, she told herself. She dropped her clothes on the lounge chair in her bedroom and fell into bed wearing the first negligee she plucked from the drawer. A tear slid down her cheek, and she told herself it was from exhaustion. But when she hugged her pillow to her, the ache behind her eyelids eased a little. And as she fell asleep, she murmured Jonathan's name and dreamed she was back in his arms.

It was the insistent banging that finally dragged her awake late in the morning of the following day. If there was any way she hated to wake up, it was to that kind of insulting, violent whacking at her front door. She struggled out of bed and blindly pulled a satin robe from the closet. Barefoot, she made her way sleepily to the door.

"All right, all right," she said irritably.

She rubbed her eyes and shook loose her shoulder-length hair, gradually beginning to feel as if she might actually be awake. She looked through the peephole in the front door and was surprised to find Gary Lord standing there. He was dressed in his usual impeccably stylish way, but he looked a little rumpled to her, as if he were still wearing yesterday's clothes. Maybe she wasn't as wide-awake as she thought. Gary made it a point never to look rumpled. She opened the door.

"Gary! What are you…?"

He pushed by her, thrusting her into the room ahead of him and shoving her with such force that she stumbled and nearly fell.

"You couldn't leave it alone, could you?" he snarled, his eyes wild. He raked his hands through his hair nervously and began to pace back and forth across the room. "Do you know what you've done?" he demanded, his voice sounding strangely high-pitched.

This wasn't a Gary that Carolyn had ever seen before. This was a man driven to the brink of madness, just about to snap.

She tried to stay calm, to avoid provoking him. This Gary was dangerous. Very, very dangerous. She tightened her belt and ran her tongue over her suddenly dry lips. "What have I done?" she asked warily.

He stopped in the middle of the room and stared at her. "All you had to do was marry me. Not ask questions. Do what I told you to."

There was a woodenness in him that was even more chilling than his wildness. He raised a hand as if he would touch her hair, then took a step toward her. Carolyn thought it might be better to stand still, and she let him approach her, but she couldn't suppress her reaction to his unwelcome, clammy touch. She flinched.

His eyes became flat. "I have nowhere to go," he said. The sudden absence of emotion added to Carolyn's alarm. He'd slipped out of control. Gary, who'd always made it a point to be a model of masculine success, who'd done all the right things for years. Almost. "I wanted to be a success in life," he went on, caressing her cheek. He didn't seem to notice her slight withdrawal, her effort to avoid his touch. "When they told me all I had to do was help set that fire, I couldn't resist, Carolyn. They offered so much money.... We could have had everything we wanted.... You would have looked so beautiful.... I could have had my name up in lights...."

He was looking at her as if she were a figment of his imagination, of his deeply selfish fantasy. His arms closed about her, and he touched her lips with his.

Carolyn couldn't stand it. She pushed against his chest with both hands and turned her face away. "No! Stop it, Gary!"

His face contorted in rage. "Gagan said you like it," he spat. "I told him he was wrong, but he was right, wasn't he? Wasn't he, Carolyn?"

"Gagan?" The horror of what he had said made her feel physically ill. She twisted hard, trying to get away, but he bent her arm back in a hammerlock until she cried out in pain.

"I wasn't good enough?" Lord asked in silky, venomous outrage. "I wasn't good enough? Let's see who's better, your stinking cowboy from Nevada or me...the man you said you'd marry...."

He dragged her down onto the floor and began pawing at her in frantic, vengeful lust. He was a man driven by overpowering emotions, and Carolyn began to scream in terror as she realized she wasn't going to be able to stop him. He was too strong for her.

She heard the thin fabric of her nightgown rip as he tore at the front of it, felt the sharp pain in her shoulders and thighs as he pinned her mercilessly down and reached for the belt to his pants.

"No!" she screamed, twisting and turning and desperate to get away from him. "No!"

The door flew open with a crash, and before Gary could turn to look over his shoulder he was being plucked off Carolyn and hauled to his feet. Carolyn saw Raider smash his fist into Lord's face and land a gut-smashing punch solidly to

Gary's middle. Lord fell like a log, already unconscious, but Raider followed him to the floor and was preparing to pound his face.

"Jonathan!" Carolyn cried out, pushing herself up and trying to cover her breasts with the robe. "Don't!"

Raider had stopped the second she'd cried out, but he held his arm ready to land another blow. He saw her through a red haze of fury, and the sight of her fumbling with her torn nightgown wasn't helping him much. His eyes glittered murderously. Gary made the mistake of trying to come to his senses, and Raider punched out his lights again with one hard blow.

Carolyn scrambled to her knees and threw herself into Jonathan's arms. Tears were flowing down her cheeks, and she was sobbing wildly.

"Just call the police," she begged him as he crushed her in his embrace, kissing her face, her neck, her hair. "I don't want you to end up in jail."

He drew her up with him as he stood, and held her tightly for a long, shuddering moment. Then he tilted her face up to him and searched it, reassuring himself that she was indeed all right.

"I didn't want to let you out of my sight after what happened at the ranch," he said in a raspy whisper. "But, I didn't have much choice. I'm glad I caught the first plane out here that I could, though."

"So am I," Carolyn said with a heartfelt sigh. She wrapped her arms around his waist and pressed her face against his chest.

Raider couldn't speak for a moment. The memory of seeing Carolyn on the floor, struggling against Lord, still made him feel like breaking the man's neck. He couldn't ever remember taking a punch at someone with more pleasure. But he wasn't going to kill him. He would let the courts take care of Gary Lord.

Raider located her phone and called the police. It was an hour and a half before the authorities had finished with them and driven off in a squad car, with Lord in handcuffs in the back.

Raider shut and locked her front door as best he could. After the way he had crashed through it, it would need new hinges, but that would just have to wait. He had something more important on his mind.

Carolyn was curled up on the couch. She watched in silence as he gave himself a tour of her small but obviously expensively furnished home. When he sat down next to her, she had to force herself to ask, "Do you like it?"

He stared at her thoughtfully. "Your house, you mean?"

She nodded, holding her breath. She couldn't tell what he was thinking. The man could be a blank wall when he wanted, she thought in frustration.

He reached out and tucked a strand of pale blond hair behind her ear, then traced the line of her jaw with his fingertip. A hint of a smile played across his hard lips, and a glint appeared in his slate-blue eyes.

"My father always told me it was as easy to love a rich girl as a poor one," he said.

Carolyn threw herself into his arms and tightened her grip on his neck until he began to laugh.

"I told you I love you," he said softly, kissing her eyes, her cheeks, her lips. "And I'm not quite as broke as I look," he conceded with a reluctant sigh.

Carolyn moved back and stared at him. "Just what does that mean?" she asked in astonishment.

He looked a little uncomfortable. "Well, next month I can legally begin operating the same kind of mining operation that I had five years ago, and everything is all set to go."

"You mean you haven't just been working as a blacksmith and a ranch hand for hire in Cold Heart?" Carolyn tried to give him a wounded look, but she was still so happy to see him, that it came out more quizzical and surprised than anything else.

Raider kissed her, running his tongue temptingly over her

lips, and shook his head. "Nope. I've been doing that, all right, but I've also been prospecting."

She lay back and pulled him down on top of her, sighing as he nibbled her ear, sending the most wonderful sensation right down the center of her.

"Have you found anything?" she asked breathlessly. He certainly seemed to be good at finding things where she was concerned, she thought, as she felt his hands slide over her skin, touching her breasts and hips in a loving, teasing way that was hard to resist.

He was burying his face against her breasts and exploring her intimately. "Black opals," he muttered. "Can we talk about this later?" She felt the sofa move as he got up, and then she was being lifted in his arms and carried into the bedroom. He kicked the door shut behind them and stared into her eyes like a man burning for her.

"There's just one more thing," he said, growing serious again.

Carolyn looped her arms around his neck and looked at him in utter adoration. "You're wearing a suit," she said inanely.

"Of course I am," he growled, not pleased at her sidetracking his big moment.

She kissed his throat by way of apology. He groaned.

"I want to say something first," he protested, not too strongly, however.

Carolyn bit his jaw lightly with her teeth. He tightened his hold on her and growled warningly, "Cut that out, or you're not going to hear it. I'm only going to say this once."

Carolyn was intrigued and tried to restrain herself long enough to hear what was so important for him to say.

He cleared his throat, and his cheeks darkened. She stared at him in amazement.

"What is it, Jonathan?" she asked softly, her heart in her eyes. "Whatever it is, you can tell me. I love you. Remember…?"

His eyes darkened. He remembered only too well. He lowered his lips until they were just barely touching hers. He half closed his eyes. "Will you marry me?" he whispered huskily.

She closed the tiny distance between them, kissing him, sliding her tongue along his firm lips, gasping as he took the kiss to the limits of pleasure. He pulled back, his body tight with longing, his eyes black with desire.

"Damn it, Carolyn!" he growled, sounding as if he were being tortured. "Will you?"

She laughed softly and sank her fingers into his soft, clean hair. "I thought you'd never ask," she teased. "How could you think I'd say anything but yes?"

He shuddered and let her feet slide to the floor, pulling her into his arms and kissing her with all the abandon she'd longed for so deeply.

"How about the day after tomorrow?" he suggested as he stripped their clothes off and tumbled her back onto the sheets of her unmade bed.

She was laughing and holding out her arms to him. "That long?" she asked protestingly.

"I think it's gonna take that long for me to get out of your bed," he told her.

She moaned in pleasure as he lay atop her, warm skin to warm skin.

"There's just one thing," he said huskily.

His fingers were finding all the sensitive places again, and Carolyn raked her nails down his back in a rising agony of delight. "What's that?" she asked.

"How about a honeymoon on a beach somewhere? I want to see you in a red bikini...."

She opened her mouth to say it was funny he should mention that, but his mouth covered hers, and she decided she really didn't want to talk anymore for quite a long while.

Maybe dreams do come true, she thought.

And this dream was going to last forever.

* * * * *

SILHOUETTE *Romance*

Escape to a place where a kiss is still a kiss...
Feel the breathless connection...
Fall in love as though it were
the very first time...
Experience the power of love!

Come to where favorite authors——such as
*Diana Palmer, Stella Bagwell,
Marie Ferrarella* and many more——
deliver heart-warming romance and genuine
emotion, time after time after time....

Silhouette Romance——
stories straight from the heart!

Silhouette®
Where love comes alive™

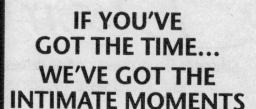

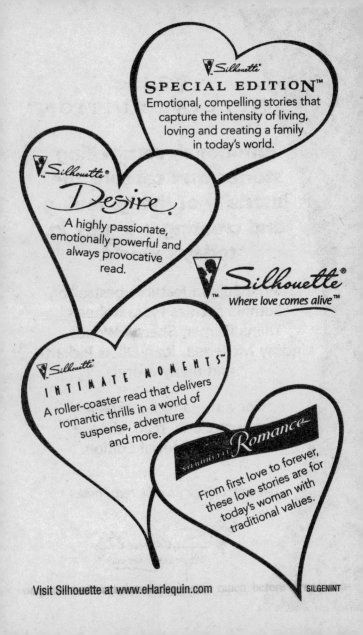

Silhouette

SPECIAL EDITION™
Emotional, compelling stories that capture the intensity of living, loving and creating a family in today's world.

Silhouette®

Desire.
A highly passionate, emotionally powerful and always provocative read.

Silhouette®
Where love comes alive™

Silhouette

INTIMATE MOMENTS™
A roller-coaster read that delivers romantic thrills in a world of suspense, adventure and more.

Silhouette Romance
From first love to forever, these love stories are for today's woman with traditional values.

Visit Silhouette at www.eHarlequin.com   SILGENINT